Double Threat

Patrick Weill

Weill & Associates

Published by Weill & Associates

Version 1.0, August 2024

Ebook ISBN: 978-1-959866-04-6

Print ISBN: 978-1-959866-06-0

Cover design by cover2book.com

Dedicated to any soul struggling to survive or fighting for a better world.

Contents

CAST OF CHARACTERS

PARK'S CHAPTERS

The Undercover team on the *Oasis*:

- Detective Tony Park: An enormous Korean American who served as a Navy SEAL in the Middle East. He's Jeff Walker's partner on the Harbor Police force and married to Carla Reyes, a helicopter pilot.

- Special Agent Scott Phillips: An FBI investigator recovering from a painful divorce who plays basketball and works on cars in his limited spare time. In this story, Phillips is drawn into a taboo romance with one of the suspects aboard the cruise ship, an exquisitely attractive vocalist. Is she as sweet as she seems or is it just another performance?

- Supervisory Special Agent John Kerr: A famous criminal profiler on loan from the Behavioral Analysis Unit at Quantico, Kerr has had a spectacular career marred only by a single slip-up, but it was a big one. Can he find redemption while working one last case, or will he fall victim to the deranged serial killer they're trying to catch?

- Chief James Richards: Head of ship security. A former soldier, Richards is the only person aboard the *Oasis* who knows the undercover team's true identities. At the beginning of the story, anyway.

The Suspects on the *Oasis*:
- Amanda Boydon: This exquisitely beautiful singer charms SSA Phillips into her bed, quickly gaining his unwavering faith in her innocence.

- Steve Russo: This clever comedian is beset by female groupies, and he's popular with his fellow men at the card tables, but what's he like when the laughter stops?

- Staff Captain Kevin Massolt: This European gentleman is a minor celebrity on the ship, which he knows like the back of his hand, and his crisply pressed uniform is immaculate. The question is, are his motives equally impeccable?

- Danielle Jackson: The kid's club manager, a young Black woman who's as sweet as they come, or so it seems. But, as the experts say, the guilty party often turns out to be the one you're least likely to suspect.

- Angelo dela Cruz: The ship's executive chef. He's got a quick temper, easy access to knives, and a knack for picking up passengers and getting them alone.

Other players
- Jessica Reynolds: A wealthy widow traveling with her son and a little white dog.

- Victor Cameron: A trusted member of Chief Richards' security team.

WALKER'S CHAPTERS

San Diego Harbor Police

- Detective Jeff Walker: Like Park, his partner, Walker has six years on the force. In this book, he joins MARTAC, the Harbor Police's MARitime TACtical team. He's married to Tina Garcia, who has so far given him two beautiful little girls.

- Sergeant Cheatham: Walker's supervisor, friend, and mentor. A Black man nearing the end of a long and distinguished career. A former drill instructor in the U.S. Army.

- Furious: A patrol officer as well as a MARTAC operator. When he's off duty, this African American powerhouse is a professional cage fighter.

- Lieutenant Bill Coffin, MARTAC commander: A former Marine Corps scout sniper.

- Sergeant Steve Ortiz: A thick-necked former soldier who is always ready for war. MARTAC's team leader.

- Detective Abbott: Like Park and Walker, Abbott is a detective as well as a MARTAC operator. He is intelligent and courageous.

Other players

- DAI (District Attorney Investigator) Dominick Taylor: Once the commander of Oceanside PD's narcotics task force, Taylor now works in the Hall of Justice alongside his better half, Chief Deputy District Attorney Lynn Peters. A former Special Forces soldier, Taylor has a dangerously short fuse.

- Sean Choi: A brilliant but timid computer programmer who works for DAI Taylor as a technical analyst and is dating one of Jeff Walker's sisters-in-law. Can he conquer his fear of fighting?

- Marcus Crawford: A supremely fit and deeply tanned individual, Crawford is the leader of the San Diego Lifeguards' dive rescue team and engaged to marry Walker's other sister-in-law. He'd love to work in law enforcement someday, but does he have what it takes?

- Ethan Hall and Jenn Fowler: Crawford's fellow lifeguards. Six years before this story takes place, Park and Walker worked on the beach with all three of them. There's always been a spark between these two, but for some reason they've never sealed the deal. Maybe now they will.

THE VILLAINS

- Chasquas: This decorated street soldier is a known enemy from a previous case. Having fought his way out of the ghettos of Honduras to work for a criminal organization in the United States, Chasquas is stronger and smarter than ever before. Now he's dropped his drug habit and is running a gang of his own.

- Stephen Baker: The only surviving member of the now-defunct North County Kings, he runs a motorcycle club that produces methamphetamine for Chasquas.

- Sammy Enright: A high-ranking member of Baker's biker gang, Sammy runs the secret meth lab and holds a deadly grudge against Chasquas.

- Ronnie Locke: A crooked, wealthy businessman being groomed for the highest office in the nation.

- Stryker Lindbloom: A thick-necked ex-convict working closely with Chasquas.

- Joshua Pope: A shaven-headed former Marine who leads a racist militia that trains at Baker's rural compound.

- Berg: Pope's second-in command. He lives at the biker compound along with Baker, Pope, and a few other guys.

- Rick Daniels: A former Army sniper and the only remaining villain from *The Mazatlan Showdown*, Daniels is sure that Walker is responsible for the death of his true love, so he wants him to suffer the same kind of pain.

1

A MYSTERIOUS SIBILANCE
IN SUBURBIA

Obviously I can't produce human vocalizations, but I do recognize some, such as *German shepherd, hot dog, walk,* and *bath.* I spend most of my days confined to a grassy back yard, which is where we are now, in fact. Though here I'm safe and never hungry, it's confinement nonetheless. My masters only let me out with a collar around my neck and only when they need to reach their step count goals.

I have one constant companion. She's one of those winged creatures that fly and sing. The former she never does, and the latter only rarely, since she's a prisoner, too, but in a much smaller cell. Then what's the point of having wings, I say! She and I don't converse, not like you humans do, but we've learned to read each other's gazes. With one look at her quick eyes, I can tell she's longing to soar through the perfect blue sky this sunny afternoon, to swoop and dive as she rides the wind. Me? I'd rather spend my time hunting for dinner, tearing through an open field in the ancient battle of will and wits for which I was created.

It's unnatural, this existence of ours; Bird and I were meant to spend the prime of our lives mating, fighting, and relaxing in the softness of nature, then to live out our golden years in peace under the protection of our offspring. Being free, above all, which is a far cry from our limited reality. Yet it's not our masters' fault; they're stuck in a similar situation, except that they don't have to choke down these disgusting pellets.

Hang on, I see something new! Something different at the bottom of the back fence, which the neighbors must have broken last night in their noisy party. I lumber to my paws and trot through the grass to have a look, running now as my excitement builds. Yes! The wood is smashed at the bottom and there's space enough to escape! I catch Bird's eye, then dig a bit, squeeze myself through, and race through the adjacent yard, bounding toward new smells. I see a fence up ahead, and it's low enough to hurdle, and that's exactly what I do. Now I'm out on the street in suburbia at dusk, and this first taste of freedom is positively delicious!

As I settle into a gallop, stretching out my limbs, I'd like to tell you something about canines, in case you aren't aware. We're more complex than we seem. For instance, you might suspect exercise is what I've been needing most, but you'd be wrong. I mean, I've been longing to get out and run, but mental stimulation is what's lacking in that back yard. It's always the same. Here, I note the sound of crickets chirping, then seek them out and make them jump. Now the noise made by fighting cats. Then motors, music, and other human inventions. Far below those, in the ultrasonic range, I hear mice, moths, beetles, and even plants talking to each other. This natural symphony has jolted me back to life like a pair of defibrillator paddles, and it's not even the best part of this adventure! You see, our circuits aren't wired like yours, not quite, anyway; the new scents I'm picking up are making my long-depressed brain explode with pleasure as I canter past the houses on both sides of the street toward the open countryside. All around me, my fellow canines burst into a jealous cacophony of barks, ruffs, yaps, and howls.

I sniff the air six times a second as I gallop along, and my visual perception appears in four dimensions, displaying multi-colored trails of scent particles that vary in brightness, color, shape, and density, providing me with a wealth of useful information. For instance, as I come to the base of a tree, green wisps rising from the soil tell me a female dog has recently made a liquid deposit here. The aroma is exquisite. She's about my age, with a similar genetic signature, in good health, currently relaxed and in a receptive emotional state, and—most importantly—in optimal estrus. The whiff of a compatible partner in heat is so intoxicating that my urethral sphincter relaxes involuntarily and I am overtaken by the need to leave a deposit of my own. Then I set off again, urged onward by the prospect of a piece of tail, yet wary of the danger foreshadowed by a second scent I'm detecting, that of a high-status male. He's big and aggressive.

By the time I reach the outskirts of the housing development, night has fallen, but I can see just fine, aided by those multicolored scent trails I told you about. Speaking of which, a few yards up ahead, I see/smell a dark purple trail wafting out from around a corner—oh crap—and a king-sized pit bull comes charging out, snarling and barking with a deadly look in his eye!

I'm off at once, feeling hot breath and fangs gnashing at my haunches, but I'm a strong runner and soon his sounds and smells fade away. Panting hard, I slow to an amble and take refuge in a dead-end alley, where I should be safe until I catch my breath because the mingled odors of rotting garbage and other waste are strong enough to mask my own scent.

"Hey, buddy," I hear someone say, behind me at the mouth of the alley. "Want a hot dog?"

Hot dog? I know that word! I turn around with happy anticipation to see a pair of male humans with violence in their scent trails and a dull, dead look in their eyes. One of them tosses the processed meat, which gives off mouth-watering aromatic tendrils as it sails through the air, but when the pink tube lands on the pavement, a toxic cloud bursts forth, signaling danger, so I bolt in the direction of freedom.

"Grab it!" one of them shouts.

The other guy drops to his knees and traps me by the neck while the first attempts to force-feed me the stinky meat. But all three of us turn toward the mouth of the alley as we detect a fourth animal present. My semi-feral rival has found me, and he's hungry! Luckily, his killer gaze is fixed on one of the humans.

"Oh shit!" says the hot dog thrower, running toward the dead end, and the pit bull takes him down in seconds.

The human trapping me shouts, "Hey! HEY! Over here!" hoping to distract the giant dog, but he also doesn't want me to escape, so he unsheathes a long knife that's glinting in the moonlight, and shows it to me to keep me from attacking, but he's not ready. I sink my fangs into his leg, realizing too late that I should have attacked his knife arm. Then I feel an icy flash on my head that blooms into a white-hot pain. The bastard's cut my ear off!

I lunge forward and bite him again, in the right place this time. As I gnash forward for better leverage, crunching his hand into an irreparable mass of bonemeal, the coppery taste of blood floods my mouth. It tastes good! Better than dog pellets, anyway.

Shrieking and cursing, he drops the blade and kicks me till I release my bite. Then he says something I don't understand; sinister and otherworldly, the words come out hissed, heavy on S sounds, like a snake would talk if it could. He spins on his heel and flees, abandoning his companion, who, I note with satisfaction, is lying on his back and no longer struggling. My high-status rival's muzzle drips with blood as he turns to catch my eye.

So I follow the scent trails—some of them mine—back to the broken fence and squeeze myself through. The yard, with its shady trees, soft grass, and never-ending supply of dog food, doesn't seem nearly as miserable as it did before.

Bird peers down at me with her beady eyes. I can feel her envy, so I do her a favor, leaping onto a planter bed and walking along the rail toward her cage. She flutters around with excitement as I launch myself into the oppressive suburban air, hitting the latch just right.

It'll be lonely, but I wouldn't have it any other way.

And what about that hissing human? Strange, don't you think? I hope someone cuts *his* ear off. Or some other, more vital part!

2

ROUGH SEAS

"I'll go with you," offered Tony Park, who needed a trip to the men's room for more than one reason.

"Perfect," Jeff Walker replied. "The closest one's in the casino."

It was day two of a week-long Caribbean cruise, and so far the efforts of these two police detectives to keep their faces scowl-free had been admirable, despite the astonishing cost of the two-family vacation. Now, however, both of them needed a break. Park especially, whose wife, Carla, flashed him a pointed look that told him he'd better return with a different attitude.

"Be right back," Walker said to his wife, Tina, who turned away from their two little girls to give him a nod and a tired smile. Tina Michelle and Mia were visibly excited for the magic show to begin, though everyone's patience was wearing thin as they stood in line, waiting for the theater doors to open.

The *Majesty* was over a thousand feet long, a hundred wide, and two hundred high, Park knew. Even so, with three thousand souls aboard, space was a precious commodity. As he and Walker strode across the gaming floor amid a cheery cacophony of electronic jangles and chimes, scanning their surroundings as was their habit, he observed that the casino was slightly miniature. Just like his and Carla's stateroom and every other part of the ship. Low ceilings, reduced aisle width, and clever placement of mirrors were just a few of the strategic elements of the vessel's design.

As they came to the cashier cage, which spanned the far wall, an overhead restroom sign pointed to a hallway leading right. They were about to take the turn when they spotted two elderly men standing at the thick polycarbonate cashier shield, on the other side of which the casino employee looked terrified.

Park and Walker stopped in their tracks.

"Do it. I won't tell you again," growled one of the older men, who, like his fellow passenger, sported a dark suit with no tie. Both were oddly muscular.

"I could lose my job," the cashier protested.

Park headed for the window to ask what was going on, but someone behind him spoke up first.

"I got this," came a deep male voice. "Thanks, though."

Park turned. The newcomer's badge read *Casino Security*.

"Can I help you, gentlemen?" said the security manager.

The wide-eyed cashier shook his head in alarm as the two passengers whirled around to face the man addressing them. "Yes, you can," said one of them, whose voice came out muffled by what was, on close inspection, a hyper-realistic silicone mask similar to the one worn by his companion. Both masked men reached into their jackets, whipped out pistols, and took careful aim. One of them shot the security manager, whose head snapped back with a red mist spraying out the rear, and the gun's loud CRACK sent the patrons scrambling for the exits.

At the same time, the second gunman panned his pistol from Park to Walker and back again. "Hands up," he ordered them.

The unarmed police detectives could only comply, but they kept their hands forward and as low as possible, ready to pounce if the crooks made a mistake.

The first gunman stooped to search the security officer, came up with a key card, and hustled to the door next to the cashiers cage. Then both of them stepped into the employees-only area, one facing forward and the other covering the rear, both with their pistols brought to bear, which Park identified as 1IK45 Compact Tacticals. *Ex-military*, he guessed, watching in dismay as they executed all the cashiers and hustled out of sight, presumably toward wherever the cash was kept. The crackling gunfire transported him back to the battlefield, to the Middle East, where he'd served as a Navy SEAL, so Park flew into combat mode, hurriedly unclipping the security manager's radio from his belt and keying up on the device.

"I'm going to the theater!" barked Walker over his shoulder, on his way out of the deserted casino.

Park nodded, then spoke into the radio. "Ship security, this is Detective Tony Park of the San Diego Harbor Police, over."

"Roger, detective. James Richards, chief of security. Over."

After Park provided a brief situation report and offered assistance, Richards came back with "Report to the security office, and stay safe on the way here. Do you know where we are?"

"Affirmative."

Park flew up the stairs and through the halls, coordinating his movement with Walker by cell phone, so when he came to the administrative offices, his fellow detective was already there. "All good?" he asked.

Walker nodded. "Yeah. Carla's in my stateroom with everyone else."

They were shown in to Chief Richards' small but tidy office, made even smaller by the presence of his security team. Most of them looked too young and too nervous.

Richards, an uncommonly large man about Park's own size, was on his feet talking to another security officer, and these two were the only people in the room, Park thought, who might have seen any combat at all, except for Walker and himself.

Richards looked up, strode forward, stuck out a hand, and introduced the other guy as Roger Lowry, his deputy chief. Then, after studying the detectives' credentials, he said, "We could use your help."

Park and Walker agreed, and Deputy Chief Lowry supplied them with ballistic vests and Glock 19s while the chief issued instructions to the rest of the team.

Park dropped out his pistol's magazine to check the load, smacked it home again, then drew back the slide and let it go, chambering the first round with a metallic click-clack. He caught Lowry's eye and gestured toward the empty weapons locker, from which only four sidearms and two rifles had been removed and distributed. "That's all there is?"

"'Fraid so," Lowry said, then seated a thirty-round mag into his M4 carbine with a push-pull motion. He was under six feet, but just as thick as Park, so his massive neck made him look like a bulldog with a rifle.

"Let's get to it," growled Chief Richards, who had sent most of his team to help the staff get the passengers into their cabins. Carrying his own M4 with both hands and the barrel pointed up, he led the way to the casino with Park and Lowry behind him, then two senior security officers and Walker covering the rear.

When they came to the cashiers cage, Chief Richards waved a key card over a sensor and got a green light, but the door wouldn't budge when he pulled on it.

Deputy Chief Lowry put his nose to the hinges and took a sniff. "It's been welded shut," he said.

"We keep all the cash in the vault," Richards explained to Park and Walker. "It's a fortified room about thirty yards back. This door is the only way in, so the crooks must be planning to blow a hole in the wall."

"Or the ceiling or the floor," said Walker. "What's above, below, and behind that room?"

Richards screwed up his lips in an effort to recall, but Park answered first. "The crew cafeteria is below us, the nightclub is overhead, and there's a souvenir shop on the other side of the vault."

"He's got a photographic memory," Walker told the chief. "Must have glanced at the deck plan while booking the trip two months ago."

Richards was not impressed. "Lowry and Park, get down to the cafeteria," he grumbled. "Walker and I'll hit the souvenir shop." Then, to his senior officers, he said, "You two stay here in the casino, keep the passengers out, and watch this door."

***

"How do you think they got the guns and tools aboard, Chief?" Walker asked Richards as they hustled through the corridors to the souvenir shop that shared a wall with the vault.

"Good question," answered Richards between huffs and puffs. "They must have had inside help."

Right then, an explosion shook the walls, blowing out a cloud of plaster dust from around the corner they were heading for, and a group of frightened passengers came from the same direction. Chief Richards ordered them back to their cabins. Then he and Walker exchanged a nod, brought their weapons up, and proceeded toward the corner.

***

Minutes earlier, Deputy Security Chief Lowry was leading Park down a wide carpeted staircase with polished-wood hand railings, which, as they came to the non-passenger decks, turned into an industrial stair system painted gray and yellow. When Lowry set off down a hallway at the first landing they came to, Park saw that he was carrying his rifle across his chest, which was strange; Park was better prepared to fire, holding his pistol at the high ready, or with his elbows bent and the muzzle forty-five degrees higher than level. Continuing along the no-frills passageway, they came to the crew cafeteria on the right, and just as Lowry stepped inside, an explosion shook the walls, but it felt far away. "Get to your rooms!" he ordered the people sitting at the tables.

"We're in the wrong place," Park said.

"Obviously," Lowry replied with an irritated frown. "Let's hit the nightclub."

Now they moved through the hallways at a much faster pace, both with their weapons at the ready, but as they hit the stairs, it occurred to Park that Lowry was making a mistake. "We should check the gangway first," he said.

"Who's in charge here?" the deputy stopped to say over his shoulder, then continued on his way.

That was Park's first clue that Lowry had a hidden agenda. The gangway was an access portal where a boat could come alongside and pick up the crooks, and it was right around the corner from where they were. How else would the bad guys get away? By helo? According to Park's calculations, the ship was too far from land to be within range of most helicopters. So instead of following Lowry up the stairs, he cut around a corner.

"Fuck!" came Lowry's voice behind him, followed by the sound of running footsteps.

Park sprinted through a long corridor, at the end of which he saw that the gangway doors had been left open, and he had a strong suspicion as to who had done it. Two hundred yards out to sea, a purple powerboat was speeding directly toward the cruise ship. Outgunned with nowhere to hide, he didn't slow down or turn to face his attacker. He commanded his big legs to take him even faster, and when he came to the gangway, he leapt into the air. Gunshots rang out behind him as he sailed toward the ocean headfirst, and the bullets snapped so closely past him that he could feel their heat. Park sucked in a breath before he sliced into the water and descended out of range, hoping Walker would have better luck.

***

Walker peered through his iron sights as he advanced, focused on reacting immediately to whatever might await him around the corner.

Chief Richards spoke to him in a whisper. "After the turn, there's a short hallway, and the souvenir shop's at the end. Let's—"

At that instant, the two masked criminals they were searching for came charging around the corner with pistols firing—BLAM BLAM BLAM BLAM!—catching Richards twice in the leg and once in the shoulder, since he was in the forward position.

The chief's big body jerked with each of the three impacts. His legs buckled and he crashed to the floor.

Meanwhile, since Walker was shielded and in a tactical ready position, he was able to line up his sights on the first man's center mass and blow him off his feet, then swing his aim onto the second guy, whose eyes flitted down to his dying partner. "Drop it!" Walker commanded him. "Get on the floor." He snatched Richards' handcuffs off his belt, restrained the second crook, searched him for weapons, dragged him to a sitting position, and hustled back to Richards to assess the extent of his injuries. Luckily, no major blood vessels had been hit.

"Take my rifle and go ahead," said Richards. "I got this guy."

"You sure?"

"Yes."

After Richards radioed for assistance, they traded weapons and Walker continued to advance toward the souvenir shop, where he encountered no further threats. Then he stepped through the hole in the wall that led to the vault and the cashier area, finding no unfriendlies and, sadly, no survivors among the casino staff. By the time Walker made it back to Chief Richards, two members of the ship's medical staff had already arrived, so he hustled off to see about Park, whom he found at the helm of a ski boat tied up to the *Majesty* at the gangway. Two scowling men sat in the aft section of the smaller vessel, bound hand and foot with dock lines, and Park looked up to lift his chin in greeting.

The ship was searched from bow to stern for the rest of the voyage, but Deputy Chief Lowry was never found.

3

THE UNDERCOVER TEAM

San Diego Harbor Police Headquarters
Six months after the incident on the *Majesty*

"All right, then. Be safe y'all," growled Sergeant Cheatham, signaling the conclusion of the morning briefing. Then he rose from the table at the front of the room, fixed his stare on Park and Walker, and said, "My office, gentlemen."

They had to hustle to keep up with Cheatham, an African American man in his mid-fifties, whose matching black pants and shirt were crisply pressed and his dress shoes polished on a regular basis. He glanced back with a rare grin. "Don't worry, guys, it's good news."

Park and Walker settled into chairs on the visitor side of their sergeant's desk as he strode to a closet, came out with three bottles of water, handed over two of them, and took a seat. "I got a call from the FBI last night," he began. "Do you know a David Pinkney out of the Los Angeles field office?"

Park and Walker shook their heads.

"I was his drill instructor in the service. You can trust him. Anyway, Pinkney's investigating a series of murders committed on cruise ships, and he specifically asked for you."

That didn't sound like good news to Walker. Even so, an hour later, he climbed into the passenger seat of Park's Toyota Tundra, under the hood of which was a 5.7-liter V8 that roared when it hit the highway. Just north of La Jolla, to their left, the Pacific Ocean glittered like a bed of diamonds under the late-morning sun, as it continued to do for the next fifty miles. At Dana Point, however, the interstate veered inland, putting an end to the scenic part of the trip.

Before long, they pulled up at the Wilshire Federal Building, where they followed a shapely receptionist down a hallway, who stopped at a door on her right, spun on her heel, smiled, and gestured for them to enter. Supervisory Special Agent David Pinkney stepped out from behind his desk to introduce himself, offering a thin smile and a quick handshake. Noting the heavy bags under the man's eyes, his paunch belly, and the stacks of paperwork on every flat surface, Walker took no offense at the lukewarm welcome.

Two other men stood to greet them, one of whom was Chief Richards. "Good to see you guys again," he harrumphed.

"Special Agent Scott Phillips," said an athletic-looking man under forty as he put out his hand.

Pinkney dropped into the chair behind his desk and everyone else followed suit. "Thanks for driving up on such short notice," he said. "I don't know how much Sergeant Cheatham told you about the case, but you must be familiar with Excelsior Cruise Lines."

"Of course," said Walker. It was the company that Chief Richards worked for, the same that had suffered the robbery attempt on the *Majesty*.

"Excelsior's had four murders this year on their Mexican routes, all with the same M.O., and they've transferred Richards to those itineraries so he can be the point of contact for an undercover team I'm putting together."

"Why us?" Park asked. "You must have plenty of capable agents."

"I recommended you," Chief Richards explained. "After looking you up. Had a chat with Lynn Peters at the DA's Office, who said Walker speaks Spanish, and we might have to liaison with the Mexican authorities on this one."

"But you're right," Pinkney said to Park. "All of our agents *are* highly capable, especially Phillips here. And John Kerr's flying in tomorrow. He's an expert criminal profiler from the BAU out of Quantico. I think you'll work well together, assuming you agree. This is a month-long operation, and the first ship sails next Tuesday."

"I'm in," Park declared.

Walker cast a sidelong glance at his massive Asian partner, who was often the first to volunteer for risky work such as this. Unfortunately, this time he wouldn't be there to watch his buddy's six. "I'm out," said Walker with a frown. "I'm starting SWAT training next week."

"That's right," Park replied. "I'd forgotten about that."

"*Es una lástima.*" This from Special Agent Phillips. "*Pero no hay problema. Yo hablo español.*"

Walker eyed Phillips and nodded approvingly. The guy's Spanish was pretty good.

"Right. No problemo," said Pinkney, rising from his desk. "A smaller operation might work even better."

Soon after that, Park, Walker, and Richards left the building together, and as they marched to their cars, Park asked Richards if there'd been any news regarding Deputy Lowry.

"Yes," the chief security officer replied. "First of all, that wasn't his name. The real Roger Lowry was an ex-cop whose identity was stolen. The man you met was Stryker Lindbloom, who was involved in two successful cruise ship robberies before the one on the *Majesty.*"

"Did you ever find out how he managed to escape?" asked Walker.

"He must have used his knowledge of the ship's layout to hide until the next port stop, where I figure he jumped overboard to avoid detection at the docks. But the crooks we *did* catch said Lindbloom was the one who smuggled the weapons, tools, and explosives aboard, and that they were all working for the same organization. Unfortunately, they were killed in custody before they could tell us anything else."

Walker raised an eyebrow. "While in custody?"

"That's right. Poisoned in their cells. This is me," said Richards, nodding at a Chevy sedan.

***

After a bittersweet weekend of Netflix and chill and beach jogs with Carla, Tony Park dragged himself out of bed at 0500 on a Monday, climbed into his prized pickup, and brought it to life with a roar. As he headed north on I-5, the sun came up over the hills to his right, painting the sky with cool blue brushstrokes. On the opposite side of the highway, white-capped waves crashed down on the sand, bringing Jeff Walker to the forefront of his mind. Park's best friend and partner had come a long way since they'd first met as beach lifeguards. Jeff's long blond surfer's mane was absent now, having been replaced by a military-style crew cut, and his attitude had also undergone a trimming of dead weight. Actually, both of them were better men than before; five years had passed since Park's last PTSD-related episode, and he felt he'd finally gotten a handle on his drinking.

As he rolled down into the Los Angeles Basin, he got stuck in heavy traffic. Practically choking on the collective mass of toxic fumes, he rolled up the windows, cranked up the A/C, and focused on his breathing to calm himself. Forty slow miles later, he came to the Wilshire Federal Building, where he found an empty parking space next to a man just getting off a motorcycle. It was a BMW R 1250 GS, a stylish but comfortable cross-country ride with advanced electronics and a top speed of 130 mph. "Nice wheels," he said to the biker.

"It's a rental," the man replied, and when he pulled off his helmet to expose a bald head and a gray beard, Park recognized him as FBI Supervisory Special Agent John Kerr, a well-known figure in federal law enforcement. Kerr's eyes brimmed with intensity and confidence, and he looked about sixty years old.

"That's what I should have gotten instead of that damn Impala," bellowed a voice from behind them. It was Chief Richards lumbering up the sidewalk in their direction. "Hey guys."

They all took the elevator to meet with the fourth member of the undercover team, Special Agent Phillips, whom they found in his office. It was a smaller version of Pinkney's, with paperwork everywhere and a bookshelf crammed with thick three-ring binders. "Operations manuals," the FBI man said glumly, offering Park a strong hand. "Good to see you again."

"There's no shortage of those in my office, either," Park returned in the same gloomy tone, but he brightened when he spotted a collection of miniature sports cars on one of the bookshelves, mostly American muscle from the '70s to modern day. "*These* look interesting. Must have taken you forever to build."

"Nah, I bought 'em like that. I like to work on the real thing."

Phillips reminded Park of Walker: both were six-one and strong, with short hair, although the federal agent's was darker and frizzy like a patch of carpet. He led them down the hall to a dark conference room, where Park, Richards, and Kerr took a seat at a table and Phillips stood beside a projection screen. Then, after Kerr had flipped open a laptop and called up the first in a series of slides, Phillips launched into his presentation. "There've been four murders on Excelsior's ships this year," he said. "All the victims were found in their staterooms. Have a look at the crime scenes."

Park cringed when he saw for himself what SSA Pinkney had meant by "similar M.O." Each of the bodies had been slashed, stabbed, ripped open, and disemboweled, yet the most striking element of all was that the victims' eyes had been gouged out and left in the resulting pool of blood, placed next to each other such that they looked back at whoever discovered the body.

"Are there clues as to the killer's identity?" Park asked while Phillips folded up and carried the portable screen to a corner, then switched on the lights and joined the group at the table.

"Yes," SSA Kerr answered for Phillips, "but we always give the profile of the unknown subject, or unsub, as we say, before we see the suspect list."

"To avoid bias," Park knew.

"Exactly. So here's my preliminary profile. The where, when, and how of these crimes are relatively clear, as they usually are, but to arrive at the who, we tend to focus on the *why*. From a behavioral standpoint, several things come to mind. The level of planning required and the forensic countermeasures taken to avoid detection indicate that our killer is psychopathic, not psychotic. In other words, he or she can think clearly, function in society, understand reality, and doesn't hallucinate. This is a sadist, someone who takes sexual pleasure in his or her victims' pain. The extreme level of violence, which we call *overkill*, indicates rage, possibly as a reaction to a stressor that might have occurred just before the killings began six months ago. And the frequency's increasing. The last three murders occurred in a period of two months, and the last two in three weeks, which means the unsub is losing control, as they tend to do in the end. Finally, in terms of victimology, I'm not seeing any real pattern. The killer's targeted a varied group in terms of ethnicity, gender, and age, with no significant connections among them."

"Thank you, John," said Phillips. "Now for the suspects. News of the murders has found its way to the national media, so people are scared to book a cruise with Excelsior. All four of their Mexican routes are running at half capacity."

No wonder they want to solve this case, thought Park after calculating the average cost of a cruise multiplied by three thousand passengers and four ships. On the Mexican itineraries alone, the company's loss came to twenty-five million dollars a week.

"And the employees are reluctant to work on a death cruise," Phillips went on, "which causes heavy staff rotation, but that's a good thing for us because there were only a handful of crew members who were present for all four murders, and those are our suspects."

"What about repeat passengers?" Park asked.

Phillips shook his head. "We've cross-checked all the manifests and there's not a single person who went on all four cruises. No repeat passengers at all, in fact. So the killer has to be one of the employees we'll be watching. Here," he said, sliding three file folders across the table, one for each of Park, Kerr, and Richards. "Your aliases and backstories, all the information we have on the suspects, and Kerr's preliminary profile of the killer."

Park stamped down his palm to stop the file, then flipped it open to read the contents. He'd be traveling as Andrew Hwang, thirty-five, engaged, a physical therapist from San Diego. Phillips and Kerr would be posing as his friends from LA, a financial advisor and an author, respectively, who were taking him on this trip as a sort of bachelor party.

"We've even printed books I can sell and sign," said the bearded criminal profiler. "They're AI-generated trash, but I published them online in case anyone checks."

"You're pretty famous," said Park. "Won't someone recognize you? Especially a serial killer, who might have read your real books."

Kerr shook his head. "I'll be clean shaven and wearing a disguise. You won't believe it's really me."

"Okay guys," Chief Richards said, "to protect your cover we'll be hopping from ship to ship at the end of every week-long cruise. You won't be meeting with me in person unless it's absolutely necessary, but we'll stay in touch by text message or video call."

Phillips rose from the table. "That's it," he said. "We'll see you tomorrow."

***

The following morning before dawn, Park, Phillips, and Kerr strode toward the *Radiance* long before any other passenger. The massive white vessel at the end of the dock was a floating city, with a full-size basketball court, a pair of deep-tank swimming pools, a grand showroom, and a world-class fitness center. Park turned to Kerr as they stepped aboard. "You were right," he said. "You really *are* unrecognizable."

The criminal profiler had grown four inches and gained a hundred pounds, his eyes were blue instead of brown, and his voice came out in a heavy southern drawl. "Ahm enjoyin' playin' the role," Kerr replied with a wink. "Takes me back to mah thee-a-tah days." They rode the elevator to deck five, then split up to get settled in their staterooms. Park's had a double bed and a sitting area crammed into half the space such an arrangement would normally occupy, but at least it offered floor-to-ceiling windows that opened onto a little balcony.

When Park had last stepped aboard a cruise ship, he'd come unarmed, but not this time. His tactical duffel bag contained a varied selection of killing tools, including his trusty P226 MK25, a Glock 19, combat knives, several boxes of 9mm bullets, and many other devices he'd thought to pack. As he unloaded it all, a familiar sense of pre-deployment dread crept into his psyche, but he shook it off. *Just one serial killer? I've fought full platoons of hostile soldiers and locked up gangs of hardened criminals. Compared to that, this might be easy.*

4

CHASQUAS RETURNS

San Bernardino, California
115 miles north of San Diego

Detective Jeff Walker was the third man of four in a line, or "stack," of police officers positioned along the wall to the right side of an open doorway, in a formation colloquially referred to as "nut to butt." While holding his M4 carbine in a one-handed ready position, he drew a flash-bang grenade out of a pouch on his tactical vest, then stepped out of line and advanced toward the doorway, pulling the pin on the diversionary device. "Bang out!" he told his teammates as he tossed it into the target room and moved back into position.

BOOM! As soon as the stun grenade went off, the lawmen poured through the doorway in single file, all with rifles leveled and each covering a different sector of fire. The point man moved toward the near left corner, ensuring no hostiles lay in wait. The second operator buttonhooked to the near right corner, clearing that critical position. Walker charged straight ahead, and was about to sweep his weapon from center to left when a member of the opposing force popped out from behind an obstacle. Walker immediately sighted on him and fired, hitting the man twice in the face.

"Run it again! This time in the dark," their instructor barked, as the "downed enemy," a fellow SWAT trainee, used a rag to wipe the water-soluble marking compound from his protective eyewear.

By the time Walker dropped his exhausted frame into the optimized ergonomic driver's seat of his Ford Mustang Shelby GT500, it was late on a Friday night. The training course was designed to include eighty hours of instruction, but if the following week progressed as this one had, a hundred and twenty hours would be closer to the total. With a long sigh, he buckled up and hit the start button, awakening the street-legal beast, and as he stopped to listen to the popping grumble of its supercharged 5.2-liter V8, a smile grew on his face. Then he stomped on the gas and blasted off for San Diego, eager to see his family after five days without them.

***

The following evening, Tina Garcia turned to Carla Reyes, her best friend, to say, "I really appreciate you doing this," while Walker dropped to a knee to hug and kiss his little girls.

"Be good for Aunt Carla," he told them.

"We will, *Papá*," they replied in unison, yet he remained skeptical. Tina Michelle, whose curly brown hair reminded him of Carla's, was three years old and delightfully spunky. Mia, who had just turned one, was walking now, with a determined confidence and strong arms and legs that made her big sister think twice before attempting any sort of mistreatment.

It was Saturday night. Walker had just completed his first week of SWAT training, and he and Tina were going to dinner with the mayor of San Diego. Carla and the girls stood at the open front door waving goodbye as man and wife strode hand in hand to the white GT500. Walker broke contact to open the passenger door, and as Tina slid into her seat, their gazes met and held. Her almond-shaped eyes were so artfully made up that he caught himself staring. And when her generous lips widened into that spectacular smile of hers, he leaned down to kiss her.

Tina took pride in her appearance. A former paramedic and now a beautician, she'd spent hours arranging her long black locks half-up in a hairstyle that would have cost her clients a hundred dollars. "You look great," he whispered as their lips eased apart.

It was a short ride to Mr. A's, an iconic fine-dining establishment that offers its patrons a breathtaking view of the downtown skyline. As they set foot on the outside balcony, awed by the glittering expanse of high-rises reflected on the bay, Mayor Pat O'Connell rose from a table to greet them, as did Chief Deputy DA Lynn Peters, a close friend of theirs. Despite his age, O'Connell's biceps still stretched his navy-blue blazer to the limit, and Lynn looked as sharp as ever, with her golden hair spilling past her shoulders onto a dark-colored dress and a string of pearls encircling her slender neck.

"Too bad Dom couldn't come," Tina later remarked over hors d'oeuvres and drinks.

Lynn nodded glumly. "I'm finally dating someone who's as busy as I am."

"You've met your match," Tina replied with a knowing smile. The subject of their conversation, DAI Dominick Taylor, formerly Lieutenant Taylor of Oceanside PD, was now an investigator for the DA's Office.

"Oh, we're a match, all right," the blond-haired prosecutor confirmed, setting down her glass of chardonnay. "We work on the same floor and I haven't seen him for a week."

"He's investigating that *so-called* syndicate," Mayor O'Connell joked. "That's what I'm calling them."

Lynn giggled politely. "It's actually *SoCal* Syndicate, for Southern California," she explained to Tina.

"Are they new?" Tina asked.

"Yeah, they are," said Walker. "Even I hadn't heard of them till recently." He leaned forward to smell the mouth-watering steam rising from the lobster strudel just set before him.

"That's riiiight," remembered the mayor. "They were behind the attempted robbery on the *Majesty*. Nice work, by the way." He held up his wine glass for Walker to clink his own against, and the two men shared a nod of mutual respect.

"But that's not all they're up to," said Lynn Peters. "We've seen a major influx of narcotics lately, and we also think they're behind the recent string of boat bombings."

"Jeff told me about those," said Tina. "The Harbor Police has had its hands full. And now that the North County Kings and the Cartel del Norte are out of the way, it makes sense that someone else would step up to take their place."

"It's a never-ending battle," the mayor grumbled, then stood to propose a toast. "Anyway, here's to—"

Those were Mayor Patrick O'Connell's last words. His head suddenly jerked back and exploded out the rear, splattering the windows behind him with a chunky red mess. For a silent split second, everyone around them froze. Then the balcony burst into noisy chaos: Walker and the mayor's protection detail whipped out their pistols and rushed to the railing to locate the shooter, while fifty screaming diners pushed and jostled each other and Tina and Lynn helped them proceed to the main dining room in a semi-orderly fashion.

Walker and the mayor's security team saw no suspicious movement or glinting optics at the windows of the nearby buildings, and no further gunfire echoed through the night. O'Connell's body had fallen to the floor, and what was left of his head was shaped like a bowl. Sadly, Walker felt, it would be a lesser man or woman who took O'Connell's seat at City Hall, yet neither he nor any other good citizen of San Diego could have suspected just how wicked the new mayor would turn out to be.

***

Finding himself with a rare quiet moment, Chasquas took the opportunity to settle onto the sofa and stretch out his long legs. Born with a rangy, wiry body with hands and feet of extraordinary size, he'd been dubbed "Sasquatch" by his best friends on the streets of Honduras, but since none of their knowledge was obtained from books, the legend of the massive gorilla man had been spread by word of mouth alone, hence the misspelling.

How far I've come since then, he thought in Spanish, sweeping his gaze over the relatively luxurious interior of one of his many safe houses as the sound of an incoming text message reached his ears. He scooped up his burner phone, read the message, grunted with satisfaction, lurched to his feet, strode out to the driveway, and brought his motorcycle to life. Lifting his boots, he rolled down onto the street, and the black cruiser bike gave an aggressive growl as it carried him off into the night.

At the National City Marine Terminal, Chasquas braked to a stop and leaned the bike on its kickstand, then headed for a superyacht moored at a private dock. Not looking forward to this encounter, but not dreading it, either, he reached under his shirt to draw his P320 Spectre XCompact and pulled the slide back enough to make sure the first round was loaded. *Never hurts to double-check*, he mused in Spanish, reholstering the pistol and adjusting his shirt to conceal it. When he reached the entrance to the dock, the two security guards—both white, of course—didn't pat him down since he was a frequent visitor, but they did blast him with what they believed were menacing scowls.

Unfazed, Chasquas stepped aboard and found Ronnie Locke in the usual spot, sitting alone on a brown leather sofa in his private domain, a study/lounge that overlooked a night-lit swimming pool. A tall, flabby man with curly black hair and a bushy mustache, Locke didn't rise to greet him or even look his way.

"It's done," Chasquas announced. He was used to dealing with rough and vulgar business associates, but still couldn't understand Locke's total lack of courtesy.

"Good." Locke snatched up a remote and aimed it at a wall-sized flat-screen TV. News of the former mayor's death was being shown on several channels.

Uninvited to do so, Chasquas took a seat beside his client on an adjacent sofa, shrugged off his backpack, and pulled out a half kilo of cocaine. After handing it over, he sat there feeling stupid as the white man pulled a knife from his pocket and sampled the delivery. Locke took his time, even sitting back between snorts to revel in the experience and refreshing himself every so often with a sip from his tumbler before returning to the task at hand.

"Help yourself to a drink at the bar," Locke muttered grudgingly.

"*No gracias*," Chasquas returned, taking to his feet in exasperation and heading for the window. There he lit a cigarette, his last remaining vice, and smoked while resting his eyes on the pool's turquoise glow. When he turned back around, San Diego's future mayor finally seemed to be slowing down.

Locke looked up. "I can only pay you half. Take it or leave it."

Chasquas immediately whipped out his pistol and lined up the greedy man in his sights.

"Can't blame me for trying," said Locke, raising his hands in surrender and faking a sheepish grin. Then he strode to his desk, pulled out a bag of money, paid his supplier, and dismissed him with a jerk of the chin toward the door.

Chasquas didn't leave right away; he stayed to count his money, and while he did, Locke picked up the phone. Chasquas wondered who was on the other end of the line, and from what he could hear, he guessed it was one of Locke's many donors. He also supposed that the purpose of the call was to confirm the assassination of Mayor O'Connell, which Chasquas had arranged for a price. The money was all there. As he spun on his heel and headed down the stairs, Locke's roaring laughter echoed in the night, following him all the way back to his motorcycle.

Chasquas shook his head in disgust. This was only the first part of the plan, he knew. Ronnie Locke was being groomed to run for the highest office in the nation.

***

Walker's SWAT instructors gave him the next morning off to serve as a pallbearer at Mayor O'Connell's funeral mass, which was so well attended that the sea of people who'd come to pay their respects spilled out of the sanctuary and into the street. He sat in the pews with DAI Dominick Taylor, who was putting together a multi-agency task force to investigate the mayor's assassination, and Taylor had asked Walker to join the team.

"You sure you can't make it work?" Taylor whispered.

"I would if I could," Walker replied softly so as not to interfere with the priest's homily.

An ex-Special Forces soldier, Taylor was nearly as big as Park but white like Walker, with black hair clipped to quasi-military specifications. "I know you would," he said. "Sorry for insisting."

"What have you got so far?"

"Not much," said Taylor. "We found the sniper's perch, but the evidence techs only bagged a couple of hairs and no match has occurred so far."

"What was the shooting distance?"

"Eight hundred yards."

"You're looking for a trained sniper."

"I know."

"And the projectile?" Walker blurted out in his normal voice, forgetting where he was for a moment.

"7.62 NATO. The ballistic tests aren't back yet," Taylor replied just as loudly.

The lawmen's passion for the subject matter earned them several angry stares and someone even shushed them. Wary of causing further offense, they dropped respectful contributions into the offertory basket when it came around, and took the conversation outside.

After the burial, Walker drove back up to San Bernardino to continue his SWAT training. Despite the heavy burden of the death of yet another friend, he made it through the program, which included vehicle assaults, hand-to-hand fighting, and complex team-based scenarios. The most important skill he developed there was tactical coordination, meaning working, moving, and fighting as a team, and the biggest lesson learned was that his unit's effectiveness in the domination of an opposing force would require continual training and refinement.

The following Monday, Walker did not report to Sergeant Cheatham's morning briefing. Instead, he drove to the National City Marine Terminal, where he rendezvoused with five other Harbor Police officers, each of whom was also a MARTAC operator. When he pulled up in his white Mustang, he would have seen one other man standing at attention on the dock, but Park was still away on special assignment, now on his third week-long cruise.

"Welcome to MARTAC," bellowed Sergeant Steve Ortiz, the team leader, a heavy-set blond man who looked like he'd been nursed from a bottle of testosterone extract. Ortiz clapped Walker on the back far too hard before the rest of the team offered their congratulations and they all stepped aboard a patrol boat. At first Walker had thought that MARTAC might subject him to a mock beat-down, as they used to do, but that was no longer standard practice, not since Park's first day, when he'd clocked Ortiz before he knew it was a prank.

The team donned full firefighting gear on the way to the Mar-Tac Trainer, which is located just offshore on a barge. Built at a cost of nearly four hundred thousand dollars, the training facility has remotely controlled burn chambers in which firefighting drills can be run in a simulated shipboard environment under real-life conditions, and that's exactly what they did all morning. In the afternoon, they switched to hostage scenarios. For this activity, MARTAC was clad in full tactical gear: green fatigues, helmets with comms, Nomex gloves, slip-resistant boots, eye protection, and ballistic vests, which was fortunate because suddenly, in the middle of an exercise, the baritone voice of MARTAC's new commander came crackling out of the radio.

Ortiz held his ear to the device as he received his instructions, then turned to his team and barked, "Code twelve, guys! This is not a drill."

5

THE OASIS

Port of Los Angeles
Embarkation day

While sailing aboard the *Radiance* on the first week-long cruise, SA Scott Phillips, SSA John Kerr, and Detective Tony Park had, in their opinion, successfully mingled with the passengers while finding subtle ways to approach the suspected employees, and nothing unusual had occurred over those seven days.

Before they boarded the *Sensation* the following Tuesday, Chief Richards proposed that he should be the one to bring the team's weapons and tactical gear aboard, and that the team should stand in line, pass through security, and roll their normal luggage up the gangway—the better to blend in with their fellow guests. Except for that one difference, the second voyage proceeded much like the first, with no attempted crimes nor any other incident.

Thus, by the third voyage, the trio knew what to expect and had established a system that worked. On embarkation day, while roasting in the cruise terminal before coming aboard the *Oasis*, a ship identical to the other two, they resolved that their discomfort should best be alleviated by a trip to the pool, where they'd sip on ice-cold refreshment and review the new suspect list. But they couldn't crack open the case files in public, of course, so Park would make use of his photographic memory to brief them on the details. After settling in to their cabins, they headed for the more secluded of the two swimming pools, took their places at a shady table, and ordered a pitcher of virgin margaritas.

"All right, guys," said Park. "The first one's a musician in the band, a singer named Amanda Boydon. She's thirty years old, with a Texas address. Charismatic and intelligent by all accounts, and I'm sure you remember her photograph."

"Oh yeah! The big-chested blonde," exclaimed Kerr, who hadn't changed into swim trunks and a T-shirt, unlike his fellows. The prosthetics he wore to create the appearance of a weight problem required him to be overdressed at all times.

"That's an easy one," said Phillips. "We'll be impressed by her voice no matter how bad it is, then buy her drinks between sets."

"Good," said Park, "but I'm supposed to be getting married, and you're a lot closer to her age than Kerr is, so you should take point on that one."

Phillips nodded.

Kerr looked disappointed.

Park moved on to the next potential perpetrator. "Angelo dela Cruz. A forty-year-old Filipino man. He's the ship's executive chef, so he has easy access to knives. He's also a frequent visitor to the passenger bars on his nights off, where he's been seen leaving with both women and men."

"Sounds like a job for a big guy like yourself," Kerr jested.

"I'll remember you said that," Park fired back. "Actually, dela Cruz plays basketball on a regular basis, so I'm thinking Phillips and I might run into him on the court. But the third suspect is about your age, and he likes to read. Staff Captain Kevin Massolt, born and raised in the Netherlands. A minor celebrity on the *Oasis*. With near-daily VIP dinners and meet-the-captain cocktail parties, plus your cover as an author, he should be right up your alley."

"Touché."

The fourth suspect was a comedian, one Steve Russo from New York City, thirty-five years of age. According to the file, they'd most likely find him flocked by female groupies after his shows, and he often played cards in the casino until late night became early morning. "I'll keep an eye on him," Park volunteered. "Watch him perform, then head to the casino to gamble with him."

The fifth crew member who had sailed on all four deadly cruises was Danielle Jackson from Arizona. The kid's club manager, twenty-five years of age. Chief Richards had spoken with her supervisor, who'd indicated that the young woman was a bit of a recluse after work, but that she was the sweetest person who'd ever set foot in the daycare facility.

"That doesn't mean anything," Kerr opined. "Serial killers are good at blending in, at working undercover, so to speak. The unsub often turns out to be the person you were least likely to suspect."

"But how can we get to her?" Phillips wanted to know. "What are we going to do, disguise ourselves as five-year-olds?"

That got him a laugh.

"Maybe Richards can help," Park suggested.

"I'll text him, see what he says," said Kerr.

Then they all rose from the table. "What do you say, Phillips?" Park asked. "Feel like a run?"

***

As the *Oasis* motored out of the Port of Los Angeles, Park and Phillips headed for the open-air basketball court on the top deck, and before long, Angelo dela Cruz did, in fact, make an appearance, showing up with a fellow member of the kitchen staff.

The four guys shot around for a bit, warming up while gauging each other's abilities. Phillips had a good three-pointer, Park noted, and he was also fairly large, while the executive chef might have measured five feet nine on a good day. The fourth player, a trim and agile Black man by the name of Wilson, was about as tall as Phillips.

When the inevitable occurred, Park suggested they mix up the teams, thinking his and Phillips' size would confer an impossibly unfair advantage.

"Nah, we're good," said Wilson. "I played in high school, and Cookie here was a college all-star."

Phillips tossed the ball to him. "Cool. You guys take it out."

Wilson took his place at the top of the key and checked the ball to Phillips, ensuring that the defenders were ready, and Phillips passed it back. As soon as Wilson caught the ball, he lobbed it over the special agent's head to dela Cruz, who suddenly materialized between Park and the basket and scored an easy layup.

Park growled like an angry dog, vowing that it would never happen again as Phillips offered him an encouraging slap of the hand.

They were playing half-court, winners' outs, so Wilson took it out again. This time he passed to dela Cruz and stood aside, far from the hoop. Phillips stayed on him, which gave dela Cruz a chance to go one-on-one with Park. The Filipino was light on his feet; in a blaze of dribbles through his legs, he whirled and juked until Park took a false step, then shot past his massive defender and darted to the hoop to attempt another layup. Phillips hurried over to block him out, but dela Cruz tossed the ball high over the basket as Wilson came soaring through the air, caught the ball easily, slam-dunked it, landed on the rubbery game tile, and bumped proud fists with dela Cruz.

Two to zero. Playing to eleven.

As the game progressed, Park and Phillips developed a successful strategy: Phillips would shoot long bombs from behind the line, which counted for two, and Park would use his size and strength to recover the shots his teammate missed. This brought the score to eight to seven. Apparently, dela Cruz wasn't used to losing; his irritation had been mounting throughout the contest, and when he tossed the ball to Phillips at the start of another point, he hit him in the side of the head.

"Sorry," said the chef with a straight face. "I thought you were ready."

"Watch yourself," said Phillips sharply.

At ten to ten, game point, Park was dribbling with his back to the basket against heavy resistance offered by Wilson. Phillips, who'd made several critical two-pointers, stood outside the line calling for the ball, which gave dela Cruz no choice but to cover him. So Park backed Wilson up to the hoop, faked a spin move—at which Wilson jumped—then went the other way and dunked.

Livid, dela Cruz stormed up to Park and shoved him in the chest with two hands.

"Hey!" shouted Phillips. "The game's over, buddy. Take the loss and shake his hand."

"Fuckin' cheaters," muttered the chef, who made like he was about to walk away, but suddenly he whirled back around and threw a front kick to Park's groin.

Park was ready for it. He caught the leg and swept the other one out from under dela Cruz, then pounced on the much smaller man and twisted his arm behind his back in a hammer-locking Kimura. "Relax," he told the angry chef.

Phillips took up a strong position between Wilson and the short-lived scuffle, and Wilson decided not to get involved. By then, a sizeable group of spectators had amassed, and one of them called for security.

As dela Cruz was led away, he fixed a molten gaze on Park and Phillips.

Later, Chief Richards agreed that dela Cruz should not be locked in the brig, nor fired, nor charged with any crime. If they were going to catch the killer, Phillips had argued by text message, all five suspects needed to remain free and under no apparent suspicion. So the chef was released with only a warning.

***

John Kerr stepped into his "fat suit," a full-body undergarment that helped to make him unrecognizable. Then he touched up his 3D prosthetic makeup, ensuring that his jowls and multiple chins looked real. Satisfied, he shrugged on an enormous dinner jacket and strode out of his stateroom, heading for a VIP event with all the senior officers. Kerr wasn't paying thousands of dollars a night for a luxury suite, of course, but Richards had gotten him on the guest list based on his status as a celebrity. It had taken the criminal profiler a week to memorize the details of the seven crime fiction novels he'd supposedly written.

On the elevator ride up to the most exclusive deck on the *Oasis*, Kerr drew a nervous breath. He was leaning toward Staff Captain Kevin Massolt as the most likely suspect, since the officer would have ample opportunity to lure the guests into a situation of vulnerability at these VIP events. And according to Excelsior's records, three of the four victims had attended at least one of these big-ticket gatherings.

Kerr's artificial jowls folded into a frown. People willing to throw away five grand a night for a bed on a boat didn't tend to be approachable or pleasant, in his opinion. But as the elevator doors slid open, he forced his scowl to retreat, straightened his tux, and headed for a private room in the best restaurant on the *Oasis*, determined to seek common ground with the ship's elite.

Every guest's name had been meticulously calligraphed on thick cream-colored cards set out on the tables, so Kerr found his place and theatrically eased himself down into an upholstered dining chair. He quickly spotted Kevin Massolt at a different table, too far away to engage in casual conversation. A well-groomed man getting on in years, the senior officer had gray hair and a gray mustache, and he was clad in formal evening wear similar to a Navy dinner dress uniform. As the meal progressed, Kerr stole glances at Massolt, watching him and his fellow officers entertain the well-dressed passengers at their table.

Kerr reached for his drink, catching the eye of an older woman at the next table over with a little white dog curled up in her lap. *Unbelievable*, he grumbled to himself, but he raised his glass to her, managed a smile, and took a pull.

After an excruciatingly long meal consisting of six bite-sized courses made from ingredients Kerr had no idea how to pronounce, he and several other men moved to an adjacent lounge for brandy and cigars. His fellows seemed well acquainted with each other, and they drifted into tight clusters of roaring laughter. So it was, whether by accident or design, that Kerr found himself excluded. He settled into an overstuffed club chair with a good view of the room, swirled the aromatic liquid in his brandy snifter, took a relaxing drink, and set his mind to work on the present case.

The killer's signature was unusual; no matching precedent had been found in the ViCAP database, and no part of Kerr's long experience was pointing him in any particular direction. With no new information and after several stiff drinks, it was easy for his thoughts to turn to another matter: his illustrious career. Weary now after thirty-five years of high-profile assignments, international prestige, and six-figure book deals, Kerr had only one regret. Fortunately, before his mind could delve any further into the tragic episode that haunted his every day and night, someone came his way.

"I hear you're an author," said Staff Captain Kevin Massolt, in halting English with a European accent. He offered Kerr a fifty-dollar cigar before dropping into a nearby club chair and lighting one up for himself.

"That's correct," Kerr replied, then rattled off a summary of the computer-generated crime thriller series that his alter ego had supposedly written instead of the nonfiction volumes on serial homicide and criminal psychology he'd actually penned.

"From where do you get your ideas?" the European inquired.

"That's the trick," said Kerr, blowing out a puff of fragrant smoke. "Real-life events, I suppose."

A thin smile played at the corners of Massolt's mouth. "Like the murders on these Mexican routes, you mean."

Kerr's heart skipped a beat. He couldn't tell whether the officer knew he was being investigated, or if he just liked to gossip after a few drinks.

"You have not heard?" asked Massolt. "It is meant to be a secret, but I think there is no problem. You seem to be—how do you Americans say? A stand-up guy."

Kerr gave the suspect a slow and serious nod. Massolt was right. Kerr *was* a stand-up guy. If it was the last thing he ever did, he was going to stand up one more time and send a monster to prison.

***

After the incident on the basketball court with dela Cruz, Tony Park took a shower and headed back out. With Kerr at the VIP dinner and Phillips off to watch Amanda Boydon and the band, he was on his own. The elevator had already come several times, always full, so finally he gave up and took the stairs, descending carefully, remaining alert to his surroundings and particularly ready for dela Cruz to come crashing through a door with a chef's knife in his hand. He was reassured, however, by the bulge of his Glock 19 in a BlackPoint Tactical inside-the-waistband holster.

The IWB rig had two small clips that curved over the top of his jeans and secured it to his belt, which he concealed with an extra-baggy short-sleeve shirt.

With time to kill before Steve Russo's comedy show, he was on his way to the kids club, hopefully to get a look at Danielle Jackson, the manager there. When he reached his destination, he ambled past the daycare room and caught a glimpse of her through the open door. Recognizing the young Black woman from her photograph, he watched for a moment as she hovered over a low table, wiping faces while the boys and girls in her charge devoured their ice cream. Like a mother hen, she looked about the room, casually at first, smiling, then studiously with a furrowed brow, then frantically as her eyes widened in alarm. "Where's Tammy?" she cried. "Tammy!"

Park popped his head into the room. "Is everything all right, miss?"

"One of my kids is missing!"

All the victims thus far had been adults, but that didn't mean a thing. Not until Tammy was found, if she was found at all.

6

COPS AND ROBBERS

San Diego, California

Walker and his fellow MARTAC operators piled into the patrol boat and raced out of the bay into open water. The code-twelve incident had something to do with a burning ship, but that's all that was known at the time, so they traveled in tactical position, kneeling at the bow with rifles ready, stabilizing each other as the vessel cut through the waves. In the wheelhouse, Detective Abbott stood at the helm and Sergeant Ortiz was on the radio with Lieutenant Coffin.

"It's a container ship," came Ortiz's voice in their comms a minute later, which was a relief since they'd all been worried the vessel in question might be an oil tanker. "And there's no sign of any hostiles. Our objective is to locate and rescue the survivors."

As the massive ship hove into view, Walker's eyes climbed fifty meters to the main deck, where raging flames were eating away at the stern and midships, and thick black smoke billowed into the air. One group of survivors stood at the bow, waving their arms in distress, and another bobbed below them in the water.

Abbott throttled back as they drifted closer, into what felt like a rainstorm because two Harbor Police Firestorm vessels were already on scene. Those larger boats were dousing the container ship with roof-mounted monitors at four thousand gallons a minute.

"Deploy the ladder!" commanded Sergeant Ortiz, at which point an operator known as Furious used a telescopic pole to attach a long ladder to the railing at the bow of the blazing ship.

"It's gonna be trial by fire, Walker," Ortiz joked, punching him in the shoulder as MARTAC started climbing up to evacuate the crew. It was a chaotic operation executed on unstable surfaces amid a cacophony of shouting voices, and they had no time to waste; if the fire hit the engine room, the explosion could kill them all.

Sergeant Ortiz, now on the ship's main deck, bellowed into the ear of the last crew member in sight, "Is there anyone else aboard?" before that crew member descended to the safety of what had grown into a fleet of patrol boats.

"Yes!" the man replied. "See that yellow crane up there? It fell and blocked the way as we were running to the bow."

Ortiz followed the man's gaze, then turned to two of his guys and barked, "On me!"

Walker and Furious hustled after their leader, scaling tall stacks of containers to reach midships. As they climbed even higher to avoid the encroaching flames, the metal seared their hands through their heat-resistant gloves, and the caustic smoke stung their eyes. When they reached the topmost container, they looked down at the toppled crane, which had, in fact, prevented a group of sailors from reaching the bow.

"Help!" the sailors cried, all with soot-blackened skin and most in respiratory distress. Worst of all, one of them was trapped under the crane, which had most likely crushed his legs.

"Our whole team couldn't drag him out from under it," Ortiz muttered.

Then, from somewhere deep within the ship, there came a series of explosions that shook the hull and threw Walker off the edge of the container. For a terrifying second, he hovered in mid-air, facing a long fall into the inferno, but Furious shot out his arm and grabbed his fatigues while dropping his own body to the top of the container. Furious hung on to Walker with one arm, then added the other, giving Ortiz time to race over and assist. As the three men clambered to their feet, the cargo ship gradually heeled to port until it lay at a sharp angle.

"Look!" said Furious, pointing at the yellow crane. It had slid free of the passage!

While Furious and Walker helped the sailors up to the top of the container and led them to the bow, Sergeant Ortiz climbed down to the injured man, hefted him onto his back, and carried him to safety even as the burning ship began to sink. At the bow, Furious stood ready at the top of the ladder, and Ortiz transferred the injured sailor to Furious's shoulders with only seconds to spare. As the ship went down, Walker and Ortiz took a running leap off the upper deck and into the choppy sea. They reached the patrol boat just as Furious did, and as soon as they were helped aboard, Abbott threw the throttle forward and headed for one of the Firestorms.

Ten minutes later, Walker and Furious were standing shoulder to shoulder on the deck of the fire boat. They were similar in terms of weight and height, but Furious was Black and Walker white. "Thanks, man," said Walker.

Furious turned to meet his gaze, grinned, and offered a fist bump. "I got you, brotha," he said.

Walker's heart leapt with emotion. He didn't know what to say. No one had called him that since David Goode had died saving his life six years ago. He wiped his cheeks, smacked Furious's knuckles without a word, and then got back to work.

***

When Chasquas rolled his right hand back, his burly ride responded, shooting onto the freeway with gut-wrenching acceleration. The 116cu, or 1900cc, machine was an Indian Chief Dark Horse Motorcycle, modified for extra speed and acceleration. Chasquas thought the name fitting, since he was the chief of the SoCal Syndicate as well as a Native American—native Central American, to be precise—and he had *always* been a dark horse. The two-wheeler hit a hundred in seconds, flooding him with elation, and as he sped away from the coast and into the mountains, the air whooshing past grew cool and fresh.

It had been a good day so far. The bombing of the container ship, intended to divert the authorities from their regular surveillance of maritime traffic, had served its purpose. Now that his three narcotics-laden speedboats had made it into US waters, he felt much better about their chances of reaching the Carlsbad facility without incident.

The only drug that Chasquas's organization sold but didn't import was methamphetamine. That substance was produced locally, and it was the reason for his ride up into the hills. As he pulled off the mountain highway onto a backcountry road, he steeled himself against the heavy temptation he was about to face. "Ice," or *hielo* as it was known in Honduras, had always been his drug of choice, ever since he was a young street hustler, and the bikers he'd come to visit were swimming in it.

An armed guard waved him into a gated compound with twenty rustic structures, some large, others like cabins at a campground. He rolled straight up to one of these—a motorcycle repair shop with rock music blasting through its wide-open doors—then set his ride on its kickstand and headed inside, where ten men in boots, jeans, and leathers were working on bikes, sitting at tables with beers and drugs, or sweet-talking nearby white women. To Chasquas's disgust, many of them had shaven heads and swastika tattoos.

"Amigo!" bellowed their leader, Stephen Baker, the only surviving member of the North County Kings. Less than a year before, after all the other bikers had died in the Battle of Cumbres Casino, Baker had founded his own club and dubbed it the East County Warlords.

A muscular man in his forties with a protruding belly, Baker turned his attention from the engine he was working on to his most important client. He stood up, wiped his greasy hands on a towel, and led the way to his office, where they took a seat on either side of a desk.

"I need a fast order," Chasquas said in stilted but adequate English. "Twenty pounds."

"Pickup or delivery?"

"Delivery. I text you the location. Ask for Daniels."

And that was most of what transpired on Chasquas's short visit to the rural compound. On his way back down the mountain, he reflected on his recent alliance with Stephen Baker. At first he'd been skeptical, since the biker had ties to the now-defunct Cartel del Norte, Chasquas's old enemies. And the same was true of another new associate, a former Army sniper by the name of Rick Daniels. But if those two could put the past behind them, then so could he.

As the heavy machine screamed down to sea level like a rollercoaster plunging down the tracks, Chasquas recalled how it had come into his possession. The memory of gunning down Chucky Matón and escaping on the man's brand-new Indian Chief would have caused him to burst into drug-fueled laughter as recently as six months ago, but not anymore. Chasquas was a serious professional now, a new man with major responsibilities, whose mouth was set in a hard line as he rode on to the next business meeting.

***

Duke's Bar & Grill was crowded, even more than usual, as many officers who'd participated in the container ship rescue had gone there to unwind. In fact, on any given night, the majority of the patrons at that lively joint were Harbor Police, SDPD, Sheriff's Department, or from another law enforcement agency.

"We got a NIBIN lead," DAI Dom Taylor said to the people surrounding him, referring to the National Integrated Ballistic Information Network and the bullet that had killed the mayor. "The rifle may have been the same weapon fired last year in another killing."

"Is it a confirmed match?" asked Sergeant Ortiz, who sat across from him.

"Negative. We'd need to have found the casing."

And that was the extent of Taylor's good news; little else was known about the assassination of a man whom everyone at the table had held in high regard.

"To Mayor O'Connell," said Walker. "May he rest in peace."

They all rose: Ortiz, Furious, Abbott (the patrol boat pilot), Chief Deputy DA Lynn Peters, Dom Taylor, and two other MARTAC operators, to bring their glasses together.

"Guess who's running in the special election," Furious remarked after they'd all settled back into their chairs.

Lynn Peters looked disgusted. "Ronnie Locke," she muttered, then turned to Walker. "Jeff and I were just talking about him."

Walker nodded. The wealthy businessman had made public statements condoning violence against illegal immigrants, the homeless, and race-related protesters. Locke had even gone so far as to show support for neo-Nazi groups, citing freedom of speech and the right to assemble.

"I can't believe anyone would vote for that piece of shit," Lynn Peters went on. She almost never swore, so the comment drew a laugh.

"He's popular," argued Sergeant Ortiz.

"He'd never win in a fair election," countered Abbott.

"Exactly," growled Furious. "Won't be nothin' fair about it."

Abbott nodded in agreement. Tall and wiry, the bespectacled MARTAC operator was a Stanford graduate and the only other detective on the team besides Park and Walker. He held Furious's gaze and said, "Did you know his party's been accused of hacking voting machines, gerrymandering, absentee ballot fraud, and voter suppression?"

"Both parties are making those claims," Sergeant Ortiz protested hotly. "It's hard to know who the bad guys are."

"Bullshit," Furious shot back, locking eyes with his team leader. "It's as plain as black and white."

"Come on guys. Same team," said Walker. "I gotta go."

By the time he got home, little Tina Michelle was asleep in her bed, but her younger sister, Mia, was still up with her mom. They were watching an animated movie on Walker's bed.

"She was waiting up for you," said Tina, his wife, as he leaned down to kiss her.

Walker's precious child held his gaze as he came around the bed. *She looks so much like me,* he thought, easing down to cradle her neck with his arm as they watched the cartoon musical together. He'd seen the same movie with Mia so many times that both father and daughter knew every word and every song by heart. By the time the credits came on, she was sound asleep, so he carried his treasure to bed.

When he came back to Tina, their eyes locked right away, and they collided in a frenzy of lust that ended in mind-blowing waves of relief. Then they lay on their backs and held hands as the night air blew in through open windows, cooling their naked flesh. It had been a rough six years, but at last Walker and Tina were doing better. Learning to trust each other, showing mutual respect.

Before his thoughts drifted into a subconscious jumble, Walker did something he hadn't done in years. He gave thanks to his creator for the gift of life.

And then to Furious for saving it.

7

SEDUCTION

The *Oasis*
Embarkation day
8:00 p.m.

"Try to relax, miss," said Tony Park to Danielle Jackson, who was fanning her face with her hand and unsteady on her feet. "When did you last see Tammy?"

"She was just here!" the kids club manager wailed.

"How old is she?"

"Six."

"Maybe she went exploring," Park suggested. "Today's day one of an exciting adventure for her."

Jackson nodded.

The hallway outside the youth activity room fell silent as Park thought about how best to conduct a search for the missing girl and the kids club manager hung her head. Then, the distant sound of tiny running feet grew louder, both of their heads snapped up, and a little blonde girl hurried toward them, causing Miss Jackson to brighten right away. She picked up the crying child and held her tight.

"I found her wandering around on deck five," growled a man whose name tag identified him as a member of the security team. "Victor Cameron," he said, offering a firm handshake.

"Andy Hwang," said Park. "Thanks for bringing her back."

Jackson wiped the little girl's eyes. "Are you okay, honey? What happened?"

Tammy was calm again, happily playing with her babysitter's black braids. "Brian was being mean to me, so I ran away, but then I got lost." She pointed toward Cameron. "He got me a Sprite." Then the child let out a shockingly long and resonant belch, at which everyone had to laugh.

"'Preciate you," said Jackson sweetly to the security officer.

"No problem, miss," he replied, then nodded to Park and took his leave.

The young and lovely kids club supervisor spun on her heel and hit Park with a smile that made his mouth fall open. "And I *really* appreciate you," she said. Her creamy chocolate-brown skin glistened, her ample lips came apart, and her rocking bo—

Park forced himself to look away and turned his mind to the woman waiting for him in San Diego, the one who'd cried when he'd left for LA. He made a mental note to call her later.

"Hey, do you want to get a drink tonight?" Jackson asked, drawing so close that the intoxicating scent of her perfume threatened to reel him all the way in.

The last thing Park's better self wanted him to do was get a drink with her that night, but—for the sake of the investigation—he let out a grin that was begging to appear on his face and allowed his lips to speak the words, "I'd love to."

***

SSA John Kerr, the FBI profiler in disguise, and his assigned suspect, Staff Captain Kevin Massolt, had at this point, in addition to their dinner drinks, consumed two servings of brandy and taken the third out into the open air of the observation deck. As they paced about the ship's highest level, their half-smoked cigars glowed in the night, and when a strong wind began to blow, the twin red embers burned even brighter, like the eyes of a demon.

Encouraged by Kerr's friendly manner, Massolt had shared everything he knew about the murders, or so he'd said.

"Do you have any idea who the killer is?" Kerr asked as they strolled along.

"It cannot be a guest," Massolt answered in his hard European accent. "Excelsior has already compared the passenger manifests, and they would not let a repeat guest aboard. Not now. So it must be a member of the staff or crew on one of the ships."

"Not an officer?" Kerr asked, as if he didn't know Massolt was a suspect.

"No. I was the only one aboard for all four killings."

"The staff and crew, then."

"Yes. There are five of us on the *Oasis*," Massolt explained. "All the staff know who we are. News travels fast when the same people work in the same tiny space for months or years."

"Tiny space?"

"Yes. There are over a thousand employees who live on the lower decks, most of them in extremely cramped quarters, and nobody's room is as big as yours."

"So who do you think it is?"

"Amanda Boydon. The singer in the band."

***

Amanda Boydon beamed at her cheering fans at the end of her second set. She was decked out in a white dress that clung to her luscious figure, and those cascading blond locks along with a skillful application of cosmetics sealed the deal for Special Agent

Phillips. *She doesn't just look good*, he marveled to himself. *She hit every note while dancing like a pro!*

At the break he'd asked if he could buy her a drink when the show was over, and she'd accepted, so now she caught his eye and he stood, and they headed for a secluded corner of the lounge where heavy rain was needling the windows.

When a waiter appeared at their table, Phillips said, "Ladies first, Mrs. Boydon."

"It's *miss*," she returned with an inviting smile, then looked up at the server. "Hey, Joe. Crazy storm, huh?"

Joe agreed wholeheartedly.

"I'll have a gin and tonic, please."

Phillips asked for a glass of red wine, which, along with the singer's icy beverage, was soon set before them. "You were great," he said, as they clinked glasses and took first sips.

Her face lit up at once. "Thank you, Jack! What was your favorite song?"

"*Bésame Mucho.* Your Spanish is pretty good!"

"Pretty *fake*," she said with a laugh. "So where are your buddies?"

"Oh, Andy's seasick and Mark's at a VIP dinner."

"So I've got you all to myself," she purred.

Phillips wondered how many passengers Miss Boydon had charmed into her stateroom over the years, but as he drowned in her deep blue eyes he cared less and less. In fact, he was eager to be her next victim. When she commented on his lack of a wedding ring, he told her about his recent and painful divorce, which was absolutely true, and when she asked what he did for a living, he described his fictitious nine-to-five in the financial sector. "What about you?" he asked after that.

"Me? I'm a military girl. My father was a Marine, so we used to move around a lot before he passed away."

"I'm sorry to hear that."

"Thanks. At least I've got good memories."

"Like what?"

"He used to take me hunting."

"Killing, gutting, and skinning?"

"Yep. I really miss it." She giggled. "Not that part, of course. The time we spent together. You know what I mean."

"I do. But hunting?"

"I know. But my mom wasn't around, and I'm an only child, so he just did what made him happy and I was glad to go along for the ride."

They were drawn to each other like a pair of magnets; over another round, their conversation continued to flow effortlessly, and as Phillips signed the check, she asked if he'd like to take a tour of the lower decks, and he agreed. For the good of the investigation.

When they got down there, Phillips saw that the staff's quarters were vastly different from those of the passengers. It was a functional, no-frills environment. The hallways were narrow and uncarpeted, the walls unadorned, "and worst of all are the rooms," the stunning entertainer explained, grinning playfully as she unlocked her door and stepped inside. "Most of us have to share, but not the stars of the show."

"Are passengers even allowed down here?" he wondered as he followed her in and the door swung shut on its own.

"No, but the rules aren't always enforced."

"Not for the star of the show, right?" he asked, slipping his arms around her waist and pulling her close.

"Right," she murmured seductively as their lips came together.

Miss Boydon's room wasn't large by any means, but it did contain a queen-size bed, on which they made vigorous love for the next hour or so. Very shortly after that, her mouth fell open and she began to snore, but Phillips was wide awake. He sat up to peer through the porthole. The rain was falling in sheets blown sideways by gale-force winds, and the sea was unusually rough, rocking the ship from side to side like a toy in a bathtub.

Phillips got up, made his way to the bathroom, shut the door behind him, and searched her toiletry bag, finding a dropper bottle of clonazepam, which, he knew, is a strong depressant usually prescribed for anxiety or insomnia. This explained why Miss Boydon had fallen asleep so quickly, and also why she didn't even stir when he crashed around the cabin getting dressed.

On his way out, Phillips cast a final glance at the gloriously attractive woman lying on the bed, naked as the day she was born. He couldn't bring himself to imagine her as a serial killer. *She may know how to gut an animal*, he reasoned with a quarter of a brain, *but that doesn't make her a murderer*. He tucked her in and kissed her cheek, then headed back upstairs feeling euphoric, with only the faintest sense of doubt and guilt.

***

Park set a pile of chips next to his original bet on the green felt surface of the blackjack table. The dealer looked him in the eye. Park's reply to the unspoken question was to spread out two fingers on the table like the letter V, prompting the well-dressed casino employee to split Park's pair of eights and deal him two losing hands instead of one.

The undercover detective shook his head and blew out a frustrated sigh. They were using six decks at every table in a continuous shuffle machine as well as a very short discard pile, meaning he didn't have enough information to make any money, even with his eidetic memory. He'd already done the math and the guaranteed winnings came out to a dismal two dollars per hour, but only if he stretched his great brain to the limit. *Look on the bright side, man*, he told himself. *Now you can focus on establishing rapport with your suspect, which you should have been doing all along.*

"Bad luck, buddy," said Steve Russo, who was sitting to Park's right. A handsome fellow with a strong jawline and dark eyes, the comedian waved a hand over his own cards to indicate his decision to stay with what he had, and he ended up beating the dealer.

"Thanks," Park replied. "I caught your show, by the way. You remind me of Tony Danza."

In the next hand, Park was dealt the king of hearts and the four of spades, while the dealer showed the ten of clubs and one card face down. As Park tapped his finger on the felt, he wondered whether the FBI would reimburse him for his losses, and he was promptly given the eight of hearts, busting him again. *By only one!* A flash of anger made him want to break something.

Russo, whose luck had been trending strongly in the opposite direction, turned to Park again as he raked in his chips. "Have you heard the one about the old man who kept winning at cards?"

"No," said Park with a smile. "How does it go?"

"An elderly gentleman was playing at a table like ours, but the game was poker, and he always seemed to have an ace just when he needed it. So the other players start to get frustrated and ask, 'What's your secret, sir?'

'I've got on my lucky sweater,' the man replies. 'It was a gift from my sister.'

So the game goes on, the old man's winning streak continues, and the other players flat-out accuse him of cheating. 'What do you have up your sleeve?' they demand.

He pulls up his sleeves to show them, and there's nothing there.

Muttering and grumbling, they turn back to their hands. On the old man's next play, he lays down an ace and wins again! Now, of course, everyone's furious, and they all stand up and shout, 'It's that goddamn cardigan!'"

Park burst into a badly needed belly laugh, and the dealer and the other players were equally amused.

Russo smiled. "Let me buy you a drink, bro."

Park had already watched the charismatic entertainer polish off four whiskeys, and not with a small amount of envy, *but I'll be dammed if I'm going back to my old bad habits*, he thought, so when he and Russo strolled up to the bar, he asked for soda water.

They spoke for half an hour on topics ranging from the ups and downs of Russo's career to "Andy Hwang's" profession and his upcoming wedding, but their discussion was often interrupted by other passengers who'd seen Russo's show, attractive female passengers predominating.

Just as Park was about to leave, Russo said, "There's a theater cast party tomorrow night. Do you want to come?"

"Sure," Park replied, rising unsteadily to his feet; the ship's rocking had grown violent. "Whoa!"

"Yeah! Big storm," Russo remarked, nodding toward the blasting rain on the windows. "Hey, thanks for keeping me company." He stood as well, offering his hand.

Park had to admit that Russo was incredibly likeable. The man had captured the attention of a crowded theater for over an hour with his witty, well-timed banter, then stepped offstage and won big in the casino, tipped the dealer generously, and bought a discouraged stranger a drink to cheer him up. Yet as Park hustled off to his next commitment, he couldn't help wondering what the comic was like when the magic ran out.

"Hey you," Danielle Jackson cooed, standing to greet him as he strode into the Neptune Lounge. Gone were her youthful shorts and T-shirt from earlier in the day. Now she wore a dress, a long black sequined number that split high up on the leg, showing off her muscular yet indisputably feminine features to maximum advantage. As she took his hands and leaned in for a cheek-to-cheek greeting, her soft touch and mind-blowing perfume pulled Park's mind in a direction that made alarm bells go off in his head.

"I ordered you a drink, to thank you for helping me earlier," she said, perching herself on a stool at a tall round table with a graceful self-assurance Park thought unusual for such a young woman.

He took a seat opposite her and glanced down at a double scotch on the rocks that brought to mind his and Walker's first case: on the North Shore of Oahu, a female serial killer had slipped a pill into Walker's drink and nearly succeeded in taking his life. "I'm an alcoholic," Park said.

"Oh! I'm so sorry," Jackson exclaimed, sliding off her stool in an apologetic fuss. "You know what they say about assuming. Club soda? Coke?" she asked over her shoulder on her way to the bar.

When she returned with a cold club soda and resumed her perch, she leaned in close to meet his gaze, giving Park an uncomfortably good view of her cleavage. "So are you single, or are we just friends?" she murmured.

Park's gaze fell on those spectacular breasts. He wondered what they'd look like in their natural state and imagined what he'd like to do to her, and where, and how. And how *else*. But whoever was operating the alarm bells in his head was now ringing them with such thunderous insistence that the clanging ripped him out of his fantasy and hurled him back down to the surface of Planet Earth, where he landed painfully.

Park, you moron! his better self berated him as he picked himself up and dusted himself off. *You are sitting with a person of interest in the federal investigation of a brutal series of homicides. Need I remind you of the woman of your dreams waiting faithfully in your bed back home? Whom you forgot to call, by the way. How would you feel if Carla slipped into a dress like that, sashayed downstairs, and invited the policemen stationed outside in for a drink?*

"Actually, I'm enga—" he started to say, but leapt to his feet as Miss Jackson was thrown from her stool by a patch of turbulence.

He grabbed her arm with both hands, steadying her just as a three-note melody came chiming through the PA system, followed by a commanding male voice: "May I have your attention please. This is your captain with an important announcement: a member of our crew is missing. I'm required by law to return the ship to that person's last known location at sea and conduct a reasonable search. And that means heading back into the storm, so the weather conditions will definitely get worse. At this time, there is no cause for alarm, but we do ask that you stay alert for further instructions and announcements. Thank you."

The ship was steady now, so Park let go of Miss Jackson. As he did, their eyes met and a slight smile crept at the corners of her lips.

Is she grateful for my assistance, Park wondered, *or laughing about the missing person?*

8

A BIG FAVOR

"Okay, bro. Stay safe," said Walker to Park before replacing the phone in its cradle. Then he went back to the pile of paperwork on his desk, but didn't get far at all. In fact, he'd only just picked up his pen when he got another call, this time on his cell. It was DAI Dom Taylor, who said he needed a big favor.

"Name it," said Walker with no hesitation.

"Oceanside PD reached out to me after receiving a citizen report of suspicious activity in the Agua Hedionda Lagoon. Strange men in ski boats were seen cruising through a residential inlet at four in the morning."

"And they don't trust the Port Authority to send a patrol boat."

"No, they don't," Taylor said. "And I'm stuck in court all day."

"No problem. I can check it out right now."

"Thanks. Two officers from Oceanside will meet you there. But be careful. One of the boats was a blue Mastercraft ProStar."

"The same model used by Cage's guard captains."

"Affirmative. And one of them is still unaccounted for. It could be just a coincidence, but you should take someone with you. Thanks, bro."

On his way out, Walker stopped at a neighboring cubicle. "Morning, Abbott," he said. "Are you free? I could use a wingman."

Walker drove Abbott over to Shelter Island, signed out a patrol boat, and took it up the coast, speeding past the wide mouth of Mission Bay to the right, followed by the beaches of La Jolla—which means "the jewel" in Spanish—an appropriate name for such a breathtaking location, in Walker's opinion. The vessel's hull slapped crest after crest as they continued on their northbound course, speeding by the cliffs for a mile or so, then the golden sands of the North County beaches, which stretched on and on until they came to the mouth of Agua Hedionda Lagoon. Walker veered to starboard, or right, and navigated across the outer lagoon, then passed under the freeway into the large inner body where the water was quite a bit calmer. At the far end of the inner lagoon, he motored into a tiny inlet.

While they both scanned its banks, watching for anything unusual about the fancy houses on both sides of the narrow channel, Walker said, "The report was made by a neighbor early this morning. We're looking for a—there it is!" He backed off the throttle and drifted up to a waterfront residence with three boathouse doors on the inlet.

They tied off at an adjacent dock and climbed the stairs to street level, where a police cruiser was parked a few blocks down the road. As they approached the vehicle, a broad-shouldered officer with his head shaven bald and a younger man stepped out to meet them halfway.

"Sergeant Larry Golino," said the older man, who, like his partner, wore a navy-blue uniform and a duty belt loaded with gear.

"Officer Matt Burke," grunted the younger officer.

Once everyone had shaken hands, Sergeant Golino mentioned that the citizen report had led him to suspect narcotics trafficking.

"Here in the lagoon?" Walker asked. "Oceanside Harbor's the usual place for that."

"It *used* to be," Golino said. "But after Taylor dismantled Jack Cage's operation, Internal Affairs started cleaning up the Port Authority."

Now Walker understood why Oceanside PD had requested a patrol boat: to prevent the crooks from escaping if necessary.

They sketched out a tactical plan, then set off for the target residence in a rough formation with Golino on point and Walker covering the rear. When they came to the stairs that led back to the inlet, Abbott peeled off and headed down to the patrol boat while the rest continued on to the front door with their service pistols still holstered. Seeing two black cruiser motorcycles leaning on their kickstands in front of the garage, Walker stopped to take a picture of the license plates, then rejoined the team just before Golino rang the bell.

***

"Get your asses down to the red boat," whispered Rick Daniels. "Quietly."

His visitors, two members of the East County Warlords, complied immediately.

Fucking bad luck, Daniels thought. The two bikers had arrived minutes earlier to deliver Chasquas's twenty pounds of ice; *if only they'd stopped for a beer on the way here*, he lamented, *I'd be alone, with nothing illegal (well, very little), and I could have just opened the door to see who it was. But of course they didn't*, seethed the ex-Army sniper as he crept past the front door on his way upstairs to the second floor. *And whoever it is just saw my shadow through the frosted glass. Anyway, even if it is the police, they can't kick the door in without a warrant.*

At the top of the stairs, he headed into a room on the right, stopped at the window, and looked down at the front porch. As he studied the cops' faces, his eyes locked onto one of them in particular—*Jeff Walker!*—and he finally understood why the late mayor's dinner companion had looked so familiar through the rifle scope at eight hundred yards. Catapulted six years back in time, Daniels re-lived a bloody firefight in which Miller, his mentor, had been killed by a tactical team that had somehow included Walker, a beach lifeguard at the time. But now Walker had gone into law enforcement, which wasn't surprising, since he'd been working with the police in Mazatlan when he threw Jack Cage off a cliff. But Miller's and Cage's deaths weren't the reason why Daniels' jaw was clenched in anger as he beheld his old enemy; it was because Maria, Daniels' true love, had also been killed in Mazatlan, and he held Jeff Walker responsible for it.

He eased the window open, stuck out his pistol's muzzle, and silently lined up his sights on the blond lawman.

***

While Detective Abbott waited in the patrol boat in case he had to prevent a waterborne getaway, it occurred to him that he might try to peer inside the boathouse, so he let out the tying line, drifted up to it, and put his eye to the edge of a sliding door. His field of vision was just a sliver, and darkness prevailed in the cavernous space, but he did distinguish the outline of a ski boat docked in a slip. Just then, the boathouse was flooded with light as two good-sized men sneaked down a set of stairs and silently boarded the ski boat. They waited there, rocking and bobbing, looking at each other uneasily until one of them fished a bag of powder out of his pocket and emptied it over the side of the boat.

Abbott's heart leapt. *Destruction of evidence! Exigent circumstances justifying a warrantless entry.* He stepped away to advise Walker by radio, then slipped into the water and swam under the boathouse door, propelling himself through the gloom to a far corner where he noiselessly broke the surface.

He heard no voices, just tiny waves slapping the hulls of three boats docked in a row, the farthest of which was the one he'd spotted through the crack. He unholstered his Glock 22 and held it in the air, treading water while moving along the hull of the closest boat. When he came to the edge, he chanced a peek and saw that the suspects had left the boathouse. *Maybe they heard me,* he speculated, clambering up onto the dock. *But if they did, why didn't they stay and fight?*

Abbott ejected the round from his pistol's chamber, caught it in mid-air, popped out the magazine, blew the gun dry, then pushed the round into the mag, which he slapped back in with a click. Next, he pulled back the action to chamber that round and prepared to enter the residence.

Straight ahead, a set of stairs led up to an open door. He extended his arms and peered through his iron sights at a sitting room with two couches and a TV. It was a corner-fed space, meaning there was only one blind corner to the left and nothing to the right but a wall. Still looking down the barrel of his gun, Abbott headed up the steps and "pied" the left edge of the doorway, gradually increasing his angle of vision until only a tiny slice of the far corner remained out of sight. Being careful not to expose his legs, he took a knee and cheated his gun to the right while leaning right, ready to pull the trigger in an instant, but the corner was clear.

Silently, he rose and hustled to the only other door, which was set in the middle of the far wall. This one was shut, and it appeared to lead into a center-fed space, meaning two blind corners, one on either side. With his Glock still leveled, Abbott steadied himself with a breath, threw the door open, and buttonhooked to the right. The corner was empty, but as he swept his sights toward the opposite side, he found himself in a slow-motion gunfight.

CRACK CRACK CRACK CRACK! came four shots from the left corner as Abbott swiveled onto two targets in ambush position. As he spun, he squeezed the trigger twice, dropping both hostiles before they could fire again. His first forty-caliber bullet drilled through the closest man's face, splattering the wall behind him with a chunky red mess, and the second round pierced the other guy's neck, producing a gushing, spurting wound that would quickly claim his life.

Abbott had been hit only once in the lower leg, and it wasn't a serious wound. He panned his pistol left and right, then all the way around to check his six.

Clear.

***

Sergeant Golino rang the bell several times, loudly identifying himself as a police officer, but no one came to the door. "Hey!" he barked, after a silhouette flew past the frosted glass. "We know you're in there!"

That's when Abbott came up on the radio advising exigent circumstances. "Roger that," said Walker, who happened to glance up at the second-story window to see the muzzle of a gun! He leapt to the side just as two rounds snapped past his head, then drew his Glock and returned fire, as did his fellow officers. Shattered glass rained down on them, and the man at the window slipped out of sight.

***

"Dammit!" hissed Daniels. It was a question of seconds before the cops kicked in the front door. Not only that, but judging by the gunfire coming from the ground floor, there was at least one other badge already in the house. He pulled open a drawer and scooped up a frag grenade. Darting silently out of the room with his big .45 in one hand and the explosive device in the other, he dropped into a crouch position at the top of the stairs. If the bikers were alive, they'd be waiting for him in the boathouse. *If not, then they won't get any deader*, Daniels reasoned, so he pulled the pin and threw the grenade at the far wall, off which it bounced into the entryway and detonated in close proximity to anyone who might be down there.

BOOM!

Daniels descended immediately, stopping at the wall's edge to slice the pie, and quickly identified the intruder. *A cop for sure.* The man was sprawled out on the floor, sopping wet and missing a large part of both his legs. Daniels strode forward to execute him, with no time for any last words and nothing more than a passing glance at the dead bikers.

A minute later, he was backing his blue Mastercraft out of the boathouse with a bubbling grumble. Just as Walker and the other cops burst into the boathouse, he threw the throttle forward and raced away, cutting across the two lagoons before hitting the open sea.

This was a major setback, of course. The Carlsbad facility, all three boats, and the armored Jeep Cherokee he'd left in the garage were useless now, and Chasquas would insist on being reimbursed for the missing drugs. Yet as Daniels steered the blue Mastercraft for the last time, he told himself he was still in good shape. Better than ever, in fact: he had plenty of cash after killing the mayor, and now that he'd found Jeff Walker, he'd finally take his revenge.

9

BACKSTAGE BLACKOUT

The *Oasis*
Day 2
8:00 a.m.

"The missing crew member is Angelo dela Cruz," said Richards, chief of security on the *Oasis*, speaking by videoconference with the three undercover investigators, who were gathered around a laptop in Special Agent Phillips' stateroom. "The executive chef. He was seen at the piano bar after the dinner shift, but he didn't make it back to the kitchen to close it down at two a.m."

"Was he with anyone in particular?" Park asked Richards' image.

The security chief shook his head. "The bartender said he was sitting with a group of random passengers, then left alone around ten."

"Were there any other staff or crew in the bar?" asked Phillips.

"None that he could recall, but the place was packed."

"The piano bar," John Kerr mused out loud, remembering Staff Captain Massolt's assertion that the singer was most likely to be the serial killer. "Isn't that where Amanda Boydon was performing?"

"No," said Phillips. "She was up in the Raven's Nest, and I can vouch for her after that." He proceeded to admit that he'd been in the singer's room and left her fast asleep at one in the morning.

Eyebrows were raised but no comments made, and everyone agreed that unless Miss Boydon had roused herself from a drug-induced slumber immediately after Phillips headed upstairs, she was probably above suspicion.

"But only with regard to dela Cruz's disappearance," clarified Chief Richards. "Not for the serial murders."

Everyone nodded.

"I was with Massolt until ten," said Kerr, "but that doesn't give him an alibi."

"And I left Steve Russo about eleven," added Park. "Then I met with Danielle Jackson, but only for a half an hour. So either of them could have gone after dela Cruz." Park's mind drifted back to the youth counselor's revealing black dress and intoxicating perfume, wondering if she'd literally been dressed to kill. "I like Miss Jackson for this."

"Do the suspects know about each other?" asked Phillips. "I mean, are they aware that dela Cruz was aboard when the killings occurred, just like them?"

"Yes," answered Kerr. "Massolt told me everyone knows."

"But why would the killer eliminate another suspect?" asked Park.

"I agree with you," Kerr replied. "That's counterintuitive. Remember, the unsub displays psychopathy, not psychosis. In other words, he hasn't lost touch with reality."

"He or *she*," said Phillips, "is not crazy. I get that. Not in the traditional sense of the word, anyway. But what's a psychopath again?"

"Psychopathy is a disorder characterized by shallow emotional responses, lack of empathy, impulsivity, and a propensity for antisocial behavior," Park quoted from an article he'd read in preparation for this assignment.

"Very good," said Kerr.

"Listen, guys. We've got another problem," said Chief Richards, who looked alarmed. "We were set to outrun a major storm system, but only barely, and now that the captain's turned the ship around, we're going to get caught in it."

"The weather's already terrible," said Kerr. "You mean worse than *this*, like a hurricane?"

"Yes."

****

"I miss you," said Carla sadly on the other end of the line.

"I miss you *more*," Park replied. "Are you gonna fly today?"

"No. I had a tour booked, but the weather's bad."

"So you're grounded. I hope *you* haven't been bad."

She giggled. Before he could suggest a spanking, she said, "So I don't know. Maybe I'll head over to Tina's house, play with the girls for a while."

Park's phone vibrated on his ear. It was a text message notification from Danielle Jackson, letting him know she'd just taken her break. "I gotta go," he said.

"Okay, honey. Be safe. I need you back here for happy hour." That's what they called their Netflix and chill sessions.

"Roger that. I love you, babe."

"Back atcha, Big T."

Park ended the call and hustled up to deck ten. His objective was to ask Miss Jackson what she'd been doing between ten and eleven the night before, prior to their meeting in the Neptune Lounge, and also where she'd gone after they parted ways. *Would those time windows have given her the opportunity to throw the chef overboard or stuff him in a crate?* he wondered as he came to a door at the top of the stairs and pulled it open. *Absolutely. Would she have been physically capable of it? No question; she outweighs dela Cruz by thirty pounds. But would she have wanted to?* That's where Park wasn't sure. All four victims had been passengers, not employees, so if Miss Jackson had killed the chef, it was a deviation from the pattern. Plus, Park saw her as gentle and sweet, not at all likely to have committed such violent crimes. On an unrelated note, she was drop-dead gorgeous.

He went over the plan as he strode toward the youth activity room: he'd pretend he'd changed his mind about her suggestive behavior of the night before. This would improve his chances of gaining information, but also plunge him back into temptation. As he rounded the final corner, he vowed not to cheat on Carla in thought, word, or deed.

Miss Jackson was waiting for him just outside the door, looking young and wholesome in a long pair of shorts and a kids club T-shirt.

"Hey you," he crooned, just as she had done, using the same words and the same seductive tone. "Can I buy you a Coke or something?"

"Sure," she replied, but not with any excitement. Then, as they headed for their destination, she grew increasingly sullen, providing ever shorter and more reluctant responses.

Is she playing with me? Park couldn't tell. He watched for her reaction when they came to the piano bar, which he'd selected in advance as the best place to speak to her, figuring that if she were involved in dela Cruz's disappearance, it might shake her up to visit the place where he was last seen and possibly where she'd picked him up.

Their sodas were set before them on a countertop that looped around a baby grand piano with no entertainer at the keys. Not this early. The only other people there besides the barman were two older women sitting in a corner sipping Bloody Marys, watching through the windows as the rain poured into the wind-whipped ocean.

"Do you know if they found the missing crew member?" was one of Park's first questions.

"No."

He wasn't bothered by her unresponsiveness; he already knew the answer—namely, that dela Cruz had not been spotted in the sea—and more importantly, her behavior was speaking volumes even if she wasn't willing to talk. Miss Jackson was obviously upset. *But by what?* "Are you okay?" he asked.

Silence.

"I heard a rumor," he persisted.

"Is that right."

"Someone said the passengers keep dying on Excelsior ships."

"Not as far as I know," she said, which couldn't possibly be true, then set down her Coke and swiveled in her stool to look him in the eye. "Listen, I don't want you to get the wrong idea. I'm not interested in anything romantic, and I want you to leave me alone."

Park was astonished, but he didn't let it show. "No problem," he replied. "It was nice meeting you."

"I have to get back to work. Goodbye," she said, then strode out the door with cold determination.

As he watched her go, Park wondered what could have led to this sudden reversal. Had she discovered she was under investigation? That he was working undercover? Perhaps, but he'd been exceedingly careful. Maybe she'd been disappointed by the "fact" that he was engaged, although when they'd said good night only nine hours before, she'd still seemed eager to take the encounter to a secluded location.

Park stayed by the piano to brood on the matter for another half an hour, and the only conclusion he was able to reach was an obvious one: she'd lied. Of *course* Excelsior's employees knew about the bloody murders. Frowning, he raised his glass to the older women at the window, who mirrored the gesture with the same absence of enthusiasm.

***

By that afternoon, the *Oasis* was pitching twenty feet between the crests and troughs of the surrounding waves, and while daylight would reign for several hours more in that part of the world, the seascape was so enveloped by the storm that the sun seemed to have already set. However, the captain had returned the ship to its original southbound course, heading for a port as fast as was safely possible, and despite the towering whitecaps' assault upon the vessel, with much more force than it was designed to withstand, no damage had been sustained so far.

Since Steve Russo was not scheduled to perform that evening, he and Park agreed to meet at the blackjack table, where Park won back what he'd lost the night before and then some. Conversely, the comedian was a shell of the man he'd been only twenty-four hours earlier: no witty banter, no luck at cards, no jokes, just slurping whiskey with his head down. As Park laid his final bet, he tried to make sense of the reversal, thinking Russo might swell with adrenaline before his shows, then crash for a day or two while his body recovered. The magic had, in fact, run out.

They cashed out their chips and proceeded to the theater, which they found visually empty, but raised voices and whooping laughter spilled out from behind the red velvet curtain to fill the auditory space.

"The cast'll be rowdy tonight," Russo remarked on their way down the aisle, "since the entertainment manager made them go on under dangerous conditions."

Park nearly stumbled as the ship listed to starboard. "I see what you mean," he said, reaching for the closest seat to steady himself.

"Plus, everyone's upset about dela Cruz, so they'll be drinking more than usual," Russo went on, looking suddenly ashamed. "I'll fit right in."

On the other side of the curtain, the stage was crammed with dancers and actors, many of whom were lounging on the set. Park spotted Amanda Boydon and Agent Phillips sitting in the center of that group.

"She's not a regular member of the cast," Phillips had told him earlier, "but she's the second-best singer on the ship, and the star of the show is seasick."

"Literally under the weather," Park had joked at the time.

Miss Boydon was wearing a blue dress with heavy stage makeup, and Phillips clad in a sport coat over khakis. As soon as the latter noticed Park, he lifted his drink in welcome and grinned like an idiot. Conveniently forgetting about his own brush with temptation, Park was incredulous that Phillips could have been so quick to kindle a romance with anyone while on the job, never mind that she was one of the suspects. Nearby, Staff Captain Massolt was standing in a different group, accompanied by a well-dressed older woman with a little white dog on a leash.

"They're not supposed to let her take it out of the kennel," Russo grumbled. "Classic rich bitch." Then Boydon and Phillips came threading their way through the crowd.

"He-ey!" the blonde vocalist called out, greeting them in an appropriately sing-song manner and wrapping her arms around Steve Russo. "You must be Andy," she said as she pulled away. "I'm a hugger." So Park got squeezed as well.

After Phillips and Russo had introduced themselves to each other, Miss Boydon led them down the hall to a dark-green door. "It'll be nicer in here," she promised.

It *was* nicer in there, with sofas, sandwiches, drinks, and a big bowl of fruit set out, but the ship's violent heaving soon tipped the bowl over, spilling apples and oranges onto the floor.

"This is our dressing room," Miss Boydon explained with a nervous smile, trying to make the best of a bad situation. "The other girls and I were allowed to invite three people each."

Park recognized one of the other guests from across the room: Danielle Jackson, perched on a sofa in her sexy black dress, surrounded by an eager bunch of young men. He tried to catch her eye but was coolly ignored.

Miss Boydon gestured toward a cluster of plush upholstered chairs, then produced a bottle of whiskey and poured them each a dram, but none for herself. A lively exchange ensued, with only one exception: Russo's persistent foul mood. In an effort to repay the comic for cheering him up the night before, Park told the joke about "that goddamn cardigan," but it didn't seem to do much good; at the punch line, the best Russo could do was a sad little smile.

"Why don't you favor us with a song?" Phillips asked Miss Boydon.

"They should have come to the show," she replied, laughing as she poured him and Russo a third dram, which Park respectfully declined.

At Phillips' insistence, Miss Boydon finally agreed, and she stepped away to ask her castmates to accompany her, at which point Park turned to Phillips to ask about the show, but Phillips was too drowsy to reply. And Russo was nodding off as well!

An icy wave of fear washed over Park, but only briefly, as his eyelids grew irresistibly heavy and his mind was plunged into oblivion like a mob victim sinking to the bottom of the sea with cement shoes on his feet.

"Ready Freddie!" said Miss Boydon on her way back to the group with her castmates close behind, only to see her guests slumped over in their chairs. Then, making matters much, much worse, the ship's power cut out and the room went totally dark.

***

John Kerr had also been invited to the backstage party, but he'd be arriving later than his fellow undercover operatives. Like Staff Captain Massolt—who had asked him to attend—Kerr was getting on in years, so he wasn't expecting to match or even enjoy the cast's youthful energy. And Massolt had said he'd be bringing a date, so Kerr, knowing he might not get a chance to speak with the suspect alone, took his time adjusting his padded undergarment and applying his 3D makeup. That done, he looked at his altered reflection in the mirror, which caused a conflicted mix of emotions to swell within him; on the one hand, he saw an eminently successful behavioral analyst, responsible for the apprehension of a long list of serial murderers. Few had managed to elude him, and he'd done most of the work single-handedly. On the other, "single-handed" is a synonym for "alone."

John Kerr was alone. Now, in his stateroom, as he had been for most of his life. At the bureau he was known as a person who always put himself first. Before his partners and before the case. In the hallways back at Quantico, he'd heard whispered words such as "selfish bastard" and "arrogant prick."

Before his mind could reflect on how he'd earned that reputation, Kerr headed out to the cast party. As he strode through the carpeted corridors, however, he couldn't help thinking about his wife, who had long since left him. His children, too. There was little hope in that regard. Yet with this last assignment, he had a chance to redeem himself professionally. To show that he *was* capable of being a team player, and he'd be *damned* if he was going to fail in that.

Minutes later, he pulled the red velvet curtain aside and scanned the crowd of partygoers in the backstage area. Staff Captain

Massolt was among them, joined by the older woman Kerr had met at the VIP dinner. "It's so nice to see you again," he told her on approach. As the pleasantries progressed, he learned her name—Jessica Reynolds—and that she was a widow and a retired neurosurgeon. A very successful one, if the size of her diamonds were any indication.

Soon after that, the entire ship was plunged into darkness. An uncertain silence gripped the backstage area. Then the party guests began to whisper among themselves, and their voices rose as they stumbled and jostled their way around.

"Stay calm!" Kerr bellowed into the darkness. "The lights will come back on. Everyone just sit down and relax."

He was right. The power was restored in less than fifteen minutes, but again the stage was silenced when piercing screams rang out from down the hall. Resisting the urge to draw his weapon, Kerr sprinted toward the noise and burst into the dressing room, where a crowd had gathered around three people sitting in a cluster of upholstered chairs.

Park and Phillips were passed out in their seats, still breathing, but Steve Russo's throat had been viciously slashed. Crimson tears streamed out of his empty eye sockets and onto his chin, merging with the blood pouring out of his neck.

The comedian's eyeballs lay at his feet in a spreading crimson pool, carefully placed such that they stared back at Kerr with a beady gaze that chilled him to his very core.

10

BAD NEWS

Detective Jeff Walker stayed at the Carlsbad boathouse facility for some time after the disaster that occurred there. Having seen the medical examiner stuff Detective Abbott in a body bag, starting with the torso (including the head with a hole in it) and continuing with the lower legs (one at a time), he was having trouble letting go of the memory.

Eventually, Walker heaved a final sigh, trudged down to the patrol boat, and piloted it back to San Diego Bay. It was a rough and rainy voyage, due to the hurricane happening off the coast of Baja California—the same one Park was caught in—but Walker wasn't bothered by the choppy water and low visibility; he was reminiscing about all the friends he'd lost, far too young, most of whom had died in the line of duty. Unshed tears burned in his eyes, but he blinked them back, resolving that if he had to brood about something, then it ought to be the facts of the present case.

The crime scene unit had gotten several good lifts, but Walker didn't need to wait for the fingerprint results; the armored Jeep Cherokee he'd discovered in the garage with its coffin-like compartment under the second row of seats was evidence enough. That vehicle was registered to Jack Cage, though as far as Walker knew it had only been used by Cage's guard captains, and only one of those goons was still alive: Rick Daniels, ex-U.S. Army infantryman and marksman. At the very least, it was an interesting coincidence that Daniels was a trained sniper because Mayor O'Connell had been killed by one.

The two bikers Abbott had shot were still unidentified, but Walker had called in their license plates. One had come back as stolen; the other was registered to one Samuel Enright, whose criminal record was extensive.

It's plenty to go on, Walker concluded as he tied up the patrol boat at Shelter Island, *but it'll have to wait until tomorrow*. His first priority was to get home and cuddle with his wife and daughters.

The cuddling turned out just as he'd hoped: warm and comforting after the tragedy, although the setting in which it occurred left much to be desired. The whole family watched part of a television program for which mayoral candidate Ronnie Locke had been given a full hour to promote his agenda and defame his opponent. Disgusted by the network's obvious support of such a man, Walker grabbed the remote and switched to cartoons.

"Daddy loves you," he told his little girls a few hours later, kissing them goodnight after bedtime stories. He and Tina stayed up to discuss that day's disaster and how best to support Abbott's family. Then they fell asleep in each other's arms.

The next day, Sergeant Cheatham drove Walker in an unmarked unit out to East County, where they pulled up at the residence corresponding to the bike that wasn't stolen.

"Sammy's not here," said a horribly thin woman who identified herself as Samuel Enright's wife. She held an infant girl in her arms, and two other children were running around behind her. "He hasn't been home in two days."

"Do you know where we can find him, ma'am?" asked Sergeant Cheatham.

"I'd try Baker's place."

She gave them directions as well as instructions to tell Sammy to get his ass home if they saw him, so it wasn't long before they rolled up on a large rural property, the gate to which was guarded by a man dressed in military fatigues. Walker recognized the rifle slung over the young man's shoulder as a Zastava PAP M70, a California-legal AK-47 derivative with an all-black finish. After he and Cheatham identified themselves, the guard stepped away to use his handheld radio. Then he came back and let them pass.

"I have no idea where Sammy is," said Stephen Baker, a bearded biker who led them through a garage to an office in the corner. He gestured toward two visitor chairs on one side of a desk and took a seat opposite them. "He hasn't been around in a few days. Why? Is he in trouble?"

"No," replied Sergeant Cheatham, staring hard with bulging bright-white eyes that contrasted markedly with his pure-blooded African skin. "We jus' wanna ask him a few questions. But since we came all this way, why don't you tell us about this place."

"Sure," said Baker, blinking uncontrollably, which Walker suspected was a symptom of hard drug use. Either that or a nervous tic. "It's fifty acres, all mine, and I live here with a few of my guys."

"Y'all a motorcycle club?" asked Walker.

"That's right. The East County Warlords." Baker nodded toward the garage. "This is where we work on our bikes."

The man looked familiar, but Walker couldn't remember where from, so he gave up trying and watched for signs of lying. "You're not an outlaw club, are you?"

"Of course not."

"I've never heard of you."

"We're new. I just bought the property and founded the club."

Sergeant Cheatham nodded slowly. "And Samuel Enright's a member."

"Yes."

Cheatham took charge of the interview from that point on. "Have you evah heard o' the SoCal Syndicate?"

"No."

"They're traffickin' narcotics up and down the coast, and we think they're buyin' methamphetamine from someone out here."

"East County's *famous* for meth," Walker added.

"Really?" Baker exclaimed. "*I've* never seen any. Some of the guys smoke a little weed, and we like our beers, but only after we're done ridin'."

Cheatham's features were dripping with disbelief. "The guard at the gate was wearin' military fatigues. Why is that?"

"He's a member of Bravo Company," Baker admitted after a reluctant pause.

Walker and Cheatham raised their eyebrows at each other. Bravo Company, a civilian militia, was all over the news, and the news was never good.

After a heavy silence, Cheatham asked, "Are *you*?"

"No. We have an arrangement. I let them train here, and they protect my guys."

"Protect them from *what*?"

Baker said nothing.

"Who's in charge of Bravo Company?"

Still nothing but a stubborn look.

"We can come back with a search warrant," Cheatham said, which may or may not have been accurate. "What would we find?"

"Joshua Pope's in charge," said Baker.

"Mind if we take a look around?"

***

"Dis-missed!" barked Joshua Pope at an all-white group of men in fatigues, who had been standing at attention in three rows of eight. Some threw Nazi salutes before all broke ranks and marched into the shade of an outdoor shelter, where tables, benches, and water coolers awaited. Before Pope made it to the same structure as his militia, Baker and his visitors cut across a dry, grassy field to intercept him.

"This is Detective Sergeant Cheatham and Detective Walker from the Harbor Police. They'd like a word," said Baker before stomping back to the garage.

Wearing green fatigues like his men, the militia leader lifted his cap to wipe the sweat off his head, which was shaven bald, calling attention to a large tattoo on his throat that extended to one of his temples. It looked Polynesian. "What can I do for you?" he asked haltingly, as though he'd intended to tack on the word "gentlemen" but couldn't bring himself to do it.

Joshua Pope was a rotten POS, Walker knew, having seen him in an interview. On the same network news channel that had shown unabashed support for Ronnie Locke, the heavily muscled ex-Marine had declared his belief in "white sovereignty" and used the term "genetic filth" to describe illegal immigrants and other people of color. His recruitment flyers bore the slogan "Keep America White."

"We're lookin' for Samuel Enright," Cheatham began, eyeballing a man half his age. "Do you know 'im?"

"The name doesn't sound familiar," Pope returned. "He's not one of my guys, I can tell you that."

"What are y'all training for out here?" Walker asked.

"To support and defend our community," Pope recited from memory. "As authorized by the U.S. Constitution, the California State Constitution, and the Bill of Rights. We work with the local population through outreach programs and provide assistance in cases of natural disasters. Emergency response. Pancake breakfasts. Things like that."

Bullshit, thought Walker, who'd seen videos of Bravo Company hiding behind masks, screaming at protestors, intimidating people whose only crime was standing up for their civil rights. Pope was bad news.

Sergeant Cheatham offered Pope his hand, at which the latter merely looked with the utmost disdain. "Thank you for your time, son," said Walker's sergeant with sadness in his eyes. Then he faced about and headed back to the parking area.

Walker didn't even look at Pope as he, too, spun on his heels.

Some days it seemed like he was living in hell, and this was one of those days.

***

"Have you evah heard o' the SoCal Syndicate?" said Stephen Baker, mocking Sergeant Cheatham's dialect with a theatrically stupid look on his face, causing his comrades to burst into laughter.

"Fuckin' n****r," sneered Joshua Pope, provoking similar words from the men sitting around him.

As the only person of color in the room, Chasquas had to force himself not to reply. This was a major business meeting, so for the time being, he focused on how he might benefit from it, not on how it was making him feel. *But only for the time being*, he assured himself in Spanish.

The rowdy group was spread about Locke's private lounge on the superyacht. In one section of that space, Samuel Enright, the biker Cheatham and Walker had been looking for, was seated on a sofa next to Stephen Baker. They were talking about the motorcycle seized at the Carlsbad boathouse, which Enright had loaned to a fellow member of the motorcycle club, and that friend had been one of the men killed by Abbott.

Not far away, Rick Daniels (the sniper) and Chasquas were facing each other in a cluster of overstuffed club chairs. The former handed the latter a satchel full of cash to compensate for the methamphetamine seized at the same Carlsbad facility.

Standing at the floor-to-ceiling window, looking out at the night-lit swimming pool, Mayor Ronnie Locke was speaking with Joshua Pope, explaining his plans for the expansion of the tactical force deployed whenever the mayor declared a state of emergency. (Yes, Ronnie Locke was the mayor now; only minutes earlier, everyone present had watched the results of the special election on a wall-sized flat-screen TV.) From that vantage point, Locke and Pope commanded an aerial view of the crowd packing the dock, braving the rain in hopes of a wave from their new city leader. So Locke obliged them with a friendly hand and a folksy smile.

Also in attendance was Stryker Lindbloom, Chasquas's most-trusted associate, though that didn't mean very much. The thick-necked ex-con settled into a third club chair next to Chasquas and said, "I bought the last boat today. Tomorrow I'll be working on the engine."

"*Excelente*," replied the Honduran, whose tattooed lips sketched the briefest of smiles before falling serious once again. "When you will be ready for start?"

"In one week."

Daniels rolled his eyes; he couldn't stand Stryker Lindbloom.

Chasquas and Lindbloom were referring to the new plan, which was far better than the old one because if they continued to bomb cargo ships to distract the Coast Guard and the Harbor Police, maritime border security would eventually be tightened to such an extent that there'd be no way to smuggle the drugs up from Mexico.

"They'd probably call in the Navy," Lindbloom had argued a few weeks earlier in one of the safe houses. "Listen. Why don't we run a fleet of charter boats from Oceanside to Mazatlan and back?"

Chasquas had understood immediately. "But we no carry fish."

"Exactly."

It's a solid plan, Chasquas reassured himself, now back in the present, sitting with Lindbloom in Locke's private lounge. As he watched Daniels storm away, he considered it unfortunate that the ex-Army sniper would no longer be working for the syndicate, but it had been a temporary arrangement from the beginning. Plus, the Carlsbad boathouse facility was burned, and Chasquas and Lindbloom had been working together for a much longer time.

Another point in Lindbloom's favor was that he'd worked on big ships in the past. First in the engine room, where he'd picked up the ability to customize propulsion systems for enhanced speed and maneuverability. Then in ship security, posing as a deputy officer named Lowry while orchestrating a successful string of casino robberies.

"So one week?" Chasquas asked.

"One week max," Lindbloom promised. "I have a problem with someone on that last cruise ship, and I just need a few days to take care of it."

If Chasquas was being honest with himself, he couldn't stand Stryker Lindbloom either, but the ex-con was smart, well connected, and apparently trustworthy.

Still at the window overlooking the night-lit pool, Locke and Pope nodded to each other, then headed for Locke's desk to celebrate the win with straws up their noses. A short time later, Locke looked up and gestured for Daniels to join them.

"I heard you could use a job," said the crooked city leader. "I'm sure Pope would be glad to have you on his team."

"Is that right," growled Daniels, towering over Locke from the other side of the desk, but not over Pope, who stood behind the mayor's chair like the security specialist he was.

Pope nodded. "It's a tactical unit commanded by the mayor himself. He can hire any company he wants, so he hired mine. Used to be five men but now it's twenty, and we could use a guy with your skills. What do you say?"

Daniels glanced down at Locke to refuse an offered straw, then back up at Pope. "What are you paying?" he asked, but the mayor answered first.

"More than you can spend!" Locke cackled as he rose, draping one arm over Daniels' and Pope's shoulders. "Let's get the girls in here. You like 'em young, don't you?"

11

FIGHTING BLIND

The *Oasis*
Day 3
1:00 a.m.

"Oh no," Amanda Boydon moaned between sobs. "Steve was my best friend on the ship." She darted forward to wrap her arms around the late comedian, and by doing so, smeared her blue dress with his blood.

Still in a drug-induced slumber, Park heard the singer's cries and stirred in his chair.

"You okay, Andy?" asked John Kerr, using Park's alias on account of all the people standing around.

"Yeah, man," Park mumbled groggily, but when he realized what he was looking at, namely Russo's empty eye sockets, his deeply slit throat, and the white pair of orbs set in the blood on the floor, he shot to his feet. While he and Phillips regained their faculties, a group of people entered the room: Staff Captain Massolt, Jessica Reynolds, Chief Richards, and Richards' security team.

"Nobody leaves this room," Richards ordered everyone present, although many of the partygoers had already left, including Danielle Jackson. He introduced himself, making sure to feign unfamiliarity with the undercover team, then interviewed the party guests least likely to have been involved in the crime and let them go. Meanwhile, his security team discovered a bloody chef's knife with the handle wiped clean.

Chief Richards proceeded to question the rest of the subjects, principally Amanda Boydon, whose version of the events led to a startling revelation. As she wiped her eyes with Phillips' handkerchief, she stammered, "My b-bottle of clonazepam is … missing! I had it with me in case I got nervous before the show."

Richards' eyes narrowed. "You poured the whiskey, right?"

"Yes."

"But you didn't drink any?"

"No. I'd taken a few drops of clonazepam before the show and didn't want to mix it with alcohol. You have to believe me," Boydon pleaded. "Someone must have found the bottle in my bag and poured it into the whiskey when I wasn't looking."

Richards frowned.

"And I know about the murders," the singer went on. "We all do. Did you know Danielle Jackson was in here?"

After Richards let Miss Boydon go, he spoke with Staff Captain Massolt, who said, "Amanda's not as nice as she seems. Okay, quite charming onstage, but—how do you say—haughty, yes, and *rude* in real life. I saw her screaming at Steve Russo yesterday."

Richards dismissed Massolt, Jessica Reynolds, and the entire security team, supposedly to continue with the interviews, but actually to confer with his undercover operatives.

"Massolt's in the clear," said John Kerr. "I can vouch for him before, during, and after the blackout. But did y'all see Miss Boydon smear herself with Russo's blood?"

Everyone indicated that they had not.

"Well, if we assume she's the killer," the profiler continued, "then that was a forensic countermeasure, taken to hide the stain she already had. Unfortunately, I didn't see if her dress was bloody before that."

Chief Richards looked to Park and Phillips, and both men shook their heads.

"That's a big assumption, Kerr," said Phillips. "There were lots of people in here besides Amanda, and one of them was another suspect."

"We need more information," said Chief Richards. "I'll find out who else was in here and ask them if they remember seeing blood on Boydon's dress when the lights came back on. Or red stains on anyone else's clothes. It'll be a good excuse to talk to Danielle Jackson."

"There's another possibility we haven't con—" Phillips started to say.

"Come on, man!" Park cut in. "Your judgment's compromised. Tell me you're not sleeping with the singer."

"Let me finish." Phillips nodded toward the bloody chef's knife, which was protected from contamination by a plastic bag. "We still don't know what happened to the chef."

Chief Richards leveled an impatient gaze on Phillips. "Was dela Cruz in here when the lights went off?"

Phillips rolled his eyes. "Of course not. But the power was down for more than ten minutes, right? That's plenty of time for someone to slip in and out."

"He wasn't backstage, either," Kerr grumbled.

"The blood is the key," Phillips persisted. "It would have been impossible for the killer to commit this crime without staining his or her clothes, so we need to get a look at Jackson's dress before she has time to clean it."

"I agree," said Richards, leaning into a corner to steady himself as he thumbed notes into his cell phone.

The *Oasis* was pitching and rolling even more than it had been earlier, Park observed, as a grinding noise came from belowdecks followed by a resounding BOOM! that shook the hull.

"Sounds like we lost an engine," said Richards.

Park shook his head in disbelief. Some days he felt like he was living in hell, and today was one of those days. The ship's instability caused Russo to shift in his seat, and his lifeless head to bob up and down as if he agreed.

***

Early the next morning, a familiar three-note melody came chiming through the PA system followed by the same commanding voice as before: "Attention please! This is your captain with an important announcement from the bridge. For the first time since our maiden voyage, one of the ship's engines has failed. As you may have noticed, this is affecting our speed and stability. We *are* making good headway toward the Bay of All Saints, however, and should arrive in port by this time tomorrow. Until then, all passengers and staff are to remain in their cabins. Excelsior will compensate you for this inconvenience. Once again, all passengers and staff must report to their staterooms immediately and remain there until further notice. That is an order."

Inconvenience? Park thought on his way to Phillips' room, where they'd be meeting with Chief Richards by videoconference again. He could understand why the ship's commanding officer hadn't announced the bloody murder committed just a few hours earlier (even though word of it would spread), but he strongly felt that the captain should have referred to their situation as an emergency.

The first thing he noticed when Phillips let him in was that the *Oasis* was being blasted by the rain and wind as if from a fire hose. On the other side of the floor-to-ceiling window, the tiny balcony looked like a swimming pool, and the water leaking through had soaked most of the carpet.

"The power's still out," explained Chief Richards' image once they'd all gathered around the screen. "We're operating on emergency generators."

"What about Amanda Boydon?" asked Park.

"I've confined her to the brig for the time being."

"That's good," replied the Asian detective, "because if there's another murder, we'll know it's not her. And if it *is* her, there won't be another murder."

"I'd swear to you guys she's not the unsub, but we don't have time to argue," Phillips said. "We need to narrow down the suspect list."

"And we need to do it quickly," Chief Richards added, "since by now the killer knows we're looking for him or her. If it were me, I'd disembark at Ensenada. So you guys search the ship for dela Cruz while I pay a visit to Danielle Jackson and the rest of the party guests."

Everyone nodded.

"Before we go," said Kerr, "let's not forget that all the other victims were passengers. We still don't know about the chef, but as of last night there's no question we're looking at a deviation from the pattern. Why? What are we missing here?"

No one knew.

***

Richards ended the video call, left the security office, headed for the lower decks, and knocked on Danielle Jackson's door. No one answered, which seemed unusual, but he decided to come back in half an hour. This would give Miss Jackson and her roommate plenty of time to finish up whatever they were doing and proceed downstairs.

It would have been difficult if not impossible for him to identify every person who'd been present in the dressing room when the power failed, let alone those who might have slipped in and out before it was restored. However, he had compiled a partial list, twenty-two out of an estimated thirty people, whose cabins were located in the same general area because most of them were singers or dancers. So he interviewed many of them at the same time, and all in half an hour. None of them had noticed blood on anyone's clothes, but several reported having seen Danielle Jackson dash out of the dressing room as soon as the lights came back on. When asked about the other eight party guests, they mentioned several passengers, including a middle-aged man in a blue dinner jacket, a younger guy who was there to see a dancer, and a pair of teenagers asking for autographs. Richards was mainly concerned with his five suspects—*make that four*, he reminded himself—so he made a mental note to follow up on the others later, then set off for Miss Jackson's cabin.

This time someone did come to the door: Jackson's roommate, whose eyes were red and watery.

"Good morning, miss," he said, showing her his ID. "I'm Jim Richards, head of ship security."

"Is Dani okay?" the young woman asked. "We know all about the murders, and she didn't come back after the party. I've been out looking for her."

"We don't know," said Richards. "But we'll find her. Remember, you're under orders to stay here, for your own safety. Do you mind if I come in and have a look around?"

"No, of course not."

Chief Richards searched everywhere, but he didn't find the dress, the clonazepam, or any other clue.

***

Meanwhile, Park, Kerr, and Phillips set out to scour the ship for the missing chef. They split up to cover more ground, which left them more vulnerable to attack, but all three were packing, trained to kill, and *had* killed at least one man over the course of their careers. They were communicating by handheld radio, and so far no one had reported anything unusual. Kerr continued to wear his disguise and they all kept their weapons concealed, though they weren't overly concerned about maintaining their cover. Why not? Because only Massolt needed to remain unaware of their true identities, and he was in his room and seemingly above suspicion. As for the other three suspects, Boydon was locked up, so she wasn't an issue, and if they found Jackson or dela Cruz, it would either be a rescue or an arrest, and either event would blow their cover.

Park's search took him down to the engine room, which practically spanned the length of the *Oasis*, with gigantic cylinders and machinery looming two decks high. A group of technicians clad in orange coveralls stood near one of the two engines. Busy with their work, they didn't seem to notice him.

He stalked through the cavernous space with his Glock in its IWB holster and a folding knife clipped to the inside of his front pocket, staying just as focused on his surroundings, equally as attentive to any sudden movement or noise, as an animal would in the wild. As he swiveled his head left and right to clear the spaces between the generators, he detected a flash of activity up on the second deck and the sound of a heavy door slamming. Someone was running away! Park sprinted through the rows of the machines, nearly stumbling from the rolling of the ship. The smell of smoke hit his nostrils on his way up the stairs, but he was too focused on the chase to stop and check it out. Now on the second level, he burst through the door his quarry had used, finding himself in a deserted hallway with several corridors that branched off to both sides.

The only kind of person who can make it through SEAL training is an exceptionally gifted athlete, so for Park's fugitive to have eluded him for so long, he or she had to be a rare physical specimen or someone who knew the ship inside and out. Park was betting on the latter. He strained his ears for any sound. Hearing footsteps, he was about to break right to follow them, but an explosion shook the walls. It felt like it had come from behind and below him, from the engine room, where he'd smelled smoke. *The backup generators!* Just then, all the lights cut out, and this time, Park knew, they wouldn't be coming back on for a while. Fortunately, he'd brought a piece of equipment that would confer a decisive advantage, so he shrugged off his backpack to pull out a tactical helmet fitted with ENVG-Bs, or enhanced night vision goggle-binoculars. Twenty seconds later, he could see clear as day.

Carrying his G19 at the low ready with two hands, just inches below a leveled position, he resumed forward progress through the hallways, cutting left at one junction, advancing, cutting right at the next, guided by the sound of footsteps ahead. Park knew he was gaining on the fugitive and felt he was almost upon him or her, until he heard a door crash open then saw it slam closed after rounding a corner. The suspect had gone out into the storm.

Since his NODs would be more hindrance than help in the torrential rain, he stashed them in his pack again, set the bag down, and pushed open the door. The environmental change that occurred as he stepped into the hurricane was startling. Eighty-mile-an-hour winds threatened to blow him off the ship, and he was completely soaked in seconds. Staring into the blackness, Park panned his weapon left and right, then swept it around to check his six, but visibility was nil, and the howling gusts made it impossible to track the suspect by sound.

CRACK CRACK! came the report of a gun fired at close range. At first Park thought he was on his way to the afterlife, but as he spun toward the sound he felt no pain. Then his shooting arm was forced upwards and a man was in his face, trying to swing his own pistol onto Park's center mass, but Park gripped the guy's wrist to prevent it and launched a hard knee into his testicles. With his shooting hand free again, he took aim at the standing man's heart and pulled the trigger repeatedly.

Seconds later, he dragged his non-resistant assailant back into the ship, secured the door, donned his tactical helmet, and powered on his NODs. Down on the floor, in a bloody pool of water with three bleeding holes in his chest and eyes staring blankly into the distance, lay Staff Captain Kevin Massolt.

Park searched the Netherlander's pockets and found nothing of consequence. Then he took off running toward the blazing engine room, where the technicians were trapped and screaming for help.

12

SNIPER'S HILL

Windansea Beach
San Diego, California

The sea was cold and the day gray and rainy, but the waves were outrageous and Walker's wetsuit kept him warm enough. As he bobbed up and down on his surfboard, waiting for the next set to roll in, his thoughts revolved around his mother. For as long as he could remember, they'd gone to the beach every Sunday, just the two of them, before she'd passed away far too young.

The rain on his face brought to mind one Sunday in particular, when Walker had been about twelve years old. He'd begged her to take him in spite of the weather.

"Let's go to the movies instead," she'd suggested hopefully.

"Come on, Mom, the waves are going *off* and I've almost got the forward air three-sixty."

"Going *off*?" she'd replied with a frown that broke into a grin. "Okay, big guy, you win. But only if we can get tacos afterwards."

"Yes!"

He remembered being cold and uncomfortable that day in the water, but it hadn't mattered at all. Young Walker's focus had been the fire in his heart, his desperate need to face his fears. And there was his mother, alone on the beach under an umbrella, freezing her buns off in the rain, waving with a cheerful smile.

Yet now as he peered over the back side of the breaking waves to look for her, she wasn't there anymore. His eyes burned with salty tears, and one brimmed over to join its ancestors in the sea. Walker hoped with all his heart that his mother was looking down at him with pride, and that he would always keep that fire stoked, facing his fears whenever they threatened to limit him.

Soon the next set marched into shore like endless ranks of enemy soldiers, and Walker let the first few pass him by. When his chosen wave swelled beneath him, he leapt to his feet and tipped the board forward, free-falling for a gut-wrenching moment before slapping hard and racing down the rushing wall of water. At the trough he drove his back foot around to carve a right bottom turn, and crouched to grab the rail just as a glassy sheet of water threw itself over his head. It was every surfer's dream: a crystal barrel stretching out twenty feet in front of him like the road to paradise. As he cruised in slow motion through the spinning tube, seconds stretched into minutes and he relished the natural high. Then the barrel shot him out like a bullet from a gun.

This last wave had capped off the session beautifully, so Walker leaned into a left turn and rode it back to the beach, feeling healed after one of the worst weeks he'd ever had. After Detective Abbott, his brother-in-arms, had been killed in an operation that Walker had asked him to join. Then there was the visit to Stephen Baker's rural compound, where Walker had had the extreme displeasure of making Joshua Pope's acquaintance.

He slid off the board and carried it under his arm, sloshing through knee-high water. On his way up the beach face, he spotted his good friend Marcus Crawford, who was now the leader of the San Diego Lifeguards' dive rescue team. Crawford didn't recognize Walker because he was fifty yards away and busy performing in and outs, a grueling exercise with which Walker was intimately familiar. The deeply tanned long-haired lifesaver ran into the surf and dove into a wave with his goggles on. Powering out to sea with strong pulling arms paired with a constant flutter kick, he made it past the surf line and continued for another fifty yards. Then he turned back, caught a few waves on his way to the beach—the only respite he'd get for the next fifty minutes—performed ten push-ups on the wet packed sand, sprang to his feet and hustled back into the surf. Ten repetitions had been the standard when Walker was working the towers.

It was nearly dark by the time Crawford had completed the exercise, and Walker was dry and dressed, perched on the large flat rock where he used to set his lifeguard chair.

"Hey brother!" Crawford exclaimed, still sucking wind. He was an inch taller than Walker and just as big around the chest and shoulders. There wasn't an ounce of fat on him.

Walker hopped off the rock to offer his buddy a Hawaiian handshake that ended in a one-armed hug. "I saw you do the extra push-ups at the end."

"Learned it from you," Crawford replied, grabbing a towel out of his bag to dry himself off.

They spoke about the waves and their jobs, and when the topic of discussion turned to Crawford's upcoming wedding with Maggie Garcia, Walker's wife's younger sister, it was mentioned that they'd soon have the same father-in-law.

"I've never seen him smile," Crawford remarked as he pulled on a T-shirt. "You're lucky you're Mexican. I think he likes you better than me."

"No, he doesn't."

Crawford barked a laugh.

"Hey, guess who's in town," said Walker.

"Who?"

"Rick Daniels."

"No way!"

"*Sí, güey.*"

Crawford smiled. He hadn't grown up in Mexico like Walker had, but he'd grasped the humor of Walker's double entendre. "*Güey*," pronounced "way," means "fool," or simply "man" or "dude" depending on the context, so "*Sí, güey*" had been a friendly jibe. Yet Crawford's smile fell quickly off his face, as he also grasped the significance of Daniels' being in town, having fought the man under water several years before, not far from where they were standing, in fact, just off Big Rock.

"So be careful, bro," said Walker to Crawford as the latter stored his gear in the shed. Then they both headed up to the parking area. At the top of the long white flight of stairs, Walker stopped to admire Crawford's black Kawasaki Ninja 650R. It used to be his! That, along with Crawford's sun-toasted skin and perfect muscular definition, made Walker more than a little envious. He frowned and shook his head.

"What? You're not jealous, are you?" Crawford asked. "I'll give it back."

"Of course not."

"Well, I am. I'd *kill* to be a police officer."

"Be careful what you wish for."

"Hey, how's Tina?" said Crawford as he straddled his bike.

"She's good, man. I'll tell her you said hi."

"What about Dulce?"

"Awesome. Just got a job in cybersecurity, and still dating Sean Choi."

"Nice." Crawford slipped on his helmet over long wet hair.

The guys hadn't said much about Maggie or Tina, out of respect for each other's relationships, but they'd spoken even less about Dulce, the youngest of the three sisters. Her doctors had agreed she'd never walk again after a motorcycle crash orchestrated by Maldonado, Rick Daniels' former partner in crime, and that incident was why Walker had sworn off motorcycles for the rest of his life.

Before his buddy blasted off into the night, Walker flashed him the shaka sign, then headed for his white Shelby GT500 and drove it home through the evening traffic. Twenty slow miles later, he didn't take the off-ramp to Chula Vista, opting instead to execute a surveillance detection run, meaning he got off two exits early and followed a circuitous route, making wide-open turns to watch the cars behind him. It wouldn't matter much, Walker knew. Daniels was well connected. If the former sniper wanted to know where he lived, it wouldn't take him long to find out.

***

In fact, it hadn't taken Daniels any time at all to locate the Walker-Garcia residence; he'd only had to make one quick call to his asset in the Oceanside Port Authority. So while Walker was out surfing, he had driven down to Chula Vista, set up his sniper system on a nearby hill, and waited for his target. With only time to kill at the moment, his thoughts trended back to the reason for his mortal grudge.

Six years earlier, Daniels had been sitting behind the wheel of his armored SRT in a garage at the oceanfront compound in Mazatlan, feeling as happy as a criminal can possibly feel in the midst of a deadly police raid, for as soon as Maria slid in beside him, they would drive up to Northern California and start a new life together. But ten minutes had passed, and Daniels had grown jumpy and irritable. If he and his lady love didn't get out of there immediately, Walker, Park, or some other member of the raiding tactical team would be sure to place them under arrest. *Or worse*, he thought, slamming his hand on the steering wheel and wondering how long a woman needed to take a piss and grab a bag. He gave her another thirty seconds, then hustled back into the house to encourage her verbally. But she wasn't there.

Daniels groaned out loud as he realized what had happened and why he hadn't been able to find his combat knife. The only reason important enough for Maria to have delayed their getaway was to get even with Maldonado for killing her cousin.

Daniels lumbered through the house and burst onto the oceanfront terrace. There she was, down on the grass, charging toward Maldonado's house with his combat knife in her hand, heading directly into a gunfight involving Walker, Goode, and two DEA agents on one side, and Cage and Cage's guard on the other. Four of them dropped, leaving Walker standing there alone, mourning his dead best friend while Cage escaped. By then, Maria had almost made it to the south house, but she was stopped by three cracking gunshots. Daniels couldn't tell where they'd come from, but as her body jerked under the repeated impacts, he blamed the only other person in sight: Jeff Walker. And when that final shot pierced her skull, any goodness remaining in Daniels left him, never to return.

The sight of Walker's white Mustang snapped Daniels out of his reverie. A smile curled his lips as he realized his target was performing a surveillance detection run. While the young detective was circling his own neighborhood, the veteran sniper simply waited in his hide, observing calmly through a night vision spotting scope.

When Walker's Mustang pulled in to the driveway, it dropped out of sight, since the sniper's hill was behind the house. So Daniels adopted a prone position and settled himself behind his rifle's scope, fixing his sights on the dining room window and watching as Walker stepped inside to greet his family. *For the last time,* Daniels thought, breathing slowly. He initiated the trigger press, but then Walker's wife stepped into his field of view. *Should I take the shot?* he wondered. *A love for a love. That might be even better.* He made up his mind to complete the trigger press and did just that—CRACK!—sending the bullet flying toward the dark-haired woman. The gun's heavy recoil blurred the image in his scope for a moment, and by the time the picture came back into focus, Walker had charged into the back yard and drawn his pistol!

***

One minute earlier, Walker had swung open his front door, beaming with love and pride at his pretty little daughters who ran to embrace him. And Tina wasn't far behind, glowing as she crossed the dining room to complete the family hug.

Even as Walker lifted one little girl in each of his arms, he was reminded of something Park would often say: *stay alert, stay alive*, so he lifted his gaze to the hill behind the house and scanned for any irregular glints that might indicate the presence of a sniper scope. And he saw something. *Could it be?* "Shooter!" he shouted, just in case, dropping to the floor with Tina and the girls just as a high-velocity projectile shattered the window and drilled into the wall. "Lock yourselves in the bathroom and call 911!" he growled, sprinting out the back door and pulling his Glock from its holster to lay down suppressive fire. Then he vaulted over the fence and charged up the hillside in a crouch. Halfway up, he took cover behind a tree to look and listen for signs of his target. All was dark at the crest and the only sound was the rustling of leaves in the wind. *You idiot!* Walker berated himself. *So proud of performing surveillance detection that you forgot to scout the hill.*

The thunderous CRACK! of a close-range gunshot refocused his attention on the now. Walker returned fire, then swiftly advanced with his pistol leveled. As he came to the top of the hill, a motorcycle engine grumbled to life, a back tire spun, and dry dirt flew into his eyes. With his aim thus fouled, he shot at the two-wheeler barreling down the other side of the hill until his gun ran dry, but the bike's glowing red tail light continued on its way and disappeared.

Walker yelled into the wind, swearing at himself and the shooter many times as he cleared the area. Then he picked up the sniper rifle by the tip of its muzzle to preserve as many prints as he could, carried it down the hill, and stepped into another family hug. This one felt slightly colder.

"If he found us here, he'll find you at your parents' house," he told Tina a few minutes later, handing her a stack of cash he'd been saving for an emergency. "Take the girls and your mom and dad to that hotel your cousins stayed at last year. Remember?"

She nodded. Her almond-shaped eyes were hard and calculating.

"Don't bring your phones, and pay cash for everything," Walker went on. "I'll get a prepaid cell and call your room tonight."

She was up and packing bags before he'd finished talking, but he knew she'd understood. If there was one thing Tina was serious about, it was her family, and the same was true for Walker. Daniels was going to regret taking that shot.

13

REVELATIONS

The *Oasis*
Day 4, 7:00 a.m.
50 nautical miles from the Port of Ensenada

The morning after Park's deadly encounter with Massolt, Chief Security Officer James Richards lumbered up to a separate area of the ship: a private deck that housed all of the luxury suites. As his flashlight's roaming beam guided him through the unlit stairwell—the generators weren't yet operational—Richards thanked his lucky stars that Massolt's gun hadn't been found, and he came to the conclusion that it had fallen overboard in the fight.

Approximately twenty-four hours earlier, he'd been working at his desk when Massolt had burst into the office. "Come on in, Kevin," Richards said dryly.

"I need to borrow a gun. For protection," Massolt announced in his hard European accent, closing the door behind him.

"You know that's against regulations."

"Listen," Massolt said intensely as he took a seat. "I believe that Amanda Boydon is the killer, but maybe she is not. Steve Russo is dead, and dela Cruz, too, we think. Perhaps I am next."

Richards frowned. "Are you *sure* you're looking at this with an open mind? I happen to know Amanda turned you down."

Massolt snorted. "Turned me down? Jim, I didn't want to mention this, but if you do not let me borrow a gun, I will report what I know about the girl who couldn't remember her rapist on the *Majesty*."

"It's not true and you know it!" Richards bellowed, but then he rose from his desk and headed for the gun safe. As he walked back to Massolt and handed over the pistol, the European's face lit up in triumph. For the last time, since later that night he'd be killed.

Serves him right for threatening to lie, Richards caught himself thinking as his flashlight showed him the way through the exquisitely furnished passageway. At the time of the incident in question, Richards had been a much younger man, and the female passenger even younger—though over eighteen—and both had had too much to drink. The late-night encounter had been consensual from start to finish. Then, when the young lady's father caught her sneaking back to her stateroom, the best she could come up with was a bogus story about a rapist to stay out of trouble.

Shaking his head as if to banish the memory, Richards rapped his knuckles on the door to Jessica Reynolds' suite.

"Who is it?" came the wary voice of the older woman.

"James Richards. Ship security, Mrs. Reynolds."

Massolt's lady friend invited him into a sprawling sitting room with plush wall-to-wall carpeting. The curtains had been drawn aside to let in the natural light, revealing a cloudy, drizzly sky, though the storm had passed.

"I'm afraid I have some bad news, ma'am," he began, removing his hat as he lowered himself onto the offered sofa. Before he could explain, the room was instantly bathed in bright artificial light. The ship's electricity had been restored.

"Oh!" she exclaimed, settling into a chair facing him. "What is it?"

"Staff Captain Kevin Massolt was killed in an accident last night."

Her features fell, but she didn't cry or hang her head. Richards figured her years as a physician might have thickened her skin as to the subject of death. "An accident?" she repeated, holding his gaze. "Are you sure that's all it was?"

"Why do you ask, ma'am?"

"Because I know about the murders. Kevin told me when we first met at the VIP dinner. He said he was a suspect, along with a chef, a singer, a comedian, and I forget who else."

"Yes, we're sure it was an accident, and almost definitely unrelated to the killings. Did anyone else at the dinner hear him talking about the suspects?"

The older woman pursed her lips as she struggled to recall. Then, with great reluctance, she looked Richards in the eye and said, "Only my son."

***

Amanda Boydon rested her head in her hands while sitting on a bed with her feet on the floor, mourning the death of Steve Russo. Yes, she and the comedian had argued, many times, but they'd also been very close, and now his blood was all over her pretty blue dress. It was ruined. And her job was ruined, too, she believed, though she had nothing to do with his death, nor with any of the other murders.

That's when the lights came back on in the brig, lifting her spirits only slightly. She wiped her cheeks dry, blew out the candle, lay back on the bed—if one could call it that—and cast her mind back to the night before. She pictured the dressing room and every person she'd seen since before the show to the time of the blackout. Naturally, she thought of Danielle Jackson, the only other suspect who'd been in the room when the power cut out. But the kids club manager was a friend of hers, and Jackson hadn't gone near her dressing table or her bag. So Miss Boydon moved on to the next party guest, and the next, and so on until it hit her like a slap in the face.

When Chief Richards had questioned her after the incident, she'd still been in shock, but now that she was calmer and capable of logical thought, Miss Boydon was sure there had only been three people who could have rooted around in her bag, found the dropper bottle, and doctored the whiskey—*The whiskey I'd bought for Steve!* she rued—and only one of those three had been backstage after the performance.

Staff Captain Massolt and his lady friend, Jessica Reynolds, had come to meet the cast before the show, accompanied by the woman's son, a middle-aged man with a do-it-yourself haircut and a light-blue dinner jacket.

When Massolt had strutted up with his two friends in tow, Boydon had forced a smile—*Ugh! The man was revolting*. Busy getting ready to go on, she'd shaken hands politely, then dashed off to the restroom, leaving the trio standing by her dressing table with the whiskey bottle out in the open. *It has to be the son*, she thought, *the only one who came back for the party. But why?*

Unable to relax, Miss Boydon resumed her sitting position with her feet on the floor. *It doesn't matter why*, she told herself. *No one will believe you, and you're going to prison.* Then she hung her head and wept for the rest of the morning.

***

An hour before Miss Boydon blew out the candle in the brig, Danielle Jackson found herself tied to a chair, gagged, and heavily drugged. As she slipped in and out of consciousness, she regretted not having been able to confide in the undercover policeman: Hwang, or whatever his real name was. From the way he'd just happened to show up at the kids club with no kids and by the bulge in his waistband, she'd known he was investigating her and the others, but she hadn't been able to trust him despite her best efforts. It was pathological, her fear of law enforcement; when she was a little girl, her father had been murdered by a mob of white police officers, shot thirty times for supposedly resisting arrest.

Miss Jackson raised her droopy eyes to those of her attacker. His face contorted with hate as he drew back a walking stick and swung it like a bat with deadly force. Before the solid metal rod connected, she had one last thought.

Here I come, Daddy.

***

Timothy Reynolds wiped Danielle Jackson's blood from his mother's walking stick and set it aside, taking time to ogle her perfectly formed breasts, which rose and fell with her breathing, but only slightly. He fixed his stare on the blood oozing out of her nose and mouth, and when it ran over her chin and onto her chest, his erection grew fully rigid. Eagerly, he positioned himself behind her chair, wrapped his hands around her throat, and relentlessly tightened his grip. As she wheezed and gagged, his mouth fell open and his eyes went wide, and he climaxed when her face went blue. But it was no ordinary orgasm; this was an exquisite, mind-blowing sensation heightened and prolonged by the thrill of killing.

Reynolds stood blissfully still for a minute or more, but when the afterglow started wearing off, he quickly got to work. The security staff hadn't yet come to speak with him or with his mother, but they would, he knew, and even if they didn't search his suite, they'd eventually find the bodies. So the first thing to do was dispose of the evidence while the power was still out, a circumstance he was proud to have engineered himself.

He retrieved the garbage bags and duct tape he'd brought on the trip, then hurried into the bathroom and started with dela Cruz, whose stinking corpse was still in the bathtub. As he worked, he thought ahead to the next meeting of "The Faith," at which he was scheduled to present the results of his current mission, and where he'd certainly be promoted.

Reynolds had orchestrated the serial killings by announcing the opportunity in a dark web forum for devil worshippers. The volunteers he'd selected had been honored to buy a ticket, board the cruise ships, and commit murder in the name of Satan, though he himself wasn't a believer. Yes, he and the other cult leaders did espouse a complex doctrine based on the Bible, but the members who bought that crap were feeble-minded and/or mentally ill. Tim Reynolds felt he was the brightest of them all, except for the Master. That's why he'd risen so quickly through the ranks, from acolyte, to initiate, to messenger, and now he'd be named a prophet.

Anyway, he had told the chosen ones to pick their victims from among the VIP passengers whenever possible, and provided clear instructions on how to disembowel them and gouge out their eyes. *It was a brilliant plan!* Given the same M.O. in every case, the authorities would assume the killer was a single person and therefore an employee. The information packets he had put together included the ships' layouts and comprehensive maps of the port-stop towns, which was why he'd limited the project to the Mexican routes; after investing such considerable time and effort, he'd been disinclined to repeat the process for the Caribbean itineraries.

There had been only one glitch in the execution, which had occurred on the *Sensation*. The last of the five chosen ones had contacted Reynolds to report three passengers whose appearance and behavior screamed undercover law enforcement, so Reynolds told him to abort, reimbursed him for the ticket, and booked a trip on the *Oasis* for himself. Unfortunately, his mother had insisted on coming along.

On embarkation day, after several drinks at the VIP dinner, Staff Captain Kevin Massolt had mentioned the five suspects to Reynolds and his mother, which Reynolds had seen as a major opportunity. By killing those crew members one by one, he'd give the police even more reason to focus their investigation on them. So he'd excused himself and gone in search of the chef, whom he found in the kitchen of the very restaurant they were eating in. Reynolds had thanked dela Cruz for the meal, handed him a generous tip, offered to buy him a drink after work, and, while he was at it, slipped a chef's knife into his coat pocket when nobody was looking.

Later, after cocktails in the piano bar, Reynolds had invited the chef up to his suite, where he grabbed a heavy ice bucket, smashed the man on the head, tied him up, and choked him to death, forgoing the throat slashing, the disembowelment, and the removal of the eyes since no one would ever see the body and the suite had to remain unsoiled.

Smiling at the memory, Reynolds finished bundling up the first body in the bathroom, then used a towel to wipe it off before dragging it to the near side of the front door, where he left it. Then he started on the kids club manager while reflecting on the events that had led to *her* demise.

He'd meant for the second victim to be Amanda Boydon, not Steve Russo or Danielle Jackson. *But man plans and Satan laughs,* he joked to himself. When he'd first gone down to the dressing room with his mother and Massolt, he'd shaken hands with Miss Boydon, who hurried off to the restroom, leaving them at her dressing table. That's when he saw the dropper bottle in her bag. Edging closer, Reynolds read the label, and since he knew clonazepam was a knock-out drug, when his mother and Massolt headed for a different part of the dressing room to meet some other people, he cracked open the whiskey and poured in a large quantity of the tranquilizer.

His plan was to return to the dressing room after the performance, where he'd either ask Amanda Boydon up to his suite for a drink or help her there when the drug took effect, pretending she'd had too much to drink. Unfortunately, when he went backstage for the second time, he found her surrounded by friends and without a glass in her hand. *Damn!* Reynolds thought, and he was about to scrap the mission when he realized her friends were none other than the comedian and two undercover cops, so he struck up a conversation with Danielle Jackson and watched from afar. As it happened, good fortune struck, but to a much greater extent than he'd been hoping for: as Boydon's friends were nodding off, the power failed for the first time, so Reynolds shot up from the sofa, drew the chef's knife from under his shirt, found Russo by the light of his watch, slit his throat, popped out his eyes, and placed them in the spreading pool of blood. (There hadn't been time to gut him). Working in the dark as fast as possible amid a nervous group of partygoers, he wiped the knife and ditched it, then flew out of the room. Jackson must have been suspicious, however, as she followed him out of the theater. *Gutsy girl.*

By the time the ship's power was restored—the first time—he'd made it halfway to his room, but the kids club manager was right behind him.

"Hey!" she'd shouted from ten yards back. "Why you runnin' away?" Big and strong, she reached him easily and spun him around. "What the hell?!" she exclaimed, staring gape-mouthed at all the blood on his dinner jacket.

Reynolds made a fist and threw a punch, but she recovered well and was starting to overpower him when the rolling of the ship caused her to stumble in her heels. He drove a knee into her jaw, then dragged her into his suite, where she offered little resistance as he poured a quarter bottle of clonazepam into her mouth and forced her to swallow it.

Throughout the night, Reynolds performed unspeakable acts on the poor young woman. The next day, he decided to dispose of her and dela Cruz, but didn't know how. With fifteen hundred passengers aboard, he couldn't risk being seen heaving them off his balcony or dragging bags of body parts through the halls. Recalling that darkness had come to his aid in the dressing room, he changed into different clothes, grabbed a full-face ski mask and a flashlight, tied Jackson to a chair, and used dela Cruz's key card to gain access to the engine room.

With his degree in electrical engineering, Reynolds had no trouble locating the emergency generators, nor any difficulty tampering with the wiring to start a fire. Unfortunately, Staff Captain Massolt was down on the lower decks searching for the killer, and he was armed.

"Oi!" yelled Massolt.

Reynolds took off running, leading the staff captain through the maze-like arrangement of large machines. He worried that Massolt might recognize him despite the mask, but in the end it didn't matter. Once the flames hit the generators and the power cut out again, Reynolds flicked on his flashlight and made his way outside to the promenade deck, where he scrambled into a lifeboat and hid. Massolt managed to track him there, but he himself had been followed.

Reynolds heard the shots, the struggle, more gunfire, and then just the pouring rain and the whipping wind. He waited fifteen minutes before returning to the safety of the ship's interior, where he tripped over Massolt's corpse on the other side of the door.

As always, the reality had fallen short of the fantasy, leaving him desperate for more as he dragged Jackson's bag-wrapped body to the front door and dropped it beside dela Cruz's. Then he stuffed his stained dinner jacket, a bunch of bloody towels, and the roll of duct tape into a trash bag and hauled that and the bodies outside to the private VIP deck, where he heaved them over the railing and into the sea. It took two trips, but with all the passengers confined to their rooms and the lights still out, Reynolds had no problems. The last thing he did was pull off his mask and toss it overboard, and that's when the ship's power was restored.

His lips slowly twisted into a smile. *Perfect timing*, he thought. *Maybe I <u>do</u> have a guardian devil after all.*

14

STATE OF EMERGENCY

Duke's Bar & Grill
Embarcadero Marina
San Diego, California

"It was the same rifle," said District Attorney Investigator Dom Taylor. "At least that's the opinion given in the ballistics report. But did you actually *see* Daniels?"

"No, but I know it was him," Walker replied, wiping his hands on a napkin. "First, Mayor O'Connell was killed by a sniper. Then we saw Daniels at the Carlsbad facility, which places him in San Diego at the same time, and it connects him to me."

"What do you mean by 'connects'?"

"He recognized me at the boathouse, then tried to shoot me and missed, so don't you think it's likely he went to my house to finish what he started, given our history?"

"*More* than likely. And since the rifle you found on the hill matches the bullet from Mr. A's—"

"It was Daniels both times."

"That's enough for a warrant." DAI Taylor popped the last of his burger into his mouth. "I'll submit the affidavit today. The question is who paid him to kill the mayor."

"No it's not. It's how we're going to prove it was Ronnie Locke."

Duke's was busy as usual. As Taylor finished his fries, Walker peered past the day drinkers at the bar to marvel at the spectacle on the far side of the window, which, he knew, was the main reason for the spectacularly high price of a burger there. Yet the sweeping expanse of the bay with its gentle ripples drifting in the breeze was holding most of the patrons' attention. His included. *The weather's finally nice again*, he thought as he motioned for the check and turned back to his buddy. "Any known addresses or associates?"

Taylor frowned and shook his head. "Daniels dropped off the radar years ago. It might be easier to track him down by looking for a connection between him and Locke."

"Daniels never struck me as a go-getter," Walker said, beating Taylor to the check when the waitress came. "I bet someone brokered the deal. A middleman."

***

Chasquas stepped off the superyacht, scowled at the white men guarding the dock, and stormed out to the parking lot where he'd left his bike. Having just delivered another hefty bag of cocaine to Ronnie Locke had left him in such a rage that he was afraid to start the engine. Thus, instead of racing off to his next destination and possibly causing an accident, the lanky inked-up Honduran sat on his ride and brooded over the reasons for his anger.

The police raid at the Carlsbad boathouse had resulted in many major difficulties, besides which Chasquas was still upset about Pope's racist comments at the meeting the other night. And just now, Locke had eyed the tattoos on Chasquas's brown skin with the utmost disdain, then turned up his piggish nose at him and carelessly tossed a stack of hundreds onto the desk as though both the money and its recipient were worth nothing at all. Where

Chasquas was from, that kind of disrespect would have earned the man a beating.

But survival comes before dignity, he reminded himself in Spanish as he finally hit the ignition switch and felt his 1900cc monster roar to life. Stomping it into first, he engaged the clutch and twisted the throttle, accelerating quickly off the line. When it hit the city streets, he toed up the shifter from second to third and gave it even more to drink. Gaining speed, with the salty coastal air rushing past his body, Chasquas shifted into fourth and flew up onto the freeway. This, he suspected, would be the only pleasant part of his trip out to East County.

As he grumbled to a halt at the gated entrance to the biker compound, a red-hot anger still flared within him. He locked eyes with the skinhead blocking his path and felt like forcing him to the ground, beating him senseless, and carving that swastika tattoo out of his forehead.

The guard called for authorization on his radio, got the green light, then swung the metal gate inward. With a dismissive flick of his rifle, he gestured for Chasquas to advance, but the raging Honduran was already blasting into the complex. When Chasquas came to his destination, he set his steel horse on its kickstand, strode past the gang in the garage, and charged into Stephen Baker's office.

"Ready for the tour?" asked the bearded biker boss.

Over a few snorts for Baker and a cigarette for Chasquas, they negotiated the terms of another order of ice to replace the confiscated batch. Then they hopped on their bikes and rode through the rural property, grumbling past the training facility on their left, where Pope was barking orders at his men. They also zoomed by an outdoor shooting range and a small fleet of military surplus vehicles.

Baker led the way through an intricate maze of dirt trails to what looked like a one-story power plant. But when he got off his bike, he swung open a secret door to a staircase leading down, and they descended into a large subterranean space. A laboratory, Chasquas knew, that produced much of the methamphetamine sold in Southern California. It was his first visit to the hidden installation, and it would be his last, though he didn't know it at the time.

"Where the hell is Sammy?" Baker asked one of the workers, who all wore full-face respirators, gloves, rubber boots, and protective coveralls.

The worker shrugged.

"He was supposed to meet us here," the biker boss said to Chasquas. Then he handed over a respirator, put one on himself, and set off along a well-marked walkway between stainless steel batch reactors and white vats of acid.

"We can cook up to two hundred pounds a week," Baker explained, pointing out the furnace, the filter system, the finishing tank, and the cooling room. "Place cost me six million, but I made it back in two months!" His laugh came out muffled by his mask.

Chasquas thanked Baker after the tour was over. He'd been in plenty of meth labs back in Honduras, even worked in some, but they'd all been makeshift operations, so he'd been fascinated to see such a large-scale facility. Even so, he was exceedingly glad to hit the fresh mountain air at the top of the stairs. What he wasn't glad about was the sight of Sammy Enright sitting on his Indian Chief Dark Horse!

"What you doin' with Chucky Matón's bike?" growled Enright with a challenge in his eye. He was thin but muscular, with long stringy blond hair and at least a week of stubble.

"Matón don't need it. Is dead," Chasquas replied, holding the biker's stare and walking straight toward him.

"Just like a fuckin' spick, invading our country to take what's not yours," Enright muttered, then dropped his hand to the grip of his holstered pistol.

"Sammy," Baker growled as he swung the hidden door shut.

"Is okay," said Chasquas, who'd already shot his hand under his shirt to whip out his P320 Compact. As he glared at Sammy through its iron sights, he told himself he hadn't clawed his way up from the streets of Honduras all the way to the so-called "first world" to be intimidated by an ignorant racist. *"O te quitas de mi moto,"* he said calmly with his finger on the trigger, *"o te despides de tu puta vida."*

"We speak American here," Sammy retorted, with his hands raised in surrender and his weapon in its holster. "Let's put down our guns and settle this like men."

When Chasquas nodded his assent, Baker collected both pistols and stood off to the side.

Sammy came in fast with his body bladed and his arms up in guard. Clearly, he'd seen his share of bar brawls and gunfights, but where Chasquas was from, the streets were made of shitty mud that doubled as drinking water. As a child he'd seen two women fight to the death over a chicken. At the age of twelve, he'd had to commit double murder before being allowed to join the criminal organization known as the Mara Salvatrucha. And later, as a Mara, he'd racked up the extensive kill count on his arm by fighting Honduran soldiers.

Chasquas's eyes came alive and his facial tattoos curled into a grin as he slipped Sammy's heavy lefts and rights, bobbing and weaving just out of reach. Then, while the biker was off-balance, he flashed forward with a straight fist to the throat, which he followed with a hard knee to the groin. Sammy fell to his knees. Chasquas knew he had to be quick, so he pushed Sammy onto his back and dropped into a full mount to deliver a series of cartilage-crushing throat punches. By the time Baker could pull him off, Sammy's windpipe was as flat as the road it was resting on.

Held back by Baker, Chasquas hissed and spat like a wild animal as he watched Sammy die.

***

It was only a mile back to Harbor Police headquarters from Duke's Bar & Grill, so Walker declined Taylor's offer of a ride, opting instead for a stroll along the Embarcadero. Relishing the fresh seaside air with the gentle waters of the bay to his left and Ruocco Park on the right, he was lost in the peace and quiet when his cell phone buzzed in his pocket.

"Walker, Lieutenant Coffin. SDPD SWAT needs our assistance with an emergency downtown. This is a code-three response. What's your ETA?"

"Two minutes," Walker said, already hitting his stride.

***

"Listen up, gentlemen!" barked Sergeant Ortiz as he slipped on a Kevlar vest and fastened its Velcro flaps. "As you know, there've been a lot of protests since Ronnie Locke took office, and an hour ago it all came to a boiling point. A riot's broken out in a Black Lives Matter march and SDPD and the Sheriff's Department need our help to control it."

Walker checked the load in his Glock 22, rammed the mag back in, worked the action to chamber a round, and desperately hoped he wouldn't have to use it. Then he adjusted his helmet and piled into the BearCat with the rest of the guys.

Once they were on the road, Ortiz continued to brief them. He spoke into his tactical headset, making it unnecessary to shout over the grumble of the armored vehicle's 6.7 L turbo diesel engine. "Several groups showed up to counter-protest against the BLM folks," he said. "There's a large group representing White Lives

Matter and a handful of smaller militias. Fights have broken out between the two sides, and, unfortunately, several citizens have lost their lives. Police included. Mayor Locke has declared a state of emergency."

Sitting shoulder to shoulder with his fellow operators, Walker cradled a Remington 870 12-gauge shotgun with orange plastic furniture. It had four beanbag rounds in the tube, one in the chamber, and eight ready to go in the buttstock holder. With an effective range of forty-five yards, the shot-filled projectiles would smack a rioter like a hard punch to the gut and mark him or her with green chalk to facilitate subsequent arrest. Walker was also supplied with CS gas grenades, OC spray, a ten-pack of flex cuffs, and a riot baton—but no shield. The only live ammunition he had was in his holstered sidearm.

"Our objective," Sergeant Ortiz went on, "is to disperse the rioters and arrest any leading agitators or individuals inciting crowd violence. Remember, all arrestees must be advised of the charges against them and searched for weapons, evidence, and contraband. Our area of responsibility is G Street from Sixth to Eighth Avenues."

Even before the BearCat ground to a halt, large rocks and glass bottles smashed into its side panels, but when Walker and four other well-armed lawmen wearing body armor piled out, most of the protestors gave them a wide berth. Walker swept his gaze over the streets, which were overrun with raging African Americans. He reckoned the BLM movement had made a massive call to protest, mobilizing dissenters from far beyond San Diego County. Some of them were smashing windows and looting stores, but most were fighting with counter-protestors and screaming at the police officers who'd been given the near-impossible task of calming them down.

As he and Furious marched toward the Comfort Inn, where a major disturbance was in progress, Walker recognized several members of Bravo Company, Joshua Pope's militia, by the insignia on their fatigues and the banner they'd hung up behind them. They were much smaller in number than Walker remembered, and Pope was not among them. Only ten men stood under the hotel's blue awning, screaming insults at an advancing group of protestors.

"This is gonna get ugly," said Furious, quickening his pace to a run.

Walker was right behind him. "Break it up!" he yelled at the crowd, carrying his shotgun at the high ready. "Right now! Disperse or face arrest!"

As the two mobs clashed and fists began to fly, Walker and Furious each pulled the pin on a CS gas grenade and tossed it into the fray. Not supplied with respirators, they could only stand back, watch for weapons, and wait for the protestors to move along.

The caustic gas had started to produce the desired effect when a large team of what looked like soldiers arrived. Clad in all-black tactical gear including assault helmets with built-in respirators, the approaching force stormed into the smoke and dragged out the Black men and women, punching and kicking anyone who offered the slightest resistance, and several who didn't fight back at all.

This was the mayor's tactical team, Walker knew, none of whom laid a hand on any member of Bravo Company. Some of them raised their rifles. "Hey!" Walker yelled, but it was too late—CRACK CRACK CRACK! He charged into the gas to pull out two protestors with bleeding stomachs as Furious dragged out a dead man with a hole in his head.

"Move out!" someone bellowed. As one, the mayor's men fell into formation and hustled away.

"You go!" Furious barked, then got on his radio as Walker ditched his shotgun, drew his Glock, and sprinted after the black-suited tactical team, following them into a parking lot that looked like a dirty, crowded campground. Up ahead, the mayor's men stampeded through a sea of tents, crashing into homeless people, knocking them down and shoving them out of the way. Then another shot rang out.

Walker's heart sank as he came to a gaunt, sick-looking middle-aged man with a GSW near his knee. He was surrounded by his peers, whom Walker told to put pressure on the wound as he hustled off in pursuit. "Police!" he barked, pushing his legs to carry him even faster. By then he was close enough to reach out and grab one of the mayor's men, so he leapt forward and took him down.

The guy reached back to draw Walker's pistol as they crashed to the ground. More or less evenly matched, they grappled for control of the gun, alternately pointing the muzzle at each other's bodies, but neither one managed to pull the trigger. Then the pistol skittered away. By that time, a circle of homeless men had gathered around to watch.

Both men clambered to their feet and adopted a fighting stance. The other guy's black full-face helmet made him look like a futuristic stormtrooper from a galaxy far, far away. He threw the first punch, breaking Walker's eyewear.

Walker answered with a scything elbow, but the other guy's helmet did more damage to his elbow than his elbow to the other guy's face. Walker kept his arms up to absorb the resulting barrage of punches, then spotted an opportunity and threw a low round kick that knocked the other guy's knee out of place with a pop.

"Here!" said one of the onlookers, offering Walker the Glock.

Walker took it and whirled around to cover his fallen opponent with a two-handed stance. "Face down, hands on your head!" he shouted, staring through his sights at the man. "You're under arrest!" When the other guy complied, Walker holstered, put a knee on his back, and restrained him with a pair of flex cuffs. Then he took off the man's helmet and stared into hateful eyes.

It was Rick Daniels, the ex-Army sniper.

15

A BRUTAL BON VOYAGE

The *Oasis*
Day 4, 3:00 p.m.
Bay of All Saints
Ensenada, Mexico

Before the *Oasis* arrived at the Mexican port, the passengers were given two choices: they could either be flown home immediately and receive a full refund or be put up in a hotel for a few days while the ship was being repaired, resume the normal itinerary, and receive partial compensation. In light of the bloody backstage murder, the two missing crew members, the fatal accident, and the possibility of a killer still being on the ship, it was only logical that a mere three percent of the passengers had chosen to remain aboard.

From his office in Los Angeles, SSA Pinkney told the undercover operatives to work with the Mexican police to search every passenger stateroom and crew cabin while the *Oasis* was in port, but by the time they arrived, it was too late in the day, so it was decided that the operatives would take the afternoon off and meet with the local authorities the following morning. Before they went ashore for a late lunch, Special Agent Phillips asked Chief Richards if he could visit Amanda Boydon in the brig. Richards reluctantly agreed, and took Phillips down to the lower decks.

"I still think this is a bad idea," Richards muttered in the elevator. "All the evidence points to her."

Phillips shook his head slowly, thoughtfully. "I just can't imagine her murdering her friends. And popping their eyes out?"

Richards stepped out first when the doors slid open. "That's because you're fucking her," he said over his shoulder. "Or *she's* fucking *you*."

Miss Boydon's cell, a stripped-down version of a crew cabin, was provided with a cot-sized bed, a tiny bathroom, no shower, and nothing else. The shapely entertainer was still wearing her bloody dress, and her makeup was smeared from crying.

And she still looks gorgeous, Phillips thought. "Hi," he said as Richards locked him in. "How are you doing?"

Her face lit up halfway and she rose to wrap her arms around him.

"I got you some clothes at the gift shop," he said as he held her close. "I hope they fit."

He felt her nod of thanks on his shoulder, and when he pulled away to look into her sky-blue eyes, they were so pitifully sad! He wanted to kiss her, but decided against it; then he led her to the bed and sat beside her. Just holding hands and staring at the floor, they didn't speak for quite some time.

"Do *you* think I did it?" she finally asked.

He searched her eyes for any sign of deceit. There was none. *He*, however, would have some explaining to do if she turned out to be innocent.

"I swear it wasn't me," she insisted. "Steve and Danielle were my friends. Anyway, I have to tell you something. I know who it was. There was this weird guy in the dressing room before and after the show. He was wearing a light-blue dinner jacket."

Still not sure what to believe, Phillips looked away. On the one hand, he was a federal agent, sworn under God to well and faithfully discharge the duties of his office. All three of his onboard colleagues had told him he was thinking with the wrong head. *Maybe it's true*, he admitted to himself. And if she was lying about this mysterious guy, then Richards was right: all the evidence *did* point to her. On the other hand, Phillips had never bonded so closely with another human being. He felt certain she was just as pure-hearted as he was, and that they were destined to be together. *She's like the wife I never had*, he scoffed bitterly. "What's this guy's name?" he asked.

"I don't remember," she said, "but he was there before the show with his mom and Kevin Massolt, and afterwards he was the only one who came back. I tried to tell the security chief, but he wouldn't listen. Maybe you could talk to him. His name's James Richards."

Phillips blew out a long sigh. Setting aside their emotional involvement, if such a thing were possible, he knew he could rely on his vast experience in suspect interrogation, every bit of which was telling him she was innocent. He leaned in to plant a lingering kiss on her lips. "I'll talk to him. That's a promise." Then he rose to leave. As he turned toward the door, he caught a glimpse of Richards watching angrily through the window.

The security chief opened the door in a huff and locked it again, then led the way down the hall.

"You didn't tell me about the weird guy in the dinner jacket," Phillips said, hurrying to keep up. "Did you check him out?"

"Of course I did," Richards replied, pressing the elevator button. "He is, or was, a passenger named Timothy Reynolds. I personally searched his stateroom and luggage first thing this morning and it was clean. Even had him face the wall and patted him down. His mother's filed a complaint about that, by the way."

"Did you find the jacket?"

"He showed us a blue one and it was spotless."

"Was it light blue?"

Richards turned sharply around to look Phillips in the eye. "Listen, I know you think she's innocent, but there's nothing I can do. Reynolds has already disembarked, and it couldn't have been him anyway, since he wasn't a passenger on any of the other cruises. So unless you guys can dig something up before we get back to LA, I'll be turning Miss Boydon over to the police."

***

Park, Phillips, and Kerr marched down the gangway and headed for the restaurant in the hotel where Excelsior was providing accommodations for the crew and the remaining passengers while the ship was being repaired. The three undercover operatives, along with Chief Richards and Amanda Boydon, were the only people who would sleep aboard the *Oasis*.

"What the *hell* are we supposed to dig up before we get to LA?" Phillips grumbled after they'd been seated. "The original suspects are either dead, missing, or in custody."

"I agree," said Kerr, whose 3D makeup couldn't disguise the irony in his voice. "I don't think we'll dig up anything. The facts are clear."

"That's not what I meant," Phillips retorted with a frown. "We need to take a look at—"

"If it looks like a duck and quacks like a duck," Park declared, leaving the rest of the adage unsaid.

"It's a bloody duck!" roared Kerr, in a fair impression of an English accent. He and Park clinked their beers and chuckled away.

"Tim Reynolds doesn't look good to y'all?" persisted Phillips.

"Honestly, I don't know," said Park, setting down his drink. "But I do know Richards checked him out and he came up clean. I don't even know what he looks like."

At that instant, a middle-aged man with a do-it-yourself haircut and a fancy camera covering his face passed through the restaurant taking pictures of some of the tables, including theirs. Working with a professional air, as though he were on assignment for a newspaper or a magazine, he quickly moved on to the lobby, where he snapped a few more, then stepped out of view.

"I met *Jessica* Reynolds, his mother," said Kerr. "She was more or less what you'd expect from a VIP. But I never got a good look at him."

"Me neither," said Phillips, having paid no particular attention to the photographer's homestyle haircut because Miss Boydon hadn't mentioned it to him. "Fine. For the sake of argument, let's forget about Reynolds for a minute. I still don't know how y'all can be so sure that Amanda's the unsub when dela Cruz and Jackson are unaccounted for."

"I hear you, Phillips," said Park. "She's innocent until proven guilty. Maybe something'll turn up when we search the ship."

They stayed at the table for another hour and a half, discussing non-controversial topics such as high-performance cars and bikes, which normally would have held John Kerr's attention, but not that day. As he peered through a picture window at the marina and the open ocean beyond, sweeping his gaze over the cool blue undulations that stretched on forever, a wave of nostalgia swept him up and carried him away. Just a few drinks ago he'd been howling with laughter, but now his drunkenness had stripped him of the mental barriers that kept his pain out of reach, so as his companions got to talking about superchargers and compression ratios, Kerr was whisked away to a time and place he'd tried hard to forget.

Twenty years earlier, he'd been a star at the FBI's Behavioral Analysis Unit, or BAU, shining such a bright light on the department that he'd been promoted to supervisory special agent before many of his more senior peers. He'd been given his own team of criminal profilers, with whom, over the years, he had apprehended and incarcerated some of the most prolific killers in the history of the country. Unfortunately, it wasn't the kind of job one could just walk away from at five o'clock; it had demanded all of his energy. *Or had it?* his muddled mind asked him. *Maybe I only demanded it from myself.* And since he'd fallen into the habit of sleeping six hours a night and working the rest of the time, Kerr had rented an apartment in Quantico while his family had stayed in Richmond for a variety of logistical reasons.

For him, the feeling of putting a murderer behind bars had been more satisfactory than any other sensation, including that of being surrounded by a loving family—*at least that's what I must have thought*, Kerr lamented as he consoled himself with the rest of his beer. *I was too busy with keynote speeches, award ceremonies, and book deals to see my home life crumbling before my eyes.* He looked over at Park and Phillips, who were involved in a discussion of cylinder heads and intake systems, so he called for another drink and thought back to the case that had effectively killed his career.

They'd identified the subject, a twisted individual who'd racked up a record-breaking number of victims, and after tracking him across the country, they'd cornered him in a school. At that point in Kerr's career, his self-image was so inflated that he'd pulled rank with the local authorities and announced that he would be leading the tactical operation. After a heated argument with the SWAT team leader that left everyone speechless, he'd proceeded to negotiate with the subject, stalling for time while the tactical unit and his own team of profilers initiated entry. *I thought I had him all figured out*, Kerr rued, wiping his cheeks. But while they were on the phone, the subject destroyed himself and everyone else in the building with a series of strategically placed explosive devices.

No! Kerr grieved, laying his head on the table. *The children. Their teachers. The police. My own team, my closest friends! I wish it had been me. I wish it had been me. I wish it had been—*

When a few minutes had passed and Kerr was still face down, Park knew the man had drunk himself unconscious. His heart went out to the guy; he'd been there himself, many times. "Is he okay?"

"Yeah, Kerr gets like that sometimes," Phillips replied, raising his hand for the check.

***

Stryker Lindbloom drove past the hotel in Ensenada where he'd been told Excelsior was putting up the crew and the few remaining passengers. On his left he came to a row of cars parked at the edge of the marina and found an empty space. He pulled into it, killed the engine, checked his messages on his phone, thumbed in a reply to Chasquas, then sat in the driver's seat for a spell, psyching himself up for what he was about to do. The thick-necked ex-con lifted his backside to pull out his wallet, from which he extracted a faded photograph that stirred up a raging storm inside him. The yellowed image showed two tough kids with their arms draped over each other's shoulders.

Lindbloom's face twisted into a scowl as he thought of his younger brother Erick visiting him in prison. The only one who'd taken the time to do so. And when Lindbloom had finally been released, there he'd been, waiting outside to pick him up. But now, thanks to Chief Richards, Erick was dead. At least that's how Lindbloom perceived the events of the thwarted casino robbery on the *Majesty*, which he'd orchestrated while posing as Deputy Chief Lowry.

Now properly riled up, he put the picture back, grabbed his bag off the passenger seat, and stepped out into the late-afternoon sun. Dressed in the crisp white uniform of a high-ranking officer, he strode toward the *Oasis* with the air of a man who belonged on it, and as he came to the top of the gangway, he showed his Lowry ID to the Mexican officials posted there, nodding to them and stepping aboard as though he were too busy and too important to be stopped. They didn't scan it, just as he'd hoped. Then, with the ship to himself and intimate knowledge of its layout, he had no trouble finding the perfect place to hide.

***

Chief Richards stepped out onto the promenade deck to light a cigar as the *Oasis* departed from the Port of Ensenada. It had taken the engineers three days to repair the propulsion system, which for Richards had meant three glorious days of nothing to do but watch the bikinis bouncing on the beach. Every afternoon, he'd come up to this spot to drink iced tequila and watch a distant ball of fire drift down to the horizon line. The only stain on this otherwise perfect and very rare vacation had been his duty to keep an eye on Amanda Boydon. He'd gone down to visit her twice a day, bringing her food from the kitchen, and each time he'd refused to entertain her wild explanations for all the evidence against her. "Save it for the judge," he'd said more than once.

Since Phillips, Park, Kerr, and the Mexican authorities had found nothing significant in the staterooms and staff cabins, and since there were only a handful of passengers aboard and no suspects on the loose, Chief Richards felt more relaxed than he had in a long time—at least since he'd started working with the undercover team. Puffing on sweet smoke, he strolled languidly to the aft end of the ship, where he leaned on the railing to rest his gaze on the fat white wake left behind the vessel as the dry hills of Mexico faded away in the distance.

A few hours later, he dined on a medium-rare porterhouse paired with drinks and laughs with his fellow officers, then retired to his cabin for some well-deserved rest. The door had almost shut behind him when a thick length of pipe jutted inside, preventing it from locking automatically. As the door flew open, Chief Richards whirled around, briefly catching sight of the man he'd known as Lowry, who at that instant was swinging the pipe straight at his head.

The next thing Richards knew, he was face down on the floor and suffering from the worst headache of his life. A geyser of colors exploded from behind his eyes and his porterhouse steak and drinks came surging up into his throat. He had no choice but to choke it back down, since his mouth was gagged by a fragment of one of his T-shirts.

"Bon voyage," gloated Lindbloom, with a cruel half smile and eyes that gleamed with violence. He drew back the heavy pipe and slammed it into Richards' skull, again and again. It took four such strikes to bash the big man's brains out of his head and onto the floor.

16

EXIT DANIELS

Downtown San Diego
Homeless camp near the site of the riot

When Walker pulled Rick Daniels' assault helmet off his head, he was taken aback by his and the crook's striking resemblance to each other. It was like looking in the mirror, except the hateful marksman's skin and hair were darker than his own. "You have the right to remain silent," he began.

The next day, Walker picked up the phone, placed a call, and caught Chief Deputy District Attorney Lynn Peters in the middle of a business lunch, where he imagined she'd be savoring a Caesar salad and a glass of sparkling water. Lynn wasn't a burgers-and-fries kind of gal.

"It's a tricky situation," the fair-haired prosecutor explained in relation to the crimes committed at the riot. "The Mayor's Office bears some liability, as does Pope's private security company to a greater extent, but I'd like to file charges against specific individuals."

"Which is tough to do since they were all wearing full-face assault helmets."

"Exactly," she said. "My plan is to put pressure on Mayor Locke. Maybe he'll get Pope to give up the names."

"Good luck," said Walker. "I bet Pope pulled the trigger himself. What about Daniels?"

"Oh, he'll go down for the rest of his life. Even if we can't prove he killed Mayor O'Connell and shot at you and your family, we've got him on the hook for a long list of other offenses. As you know."

Walker thanked his friend and ended the call, then headed over to the central jail where DAI Dom Taylor, Lynn's boyfriend, was waiting for him outside. Like Walker, the district attorney investigator was clad in dark slacks and a sport coat, and when they shook hands and held each other's stare, it was clear that both lawmen were fired up for what they were about to do. They charged in to the reception area, flashed their credentials, and were buzzed past the desk by a bored-looking guard.

"You finally got him. Congratulations, brother," said Taylor as he stored his sidearm in a small square locker.

"Team effort," Walker replied, placing his own weapon next to Taylor's. "Is he safe in here?"

"As safe as possible, I guess. He's on twenty-four-hour lockdown."

Another guard, this one looking more alive, led them past several checkpoints to a secure interview room. "Holler if you need me," he said before taking his post outside the door.

Daniels was already seated at a table in the center of the room, wearing a baggy dark-blue inmate uniform as well as handcuffs, a belly chain, and leg irons.

"Good morning," said Walker, taking a seat opposite him.

Daniels gave no reply.

"Trafficking in controlled substances," Walker went on. "First-degree murder of a peace officer, attempted murder of a peace officer, assassination of a government official. Possession with the intent to distribute. You're lucky Newsom repealed the death penalty."

Still standing, Taylor shot out his arm to rip out a lock of Daniels' hair. Then he dropped into a chair next to Walker. "I'm betting this'll match the DNA we found in the sniper's perch. But even if it doesn't, I've got your rifle and the bullet from Mr. A's. You're looking at federal prison for life."

"What rifle?" asked Daniels with an insolent grin.

"The one you left at my house, *cabrón*!" Walker growled. "You could have killed my wife and kids."

"Fuck your wife and kids."

Walker didn't know what to do. He felt like beating the man to death, but if he did, he'd be deprived of his job and his liberty.

Taylor, however, was unable to contain himself. He flew out of his chair to seize Daniels by the neck with both hands and squeezed with every ounce of his considerable strength, cursing him for killing so many of his good friends. As Taylor ran down the list, which included Big Don Roberts, all of Taylor's old narcotics unit, and Mayor O'Connell, Walker eased himself to his feet. Then he took slow steps around the table and halfheartedly peeled his buddy's fingers off the man's throat.

Daniels' face was still purple a few minutes later, by which time everyone had returned to their seats. "So what do you want?" the crook asked hoarsely. "Let's make a deal."

"What can you tell us?" Walker returned.

Daniels didn't just talk. He *sang*, giving the location of his own apartment as well as Stephen Baker's secret meth lab, and describing Baker's and Pope's hard drug use, the meetings held aboard Locke's superyacht, and the new mayor's donors. "CEOs of pharmaceutical companies, weapons manufacturers, for-profit prisons, private student loan companies. That kind of thing," Daniels explained.

Walker was calmer now, able to verbalize the rest of the questions he'd come to ask. "Who on Pope's squad shot the protestors and the homeless man at the riot?"

"I don't know. We were all wearing masks. And I haven't talked to any of them since the incident."

"Who hired you to shoot the mayor?"

Daniels' features grew hard. "No one. I was acting alone."

Taylor and Walker didn't get anything else out of him after that, and on the way back to the booking area, the guard who'd been posted outside the door gave no indication that he'd heard anything unusual during the interview.

As Taylor retrieved his sidearm from the small square locker, he muttered, "Lying son of a bitch. Of course he wasn't acting alone."

"I agree," said Walker, returning his own pistol to his hip holster. "But you gotta watch that temper. It's going to get you in trouble one of these days, bro."

"He deserved it," Taylor hissed, so as not to be overheard. "That and so much more!"

***

As Daniels shuffled back to his cell, walking with limited mobility due to his leg restraints, he was absolutely terrified. Aware that Chasquas had connections from Nicaragua to Northern California both in and out of the correctional system, his fear was that the heavily tattooed Honduran might order his death to prevent him from revealing that Ronnie Locke, through Chasquas, had paid him to assassinate the former mayor.

"Get your ass in there," grumbled the guard behind him, after the one in the lead had opened the door.

A few hours later, as his fellow inmates lined up for dinner outside his cell, Daniels watched in horror as a plastic water bottle came down the line and stopped in the hands of the inmate closest to him. That man stepped forward, popped the spout, and squeezed the container to hit him in the face with a pungent stream of gasoline, dousing his shirt and the back of his pants as he sprinted for the far wall, yelling for help. The inmate then squirted the flammable liquid onto Daniels' cot and all over the floor. By then, the prisoners had crowded around the bars. One of them lit a match, yelling, "SoCal Syndicate, motherfucker!" and tossed it onto the trail of fuel that led to Daniels' dripping pants, producing a soft *whoomph*.

His clothes and hair burst into flames and his mind raced to come up with a solution, but his blanket and the floor were afire, and that was by design. He could hear and smell his face sizzling and tried to pat out the pain, but his hands were burning, too. As the prison guards tried to jostle their way through the thick pack of inmates, he screamed for help again, then fell to his knees, popping like a blazing log.

***

To gain access to Daniels' apartment, Walker employed a kinetic breaching tool, which, unlike traditional forcible entry equipment, used a .45 caliber handgun blank to deliver eight hundred foot-pounds of force through a hardened steel ram.

"Nice," said Taylor, keeping his pistol leveled and his eyes forward. He entered first, clearing the right corner, then sweeping quickly toward the left side.

Walker dropped the tool and whipped up his Glock, peering through its iron sights as he headed straight up the middle, swiveling left to check the kitchen, then back to twelve o'clock as he continued to advance toward the only unexplored space. "Clear," he said.

Daniels had been careful not to leave much evidence, but they did find his Colt 1911 and the keys to a motorcycle in the parking lot, both of which gave Walker a terrific idea.

***

"It's a terrible idea," growled Sergeant Cheatham back at headquarters. "Pope and Baker will recognize you."

Taylor nodded. "I agree. We should just raid the meth lab."

But Walker was adamant. "If they're as high as Daniels says they always are, they won't remember me, 'cause I only met them once. This is our best chance to find out who shot the protestors at the riot and who ordered the hit on the mayor."

"We know who ordered the hit," said Taylor.

"You need proof, though," said Sergeant Cheatham. "All right, Walker, but you gon' wear a wire and we gon' be two minutes away."

"No sir. What if they—"

"And your duress code gon' be the word *cigarette*," said Cheatham, whose fiery eyes left no room for further discussion.

***

Daniels knows his bikes, all right, thought Walker on his way out to Baker's compound the next day. The dead crook's dual-sport Honda XR650L had a 644cc engine and high-end multi-use tires, meaning Daniels had been able to commit his crimes with equal ease both on and off the road. Walker felt sure this was the bike he'd seen barreling down the other side of the hill behind his house.

Earlier that morning, he'd dyed his hair brown, dressed himself in Daniels' Bravo Company fatigues, armed himself with the man's pistol, fired up the Honda, and met with Cheatham and Taylor, who followed him in an unmarked unit almost all the way to the compound, pulling off the road just a mile away.

The man at the gate was young, maybe twenty, and dressed in the same green fatigues as Walker was. He nodded and threw a Nazi salute.

Walker wasn't sure Daniels would have returned the gesture, since the crook had been in the U.S. Army, a successor to the men who'd liberated Europe. Then again, most of Pope's men were ex-military. Either way, he couldn't bring himself to do it.

"Where have you been?" the young man asked.

"Had to lie low for a few days," Walker replied.

"You'd better go see Pope. He's in the garage with Baker."

When the guard swung open the gate, Walker flew forward, roaring over a hill and down a slope toward the parking area in front of the garage. There he exchanged his helmet for a camouflage cap, looked down at his thigh, and said, "So far, so good."

Having already tested it, he knew Cheatham and Taylor had heard him through the device he was carrying in his pocket, which was designed to look like a keychain ornament and fitted with a GPS tracker in case he was captured.

The bikers nodded to Walker as he strutted through the garage, and when he stuck his head into the office, Joshua Pope broke into an ecstatic grin. "Hey buddy!" exclaimed the heavily muscled ex-Marine. "I thought we'd lost you."

Baker finished snorting a line at his desk, then rose in happy welcome. "So? What happened?"

Walker fed them the same story he'd told the guard, but in greater detail, having practiced it in front of the mirror.

Pope nodded. "Did you know the DA's filing charges against my security company?" His eyes were beady and unnaturally intense. "You'd think she'd show more respect to a fellow Aryan."

"She has to come down on someone," Baker opined, "'cause she's under pressure from the activists and the liberal media."

"Well, they've got their groups and we've got ours," said Pope. Beads of sweat glistened on his shaven head, even though the room was chilly. "Speaking of which, Mayor Locke's throwing a party for his donors and he told me to invite you."

"I'll be there," Walker growled.

"And you're just in time for training. It'll be great for the guys to see what a real marksman can do!"

Unfortunately, Walker was not a real marksman.

17

ON AND OFF THE HOOK

The *Oasis*
Day 8, 3:00 p.m.
20 nautical miles from Cabo San Lucas

It took the *Oasis* twenty-four hours to sail south along the Baja California Peninsula from Ensenada to Los Cabos, the local name for the ship's next destination. In Tony Park's view, it had been a pleasant journey, all things considered, with no lines at the buffet, immediate service at the bar, and front-row seats in the theater, where the singers and dancers were currently giving a well-rehearsed, if uninspiring, performance. At the intermission, he stepped outside to make a call.

"How are you guys doing?" Carla asked.

Park provided a censored account of the past few days, failing to mention the deadly shootout in the hurricane and glossing over the gory details of Russo's murder at the backstage party. "Looks like it's all over, honey," he told his wife in conclusion. "I'll be back in four days."

"I've got a surprise for you."

"Oh reeeeally," he replied.

"That's not the surprise," she said, giggling. "But it can be if you want."

"Yes, please."

When they ended the call, Park was left with no other company than the spectacular seascape off the bow, straight ahead: wispy clouds stretching an immeasurable distance to the horizon line, and the deep blue of the ocean inviting him to dive in and refresh himself. It reminded him of a surf trip he'd taken several years before, which, as it happened, was the last time he'd been to Cabo San Lucas.

One day when the waves weren't so good, he and Walker had taken the Cabo Arch Tour, an hour-long expedition to Land's End, the southernmost point of the peninsula. Both being lifeguards and competitive to a fault, they couldn't resist diving off and racing to shore, then waiting on the beach for the boat to arrive. Park smiled at the memory.

The *Oasis* was sailing close enough to shore that the peninsula could be seen to port, or Park's left. The captain would skirt around it and drop anchor on the protected side. Then, Park and his colleagues would take a tender boat to go ashore, since the marina wasn't large enough for cruise ships. He was looking forward to a plate of real Mexican food, but first he had to hurry back to catch the rest of the show.

When it was over, the three undercover operatives left the theater together. Kerr was in high spirits again, and Park was laughing with him, but Phillips, inconsolable ever since Miss Boydon had been confined to the brig, was trudging along in a miserable state of mind.

"Come on, Phillips," said Kerr. "It'll do you good to get off the ship."

"No thanks. You guys go ahead."

***

Phillips watched his colleagues step aboard the tender boat, then headed for the security office to see if Chief Richards would allow him a visit to the brig, but Richards wasn't there.

The deputy chief shook his head. "I tried to get him on the radio, but he didn't respond."

"Thanks anyway," said Phillips, forcing a smile. It struck him as odd that the head of security had failed to reply during daylight hours, particularly given the number of critical incidents that had occurred over the past week. Walking quickly now, he ventured down to Richards' cabin, where he knocked and received no answer. "Richards!" he called out.

In the heavy silence that followed, Phillips tried the door. It was locked, but that's when he noticed a trail of blood trickling out from under it, so he whipped out his Beretta, took a few steps back, lowered his shoulder, and burst into the cabin with his pistol leveled. Only after he was sure that the room was clear did he allow his gaze to drop to the bashed-in remains of Richards' head.

***

Park peered through the tender boat's hullside window as the thirty-foot craft motored in to the marina, watching as the setting sun brightened the clouds from behind, which in turn provided a kaleidoscopic backdrop for the famous rocky arch. The higher his eyes traveled, the darker the sky became, its color morphing from orange to red, to violet, to black as night descended on the popular port of call. At Park's suggestion, Kerr turned to look, and he gave an appreciative nod.

Drilled into him since his military days, Park's habit of situational awareness swiveled him back around to face the passengers traveling with them. He consulted his perfect memory and recognized the bulk of them, but there were a few he hadn't ever seen on the ship, and one of them sat alone, close to the side-entry door with his back to almost everyone. That man wore a dark-blue baseball cap and sunglasses, which was unusual, since it was fairly dark already, and he had a familiar thick neck sitting on broad shoulders that also rang a bell. It was Lindbloom, a.k.a. Deputy Lowry, the man who'd tried to shoot Park as he dove off the *Majesty*!

"He's packing," Park said to Kerr as the boat glided up to the dock. When the skipper hopped out to secure her, they rose from their seats but didn't pull their pistols.

Lindbloom suddenly bolted, shoving the captain aside as he leapt out and sprinted away.

"Police!" Park yelled, jostling through the crowd to follow in foot pursuit, drawing his G19 on the run.

Kerr was right behind him. When they came to the main street, he fired his pistol into the air, scattering the masses of slow-moving tourists. "FBI! Move!" the profiler shouted, displaying much more agility than his padded disguise would have led anyone to predict.

Lindbloom broke right, charging up a steep side street, and by the time Park and Kerr rounded the same corner, he was gone. They continued to climb the hill, but Kerr was falling behind and heaving for air. "Let's split up," Park called out over his shoulder, already setting off in the most likely direction. "We'll coordinate by phone!"

Kerr nodded and peeled off in the opposite direction.

As Park hustled along, he carried his Glock in position *sul*, a compressed technique with the muzzle canted left and facing down. It would take him a split second longer to achieve target acquisition than from the high ready, but with the large number of civilians in the area, it was the safest choice. At each wall's edge he slowed to check for an ambush, and every time he saw no sign of the fleeing suspect. Hopefully Kerr would have better luck.

***

Kerr sliced the pie at a corner, caught the suspect in his sights, and pulled the trigger—CRACK CRACK! He thought he'd hit the man, but didn't have visual confirmation, so he kept his eyes on where he'd last seen the suspect while crossing the street. With his P365 at the high ready, he continued along the sidewalk, advancing to the next wall's edge, where he took the turn and saw nothing but a dead-end alley. Cold panic hit him like a freight train. Then a gunshot rang out from above. A white-hot pain tore though the right side of his body from his collarbone to his waist, and his gun fell to the ground with a clatter.

Blood was dripping down from the sky, staining Kerr's shirt. The suspect was directly above him! So Kerr shot his left hand up, found a boot, and yanked on it with all his strength. This caused his assailant to come tumbling down from a ladder on the wall, and his assailant's arm to break when it slammed into the pavement.

Both Kerr and Lindbloom were on their hands and knees, weakly scrambling for their weapons when a commanding voice stopped them cold: "¡Alto! Policia. Las manos arriba, ¡ahora!"

A young Mexican policeman was covering them with a pistol while stooping to pick up their guns. Lindbloom's face fell in utter disappointment, but Kerr blew out a sigh of relief.

***

Park hustled through the streets toward the sound of gunfire. When he finally arrived on scene, he found Kerr wounded and with his wrists behind his back, but alive, at least, and he was astonished to see an old friend snapping handcuffs on the suspect. "Murci!" Park exclaimed, causing the Mexican policeman to turn his way.

The officer's stern features brightened immediately. "Park! You know to this man?" Murci asked in halting English, gesturing toward Agent Kerr.

Park nodded, so Murci told his fellow officers to release him.

"FBI, goddammit," grumbled Kerr, loud enough for Murci to hear. "I tried to tell him but he wouldn't let me pull out my credentials."

Murci shrugged.

"Are you hit?" Park asked, jutting his chin toward the blood on Kerr's shirt.

"Yeah. In and out. But you should see the other guy."

"Ha!"

Lindbloom was sitting against a wall with two dark patches seeping through his shirt at the level of the abdomen, and a hollow depression where one of his shoulders should have been, most likely due to an anterior dislocation.

That's when Phillips and two more Mexican policemen came running up. "Hey guys," said Phillips. "*Buenas tardes.*" He flipped open his leather cred pack, holding it up so Murci could get a good look. "*Agente Especial Scott Phillips de la efeh-beh-ee. A sus órdenes.*"

Murci offered his hand. "*Oficial Luciano Sánchez. Policia Ministerial de Los Cabos.*"

Phillips served as Murci's interpreter, verbally translating Murci's questions for Lindbloom as well as the crook's reluctant replies. Then he did the same for the paramedics, who confirmed that Kerr's GSW was indeed an exiting wound with no major blood vessels or organs involved.

When Murci's sergeant rolled up in a large police pickup, he insisted that Lindbloom be taken into local custody. Phillips agreed, on the condition that he be allowed to keep the burner phone found on Lindbloom, as it related to a crime committed aboard a ship registered in the United States. Phillips also made sure to inform the local sergeant that Lindbloom was an extremely dangerous man, even in his present condition, and that a pair of U.S. marshals would be coming to collect him as soon as the Mexican authorities approved his extradition.

At that point, emergency response settled into administrative procedure, giving Park and Murci a chance to talk. The brave young man, whose assistance had proven invaluable in Park's and Walker's last major case, hadn't changed much in just under a year; some of his tattoos had been lasered off, but his buzz cut was the same as before and his body equally lean and strong.

"I didn't know you'd moved to Cabo," Park said. "How's Nayeli?"

"More or less," Murci said, nodding but with a discouraged frown. "Thank you. She is still very—how do you say—altered?"

"Upset?"

"Yes, upset. But I think she will go to school. Private school," Murci added proudly. "And we bought a hotel. For this we moved to *Los Cabos*."

Park stopped himself from offering any kind of congratulations for the Sanchez family's newfound wealth, as it had resulted from an unspeakably traumatic experience. He merely nodded, hoping that Murci's younger sister might someday rise above her pain.

"*Gracias*, Murci," Park said a moment later. "Outstanding work. I'll make sure you get an official recommendation for this."

"Thank *you*, Tony. For everything," the young man replied. Then they bade each other the best of luck, shook on it, and never saw each other again.

In the tender boat on the way back to the *Oasis*, Agent Kerr produced a black prepaid cell phone. "I bet *this* is going to come in handy," he said, scrolling through the data on the device.

"I don't know what for," retorted Phillips. "Lindbloom's not getting out of prison for a long time, if ever."

Kerr was right and Phillips was wrong. The burner phone would turn out to be a critical piece of evidence, but the man who murdered Chief Richards would never spend another day behind bars.

***

One week later, Stryker Lindbloom opened his eyes a crack to watch a pair of U.S. marshals take their seats in the airplane a few rows forward from where he'd been seated. He was pleased to note that they weren't watching him as closely as they might have been, had he not been feigning semiconsciousness following the surgery he'd undergone. *Strike one.*

He had trained for this moment. While serving a ten-year stint in San Quentin, he'd been taught by the older inmates how to move and fight in full restraints, using ropes as makeshift handcuffs, leg irons, and belly chains. So now, as the ten-seater gathered speed and lifted its nose, Lindbloom was ready to act. Time was critical, since the hospital orderlies might have already found the spit-out pile of painkillers he'd left in his bedsheets. "I have to take a shit," he called out groggily.

Chief Deputy U.S. Marshal Blocker, the senior of the two men minding him, grunted and frowned. "Go ahead," Blocker said from his seat, which faced Lindbloom's. "The bathroom's at the back."

Lindbloom rose with counterfeit drowsiness. "How am I supposed to wipe my ass?" he said, showing Blocker his wrists, which were shackled to the chain around his waist.

"You aren't," Blocker retorted.

It was worth a try, Lindbloom thought, turning to shuffle back to the aft end of the plane. When he reached the inward-swinging door, he made a show of his supposed inability to reach the latch, even trying with his nose, which would have been comical under other circumstances.

Blocker blew out a sigh of irritation and stood up. *Strike two.* As he came striding down the aisle with a pistol on his right hip, Lindbloom studied the holster's thumb break. The thick leather loop would normally have made it difficult to disarm the man, but Lindbloom had been trained to unsnap a similar model, one-handed, in the dark, and under duress. So he moved left, flattening himself awkwardly against an empty seat, supposedly to let Blocker by, while actually planning to pull out the gun just like he'd practiced in prison.

"No!" Blocker barked. "Step to the other side until I pass."

Lindbloom complied. Now that the marshal's weapon was on the far side of his body, there was only one thing to do. As Blocker walked by, Lindbloom grabbed two handfuls of his shirt and bit into his neck, not too high since the carotid artery goes internal as it nears the brain. Blood spouted and sprayed into Lindbloom's mouth and all over his face, but he continued to bite down and shake his head like a dog to tear the flesh. As he did, he spun the disoriented marshal around and quickly unholstered the man's pistol, a Staccato P 2011, just as expected. By that time, the second marshal was on his feet with his own gun leveled, but he didn't fire for fear of shooting his partner. *Strike three. Blocker's already dead.*

Lindbloom would have to fire upwards from his waist, but he knew the Staccato would easily penetrate the soft seats between him and the second marshal, so as Blocker fell, Lindbloom took aim as best he could and pulled the trigger, catching the second marshal somewhere on his lower body. Then he shuffled forward to get a better shot, firing as he went—BLAM BLAM BLAM! The last of those rounds tore a hole in the middle of the second marshal's face, splattering the panel behind him with chunky gore.

Having visualized this entire routine in advance, Lindbloom proceeded with no hesitation.

Search the marshal's pockets.

Find the handcuff key.

Force the pilots to re-route.

Then all he had to worry about was that damn burner phone the feds had found on him in Cabo.

18

A BLOOD-CRAZED WARRIOR

Stephen Baker's rural compound
East County
San Diego

"Shoot that n****r," Pope muttered to Walker, much to the delight of the all-white company of men standing around.

Walker would have liked nothing more than to force the muzzle of his sniper rifle into the militia leader's mouth and blow his tiny brain out the back of his head, but, he reminded himself, he was there to catch a bigger fish, impersonating Rick Daniels to collect evidence regarding the assassination of Mayor O'Connell and the shootings at the riot. And the recording he'd just obtained would help in the latter regard.

From the prone position, Walker put his eye to a range finder, a handheld device that measured the distance to the paper target Pope had just described as an African American; it was six hundred yards away. Based on that information, Walker adjusted the dial on his rifle scope to make the corresponding elevation changes. Luckily, there wasn't much wind, because if he missed, Bravo Company would wonder why a trained marksman had failed to hit such an easy target, and fortunately, Lieutenant Coffin, who had been a Marine Corps scout sniper, had given Walker a crash course to prepare him for this undercover assignment.

Walker settled himself behind the scope and slowed his respiration as he lined up the paper silhouette in the crosshairs, then applied slight pressure to the trigger. At the natural pause between breaths, he completed the press—CRACK!—and the rifle leapt back into his shoulder as the round exploded out of the barrel. When he got the scope back on the target, he saw a hole in the paper man's head. Not at dead center, but close enough. "All right, guys," Walker bellowed with extreme relief. "Your turn."

He had all the men, including Pope, practice proper technique for shooting in the prone. Then they switched to pistols and worked on the holster draw, malfunction clearance, and the failure-to-stop drill, in which the shooter quickly draws, presents, and places two rounds into the target's center mass followed by a head shot, all while backpedaling.

The final exercise was an hour-long run with their packs on. "Good!" Walker hollered once most of the men had made it back to the outdoor shelter. "Now get some water." Sweat pooled in the small of his back as he filled a cup for himself.

Some of the guys cracked open a can of beer, Pope being one of them. He pounded it, crushed the empty with his hand, and tossed it accurately into an open-head steel drum. "Fall in, girls!" he nearly screamed.

Each member of the company hustled forward to assemble in three ranks of eight. Walker stayed up front with Pope, facing the rest of the militia.

"Let's thank Corporal Daniels for the training today!" Pope bellowed.

"Oo-rah!" they bellowed back as one.

As they all marched back to the parking area, a cluster of cabins came into view on the left. Berg, one of the older guys, meaning close to Walker's age, asked Pope and Walker if they wanted a beer.

Pope declined, saying he had to take care of something, but Walker agreed and followed Berg into one of the small wooden dwellings.

"Have a seat," said Berg, pulling open the fridge and tossing a can to Walker. Then he stripped off his sweaty T-shirt and headed into the bedroom for a clean one. Berg was tall, wiry, and bearded, with a tattoo that covered most of his back: the head of a goat with beady red eyes. That and one of the posters on the wall, which featured an inverted pentagram within a circle, left no doubt as to his religious leanings.

When Berg reappeared, he dropped onto the same couch as Walker and put his feet up on the coffee table. He offered his can to clink against, which Walker bumped with his own, and the guys drained a good amount of their contents.

"Does the whole company live here?" Walker asked, wiping his mouth with the back of his hand.

Berg shook his head. "Only some of us. Me, Pope, Baker, and a few other guys."

Later, halfway done with his second beer, Walker jutted his chin toward a different poster. This one showed a scantily clad young woman straddling a motorcycle. "You ride?" he asked, hoping the topic might lead to a discussion of Stephen Baker's business relationship with Joshua Pope. Directly below that poster, Walker didn't fail to notice, there was a desktop computer sitting on a table.

"Berg, front and center!" someone barked from outside the cabin. It sounded like Pope.

"Yeah, I do ride," Berg said, then stepped out to speak with his visitor.

Walker flew to the window and peeked through the curtains. Pope and Berg were standing on the dirt road with their heads close together, conferencing quietly. Certain they'd discovered his true identity and were planning to attack, Walker prepared to utter his duress code and draw Daniels' pistol.

Berg nodded and headed back to the cabin. By the time he burst through the door, Walker was back on the sofa.

"I'll be back in fifteen," said Berg, slipping on a tactical vest. "There's more beer in the fridge."

"Roger that," said Walker casually, despite his racing pulse. When the door clacked shut, he made for the window again and watched as Pope and Berg jogged away. Then he pulled a portable hard disk out of his pocket and plugged it in to the desktop computer.

Berg's old machine took forever to clone itself. By the time Walker moved on to the second step, the installation of a piece of software, his heart rate had been in the red zone for so long that, aside from being caught and killed, he was afraid he'd die of a heart attack. Finally, he got the green check mark and shut the computer down. Shoving the hard disk back into his pocket, he hustled to the fridge for a couple of beers, cracked them open, poured them down the sink, carried the empties to the sitting room, and tried his best to relax.

"Sorry about that," said Berg, crashing back into the cabin less than a minute later. "Bunch of nosy trespassers." Walker doubted that explanation, but made no mention of it as he and Berg proceeded to knock back a couple more cold ones. Their conversation revolved around Berg's service in the Marine Corps, which was where he'd met Joshua Pope.

It was as friendly a sit-down as two trained killers can have, Walker reckoned. But since he'd never served in the military, he was worried that Berg might ask him about Daniels' time in the Army, and he didn't want to give himself away. So he said, "I gotta go. Thanks for the beers. Next time they're on me."

The next time would be at Ronnie Locke's party on the superyacht, a festive ocean cruise. *I'll meet the new mayor and a bunch of other crooks*, Walker thought as stomped the Honda into gear, *but it'll be tough to get out of there if something goes wrong.*

***

"I'm sorry to hear that," Walker said into his cell phone a few days later.

"Richards was a good man," came Park's voice in his ear. "And Lindbloom got away. He took out two marshals on a JPATS jet and forced the pilots to fly him to safety."

"Any idea where he is now?"

"They landed in Las Vegas, but we're assuming he went from there to San Diego, since he's colluding with Chasquas."

"No way!" exclaimed Walker.

"*Sí, güey.* There were only a couple of messages on Lindbloom's burner phone, but one of them gave the location of a safe house in Lemon Grove. Looks like Chasquas is smuggling narcotics into the country from Mexico."

"So he's running the Cartel del Norte's old routes."

"Apparently so. I'll email you all the information."

"Thanks, bro," said Walker. "Hey, I've got a surprise for you."

"That's what Carla said."

"Listen. I'm guessing you had no luck with any of your suspects. Right?"

"More or less. We've got one of them in the brig, but Phillips doesn't think it's her."

"It's *not* her," Walker said. "Remember that new biker gang out in East County I told you about?"

"The East County Warlords, run by Stephen Baker, the last surviving member of the North County Kings. Headquartered on a fifty-acre compound where Bravo Company trains under Joshua Pope."

Of *course* Park remembered. Walker shook his head at himself. "Correct," he said. "And there's a huge underground meth lab there, but that's another story. Anyway, posing as Rick Daniels, I got into one of the cabins, found a computer, and installed Choi's remote access program. Turns out the guy who lives there frequents a dark web forum for devil worshippers, and Choi went through all the message boards. He didn't find much, since most of the details were communicated by direct message, but he did learn that the killings on the cruise ships were orchestrated by someone traveling on the *Oasis* with his or her mother."

"Tim Reynolds," Park said slowly. "So Miss Boydon *was* telling the truth."

"Who?"

"I'll tell you the whole story when I get back. I gotta go, brother. Appreciate the call."

"Likewise, man. See you soon."

***

Acting on the intelligence provided by Park, Walker applied for a warrant to search Chasquas's safe house. Then he, DAI Taylor, Sergeant Cheatham, and Furious drove out to Lemon Grove in an unmarked unit.

"I doubt there'll be anyone there," Walker said from the passenger seat.

"Me too," Taylor replied from behind him as he secured his tactical helmet. "If I were Lindbloom, I would have warned Chasquas as soon as I lost that burner phone."

Behind the wheel, Sergeant Cheatham looked furious, as did Furious, of course, who sat behind him. With the lights and siren off, Cheatham pulled up to a residence two houses down from the target location. They stepped out quietly, closed the doors softly, advanced at a run, and stopped at the front door, two of them on either side. Each wore a ballistic vest, and all but Furious held an M4 carbine at the compressed low ready position. Taylor was on point, Walker on cover, Cheatham had lead, and Furious played the dual role of breacher and rear security.

Taylor rapped his knuckles on the door and shouted, "Police!"

Furious turned to look across the street. Several neighbors had come out to see what was happening, so he made a one-armed gesture in the air, waving them back into their homes. Then, since a reasonable amount of time had passed after Taylor's announcement of police presence, Furious stepped forward with the kinetic breaching tool, defeated the lock, and pushed the door open.

Taylor and Walker entered immediately, crossing to the far right and near left corners, and Cheatham and Furious were right behind them, covering parallel sight lines straight down the middle. For a moment, all was clear and quiet. Then three consecutive explosions in the middle of the room hurled them against the walls like open hands swatting flies.

Walker's ears were ringing as he clambered to his feet. Surrounded by flames and smoke, he figured the only place from which the attack could have originated was an ascending staircase to his right, so he brought his M4 to bear and targeted the highest step he could see. Sure enough, three men came charging down with their rifles leveled, so he squeezed the trigger immediately and caught the first one in the head with a three-round burst, dropping him like a stone. But that man also fired on sight, blasting Walker off his feet once again.

Amid the crackling gunfire, Walker lay on his back, feeling like he'd been hit in the chest by a truck. With great difficulty, he sat up to sight the staircase, but the two remaining suspects had already escaped through the front door. Furious took off after them.

Taylor lay unconscious at the base of the wall opposite the stairs. Walker could see him breathing. But Sergeant Cheatham was sprawled out on the floor with a jagged, stringy crater where his left shoulder should have been, and with far too much of his lower body missing for him to have any chance of survival.

"Sarge!" shouted Walker, racing to his mentor's side and dropping to his knees.

Cheatham was fading in and out. It was all he could do to hold Walker's gaze. "Be good ... to your ... good self, son," he managed before the twinkle drained out of his eyes.

"No!" Walker screamed, seeing red. He snatched up his rifle and charged out the front door, spotting two men on motorcycles racing away in the distance and Furious hurrying back toward the house.

"They shot out our tires!" shouted Furious.

Walker searched the man he'd gunned down and found a set of keys. An instant later, he was starting up the last of the motorbikes in the side yard. "I got 'em. You get on the radio," he said to Furious, then accelerated down the driveway and carved a hard left turn, shifting quickly through the gears as the bike leapt up to speed, screaming into the wind like a blood-crazed warrior.

19

THE BLACK MASS

Hacienda Heights
Los Angeles, California
115 miles north of San Diego

Tim Reynolds cranked up his car stereo and grinned with pride as he drove to the music of Mozart, his favorite composer. Nothing like those awful hissed incantations or screams of the damned they played at the rituals.

Reynolds' internet recruiting strategy had far surpassed his wildest hopes. In a span of only six months, his "serial killer" sprcc had earned him hundreds of followers in the dark web forum, dozens of whom lived in LA, so he'd invited them and everyone else within driving distance to the next black mass, his current destination.

Regrettably, there was unfinished business to attend to. Amanda Boydon had certainly told the *Oasis*'s security team about his being in the dressing room before Russo was killed, since they'd searched his room and patted him down. Consequently, the three undercover operatives would also be looking for him, but with the picture he'd taken at the restaurant in Ensenada, a hacker had found the three agents' identities and provided Reynolds with their home addresses.

Miss Boydon had been even easier to track down, the hacker had said, because she'd used her credit card to pay for three nights at a hotel. *And now that I've got so many local followers,* Reynolds thought, *there's no shortage of weak-minded bootlickers just waiting for me to give the order to take her out.*

He steered up a canyon road and stopped at the top of a hill, close to the head of a hiking trail. The light of the full moon was more than enough for him to follow the stacks of rocks that showed the way to the old pumping station, which took twenty minutes to reach, and which was tough to spot through all the overgrowth, but the steel door was oiled at the hinges. It swung open to reveal a dark, musty space that stretched fifty yards to the far end. Burning torches lined the side walls, so flames flickered and shadows danced as Reynolds made his way to the front of the unholy temple.

The chairs had been set out already, but there was no one in them as he came to the altar, which stood on a raised platform surrounded by burning candles. The far wall was adorned with the head of the Devil, inverted pentagrams, the German SS lightning-bolt insignia, and the words "THOU SHALT KILL" all painted in red.

"Brother Tim," the priest at the altar intoned. "Thank you for coming early." Known only as Father John, the man wore a long black robe and a matching peaked hood with eye slits. He looked like a member of the Ku Klux Klan dressed in black instead of white. "Ave Satanas," he said.

"Ave Satanas," Reynolds returned.

"Are you ready, Brother Tim?"

"Yes, Father."

"Good. I'm excited for you." The priest handed Reynolds a folded robe and hood just like his own, a privilege extended only to prophets, priests, and the Master. "Would you turn on the music for me?"

"Yes, Father John."

Soon after that, the congregants began to trickle in, with recorded screams and hissed incantations playing in the background. Then, at the appointed hour, Father John and the Master emerged from opposite sides of an ornamental partition, stepping solemnly onto the raised platform, or chancel, as it was called. They were dressed exactly alike except that the Master's hood and waistcord were red, not black like Father John's.

The Master took his place at the altar and raised his hands in the air. "*In nomine Dei nostri Satanas Luciferi Excelsi,*" he called out, in a deep voice that echoed throughout the hall.

"Amen," the congregants responded as one.

"The grace of our lord Satan, and the hate that he provides, and the communion of the demons be with you all."

"And also with you."

It's time, thought Reynolds, who was sitting in the front row wishing he had a German shepherd on a leash. At the start of every mass, Satan was supposed to be invoked by the murder of an animal or a person. Unfortunately, through no fault of his own, that part of the service had been canceled at the last minute. Cloaked in his new robe and hood with a white waistcord that identified him as a prophet, he rose and took his place on the chancel steps, turning to stand before the congregation. He smiled thinly but ground his teeth in embarrassment as he turned to Father John, who at that point would have brought down an empty silver chalice. Reynolds would have slit the drugged dog's throat and filled the vessel with spurting blood, then nodded to two acolytes, who would have dragged the dog away to be butchered, and the resulting raw flesh and blood would have been eaten and drunk for communion. However, only one of those two acolytes was in attendance, and at the moment he was holding up the severed ear of the German shepherd he and the other one had tried to capture, as though Reynolds might be aided or appeased in some way by the sight. *Idiots!* he thought, still smiling thinly. The second acolyte had been eaten by a pit bull in the attempt. *Good thing there'd been reserves in the freezer.*

As Reynolds made his way up to the chancel and stood behind the pulpit, Father John led the assemblage in a grating hymn, purposefully sung in deep and out-of-tune voices. Once the song had come to an end, Reynolds called out, "Ave Satanas."

"Ave Satanas," the congregation replied in chorus.

He proceeded to introduce himself and explain what he'd done to earn his promotion. Then he asked his four killers, the chosen ones, to rise and receive a standing ovation. Reynolds also mentioned the man who'd had to abort his mission, and that person was politely rewarded with a smattering of applause.

They sang another hymn, after which the members of "The Faith," as the cult was called, were invited to come forward to publicly admit as sins the good deeds they had done since the last gathering, and the evil deeds that they had failed to do. Then Reynolds assisted Father John and the Master with communion, which was followed by a collective recitation of The Lord's Prayer, but not the original version. This one started with "Our Father, who art in Hell."

The Master closed the ceremony with *"Ego vos benedico in nomine Magni Dei Nostri Satanas,"* at which point the congregation was free to go.

"Brother Tim," boomed the Master, motioning for Reynolds to join him and Father John at the altar. "You did an outstanding job tonight." He shook Reynolds' hand and involved him in the succeeding conversations until every member had left the premises. Then the Master handed Reynolds an envelope stuffed with cash and produced a sizeable bag of cocaine, which the three men divided into lines and snorted off the altar to their hearts' content, lifting the front flaps of their pointed hoods just enough to do so.

In the middle of that process, Father John turned to the newest member of the High Command and said, "You are now in charge of distribution. I'll be moving on to bigger things."

"Thank you, Father. It's an honor," Reynolds replied. It would be easy. He was popular now, with a hundred mentally ill followers eager to carry out his orders, even if that meant selling narcotics and murdering federal agents.

"Excellent," the Master boomed. "Then you're invited to a party. A good friend of mine owns a superyacht. Or should I say a *bad* friend?"

The three men's belly laughs erupted from the abyss of darkness, echoing powerfully throughout the torch-lit room.

***

Special Agent Scott Phillips strode out of the LA field office, shaking his head in disgust after a long day of meetings with difficult colleagues, but when he spotted his fully restored 1977 Ford Mustang Cobra II in glossy black with gold racing stripes, he, too, was fully restored. That model year hadn't been anyone's favorite Mustang, especially not with the standard 2.3 L V6, but just before the undercover assignment, Phillips had expertly installed a 5.7 L stroker V8 and a modern sound system.

His best friend grumbled to life at the turn of a key. Then, with the inspirational sounds of classic rock pumping through an array of high-end speakers, he roared away from work as fast as he safely could. But he didn't head west on Wilshire to his crappy little duplex. (*At least it's a crappy little duplex located three blocks from the Santa Monica Pier*, Phillips told himself.) Instead, he hopped on the 405 south and crawled through rush-hour traffic to a Residence Inn near the airport, where Amanda Boydon was staying before leaving for her next gig in a few days.

Phillips hated traffic. It was one of the worst things about life in LA. Ordinarily, he'd be fuming and cursing and tailgating the car ahead, braking hard and often so no one could cut into his lane. But not today. Excited to spend time with the stunning entertainer and grateful for what Walker had done to make that possible, he just cranked up the music and sang along. Another thing Phillips was glad about was that he'd already come clean, telling her his real name and occupation, and she'd forgiven him right away.

"Hey Scott!" Amanda exclaimed, flashing that brilliant smile of hers as he stepped in to the lobby. They shared a modest kiss and a long embrace, then headed straight for the Cobra II. As he drove, he kept his eyes on the road for the most part, but at times he'd turn to glance at her. Whenever that happened, his face would break into a grin that wouldn't go away. She wasn't heavily made up or wearing a fancy dress like she had on the cruise; this evening she'd opted for tight-fitting jeans, a touch of cosmetics, and a white blouse, onto which her lustrous blond locks spilled past her shoulders.

They made it to Playa Del Rey Beach just in time for the sunset, which they watched from a booth in a cozy little hamburger joint.

"So you're headed to the Caribbean," he said, setting the menu down. He knew what he wanted, and it wasn't on the laminated list of dishes served.

"Thanks to *you* I am," she replied, reaching across the table for his hand. "You were the only one who believed me." Then her face fell into a pouty frown and she hit him with those liquid blue eyes. "Am I ever going to see you again?"

"Of course you are," he answered truthfully. "But it's a good thing you're going away. At least for now. Reynolds is still at large."

"Are you going to go after him?"

"*We* are going to go after him. I've got an early meeting tomorrow with Park and Kerr."

"I knew they weren't just your buddies."

Outside, the shifting display of colors over the vast expanse of the ocean made for a perfect backdrop to the meal. They both knew what was going to happen back at the Residence Inn, but they took their time, strolling along the beach after dinner with their pant legs rolled up, carrying their shoes and holding hands as the waves thumped in and slid up the sand, over and over again.

"Stay in touch?" she murmured at six in the morning when he leaned over to kiss her lips.

"Count on it," he promised, slowly pulling away, holding her heart-stopping gaze in the faint light of the early morning. But he didn't look back when he turned to leave, striding out the door, down the hall, and to his car with determination. It wouldn't be easy to catch Reynolds, Phillips knew, but he wouldn't stop until he did.

***

Three hours later, Amanda Boydon stirred and stretched in bed, feeling encouraged for the first time in years. *Maybe I can convince Scott to join me in the Caribbean. He'd make a great security chief.* Her features brightened as she swung her legs over the side of the bed and stood. *There's no "maybe" about it,* she concluded. *He loves me.*

On her way to the bathroom, someone knocked on the door. "Housekeeping," a female voice called out.

"Just a minute," Boydon replied in a cheery sing-song voice, stepping into her jeans and pulling on a blouse. She smoothed her hair as she peered through the peephole to see who it was: a woman in uniform with a name tag on. "Yes?" the singer said as she opened the door, and two masked men burst into the room, charging past her with the housekeeper in tow.

"You said you were going to let me go!" the room cleaner protested.

"I lied," one of the intruders sneered as he plunged a knife into the housekeeper's belly. "Ave Satanas."

***

One hundred and twenty miles south of LA, down in San Diego, Park and Carla had had a date on the same night as Phillips and Miss Boydon, but theirs was an evening in.

"Ready Freddie?" Carla called out in a melodious tone that sounded sweeter to Park's ears than the most exquisite classical music ever composed. He finished washing his hands and stepped into the bedroom, where his sweetheart was waiting for him on the bed. Her wavy brown hair fell in cascades, framing exquisitely delicate facial features, and her tender smile reassured him of her undying love. Plus her sweat shorts were riding so high up on her thighs that he could see her thong.

They held hands as they watched the show, stealing kisses at slow moments in the story. *If there's a heaven*, Park told himself, *this is it*. Before long, those quick smooches developed into something more and the program was put on pause; Park made good use of his athletic talent and Carla had no trouble keeping up with him. Then came a second episode of the series, with more kisses followed by further athleticism. This cycle repeated itself until two in the morning, when they lay on their backs in the moonlight, naked, sweaty, and heaving for air. "Ready for the surprise?" Carla asked, with a delighted smile the size of Texas. "I'm pregnant!"

Having wanted children for years, they both cried tears of joy and smothered each other with hugs and kisses. But they froze when the security system began to shriek.

Park was startled but he didn't let it show. "It's probably nothing," he said, pulling away gently. But he flew into a pair of jeans, grabbed his Navy Sig, and chambered a round as he hustled down the stairs. If there was anyone outside threatening to hurt his pregnant wife—a team of intruders, even—then they, too, were in for a surprise: a big nine-millimeter surprise fired by a seasoned killer.

20

WALKER VERSUS CHASQUAS

Lemon Grove
Just east of Downtown San Diego

Chasquas loved coffee. He drank it all day, every day, with no special regard for quality. The important thing was the continuous intake of its active ingredient, since after decades of hard drug use, his last remaining vices (caffeine and nicotine) marked the only line between him and insanity. *And it's a thin line,* he joked to himself in Spanish while sipping on a fifth cup of java. A highly intelligent man, Chasquas knew his brain had suffered permanent damage.

What he didn't know was that the safe house he was sitting in would be raided that day by a tactical team comprising Walker, Cheatham, Taylor, and Furious, so it was with a casual air that he caught his shaven-headed lieutenants' gazes, lifted his chin in farewell, shouldered his backpack, and headed for the side yard, where he prayed to Our Lady of the Holy Death. He always asked that deity for her blessing whenever he rode into danger.

He mounted his 1900cc Indian Chief Dark Horse and eased it down the driveway. When he hit the street, he accelerated into a turn and shifted through the gears as the two-wheeler gained momentum. Bound for Ronnie Locke's superyacht with yet another kilo of pure cocaine, Chasquas wondered if the so-called city leader had ever worked a day in his life.

"Lanky!" Locke exclaimed, looking up from his desk with a grin as Chasquas strode in to the study, but his smile faded as quickly as it had appeared. "Search him," he snapped.

Joshua Pope barreled forward to put his hands on Chasquas, but the latter pushed him away. "*No me toques, pendejo,*" the indignant visitor growled, reaching under his shirt for his P320, not to fire it but to hand it over.

"Easy!" Pope barked, instantly presenting his own pistol with both arms extended, his finger on the trigger, and his eyes wide with drug-fueled violence.

Chasquas frowned at the big militia leader and proceeded to drop out his gun's magazine and cycle the action to eject a cartridge, which he caught in mid-air. Then he surrendered the firearm, butt forward.

"Fuckin' beaner," Pope muttered, still aiming his pistol at Chasquas's chest.

"What you say?" Chasquas replied, inching closer, fairly certain he could disarm this drug-addled loser. After that it would be easy to murder both him and Locke, defend himself against the guards, and steal everything of value.

"Just get your ass over here," Locke commanded. "I'm busy."

Locke didn't look busy, but Chasquas swallowed his pride—again—and strutted to the desk where the fat man sat. He reached into his pack and handed over a white brick wrapped in plastic. In return, Locke gave him a manila envelope containing what felt like three bundles of bills, not four.

Chasquas closed his eyes for a moment and drew a calming breath. *I knew I should have killed this motherfucker when I had the chance.* Then his eyelids flew open and he stared at Locke, growling, "This is too small."

"First of all," the crooked statesman retorted, "you'd better use some of that money to pay for English classes. Secondly, it's only a tiny adjustment, twenty-five percent, and it's nothing personal, just how I do business. Take it or leave it."

"Leave it," Chasquas replied.

Locke smirked and shook his head. "I don't think so. What are you gonna do? How many men you got in your little gang, like five?"

"Four," said Pope. "Now that Daniels is working for me."

Chasquas whirled around. The hate group leader still had his pistol trained on his center mass.

"Oh, you didn't know?" Pope's grin widened. "Yeah, he came out to the compound just the other day. Wasn't as good of a shot as I thought he'd be." Then Pope's face fell deadly serious. "Give the mayor his money back or you're dead. And you can forget about your gun."

"Just get the fuck out of here," said Locke, waving Chasquas away. "Better yet, get the fuck out of town. I don't ever want to see you in San Diego again."

Chasquas stared at Locke in disbelief. Then he turned back to Pope, dropped the envelope on the floor, and stormed off the ship. On his way down to the dock, he heard Locke mutter, "Fuckin' beaner," then explode into roaring laughter, which, along with the words "What are you gonna do?" echoed in his mind all the way back to the safe house.

An hour later, while relaxing in his sitting room with his shaven-headed lieutenants and a sixth cup of coffee, Chasquas was startled by a knocking at the door and a strong male voice: "Police!"

In Spanish, he turned to his men and whispered, "Defensive positions."

They took quietly to their feet, donning tactical vests and readying rifles: new prototypes of the FX-05 Xiuhcoatl with 40mm under-barrel grenade launchers, a recent gift from the

Sinaloa Cartel, which Chasquas had been waiting for a chance to try out. "Let's see what these motherfuckers can do," he hissed in his native language as they sneaked up the stairs and took ambush positions on the second-floor landing.

When the police crashed through the door, he and his men let loose with the 40mm grenades, firing down at the first floor. BOOM!—BOOM!—BOOM! Then, with rifles blazing, they charged down the stairs and out to the side yard, losing one man before they came to the bikes. On his way out of the neighborhood, Chasquas looked back to see an officer chasing him on the one bike he'd left behind. He cursed himself for failing to shoot out its tires, although, to his credit, he *had* thought to disable the cops' unmarked car. *Wait a minute.* Chasquas swiveled his gaze onto the angry lawman again. *Is that Jeff Walker?*

Weaving his way through the morning traffic at a hundred miles an hour, Chasquas whipped out his phone. "*¡Oye!*" he bellowed when a trusted associate answered the call. "Can you be at the farmers market in ten minutes?"

***

Screaming into the wind like a blood-crazed warrior, Walker also hit a hundred on his bike, the one he'd just commandeered. It was a mid-size cruiser, a black Kawasaki Vulcan 900. When he hit the freeway, he was only fifty yards behind, so he managed to identify one of the fleeing suspects as Chasquas, but then they accelerated into the distance, pushing his anger meter even deeper into the red zone.

Walker saw them take the Fourth Avenue off-ramp, but he lost them after that. Fortunately, they'd just dropped into Chula Vista, his neck of the woods, so it wasn't difficult to find them. He zipped along the boulevard with palm trees whipping past, then leaned into a turn, feeling the centrifugal force lock him down, and that's when he spotted the suspects in front of the farmers market. Chasquas was standing far away from his bike with a phone held to his ear.

When Walker was thirty yards out, Chasquas looked up. *Why hadn't he jumped on his bike and raced away?*

Twenty yards out.

Ten. Walker pulled his pistol.

Five.

As Walker braked to a stop, he caught a flash of motion to his right. A heavy pickup had run a red light to blindside him, smashing into the Vulcan at a deadly rate of speed! He leapt off the bike just in time to save his leg, but the impact threw him onto the pickup's hood, and his unprotected head smashed into the win—

Later, out of a vague sense of semiconsciousness, Walker grew gradually more aware of a blinding pain in his head. He lifted his eyelids to see two blurry shapes: a pair of men speaking Spanish, whose words he could understand as well as if they were speaking English. He opened his mouth to check for a broken jaw (it wasn't broken), but he couldn't lift his hands to assess his head injury. Now fully conscious, Walker found that his wrists and ankles were bound to the chair he was sitting in, and that the chair was bolted to the concrete floor.

He was confined to a residential garage with a bay door straight ahead, a washer and dryer to the right, and two dirty sofas in an L shape to his left. That's where the two men sat talking, and when he blinked his eyes into focus and recognized one of them, he felt even worse than he already did. It was Chasquas, his old enemy, whom Walker thought he was seeing for the first time that day since he didn't remember anything after pulling up at the safe house with his team.

"*Buenos días*, Walker," said Chasquas, rising from the couch and stepping closer. The other guy stayed where he was and made a point of showing Walker the rifle in his lap.

Walker met his captor's gaze. The last time he'd seen the man was over six months ago, or so he thought, when he'd nearly defeated Chasquas in bare-handed brawl in a crematorium. He looked better than before: more muscular and with brighter eyes, but still tall and thin with grisly tattoos and battle scars on his hands, arms, neck, and face. One feature Walker hadn't spotted on their last meeting was a running tally of some kind on his right arm, a count kept in sets of five, each set made up of four vertical lines intersected by a diagonal slash. This tally extended from Chasquas's upper arm to his hand, and that hand currently held the traditional weapon of the Mara Salvatrucha: a razor-sharp machete. So, Walker supposed, the tally was a kill count. Their conversation was conducted entirely in Spanish.

"You caught Lindbloom, no?" the Honduran began. "That's the only way you could have found me. Did he give me up?"

Walker offered no reply.

"You and I are awfully similar, you know," Chasquas went on.

Walker spat on the floor. "Except for those hideous tattoos."

"Easy to say for a white boy born into ill-gotten privilege."

"We've got nothing in common. I fight crime and you commit it."

"Not true," Chasquas argued, wagging a finger in the air. "Call me a crook if you want, but I'm dealing with the kind of people who would have killed you already. Or worse."

It all came back to Walker in a flash: the explosions at the safe house, Sergeant Cheatham's last words, the motorcycle chase, and the crash at the farmers market. His face ran hot with anger as he strained against his bindings.

Chasquas laid down his machete and took a knee. "As for what happened at the safe house, we were defending ourselves. We lost a man, too."

"Bullshit," Walker growled, wincing from his headache. "You're not doing this country any good by bringing drugs into it."

"Point taken. But it was the only way out of the ghetto."

As Chasquas spoke, his head swayed and his eyes rolled involuntarily, a symptom of neurological damage due to drug use. And what he was saying rang true to Walker, who saw a painful history written all over the man's scrawny body.

"Let's make a deal," Chasquas proposed, grabbing his weapon and springing to his feet. "I'll let you go if you swear not to come after me."

"You know I can't do that."

"Then I'll hack you to death right now."

"Did you pay Daniels to kill the mayor?" Walker asked.

"On Locke's order."

"For money."

"Yes."

"No deal," said Walker. "You tried to kill my best friend at the crematorium, you ordered Mayor O'Connell's death, and you murdered my sergeant at the safe house. I'll be chasing you till the day I die, if that's what it takes."

Chasquas rolled his eyes, then stepped behind Walker and said, "Bow your head and I'll make it quick."

Walker let out something between a roar and a scream. The room fell silent. Then he muttered, "Two weeks. After that, all bets are off."

Chasquas came back around to face him. "You're not as stupid as you look. I suppose you're going to Locke's party as Daniels?"

"What makes you say that?"

"Pope told me he'd just seen Daniels, but Daniels is dead. Plus you look exactly like him, especially with your hair dyed brown."

"A brilliant deduction," said Walker dryly. "Yeah, he was burned alive in his jail cell, as I'm sure you know."

"I had no choice, unfortunately. I liked him. But I *hate* Ronnie Locke, so I'm going to sink his fucking ship." Chasquas scrunched up his lips and gazed absently at the floor, thinking for a good thirty seconds. Then he looked up and said, "Here's the deal. I'll set the bomb to go off at six p.m. Don't interfere with me or my men from now until that time. After that, as you said, all bets are off."

"Fine."

"There's just one more thing," said Chasquas, gesturing for the rifle.

Walker groaned. He knew what was coming.

Chasquas took the weapon from his lieutenant. "How did you know where to find the safe house?"

"Lindbloom's phone," said Walker. "We caught him, but he escaped."

"So he didn't give me up, but he *did* choose not to warn me you were coming, which is just as bad. I'll bet he's after my business," said Chasquas, who then scythed the rifle's buttstock into Walker's head, knocking him out again.

***

Chasquas sat shotgun in a minivan as his lieutenant drove him back to the farmers market, where they laid Walker's unconscious body on a bench. Then, en route to another safe house, his cell phone rang. He didn't recognize the number, so he took the call without a word.

"Hello?" came a deep, gravely voice. "Boss?"

Boss my ass. There was only one thing Chasquas hated more than a racist, and that was a traitor. "Hey!" he exclaimed, acting as happy to hear Lindbloom's voice as if the man were his long-lost brother.

"Hey, boss. I'm back in town and ready to get to work."
"Perfect. When can we meet?" Chasquas replied warmly.

21

MISS BOYDON FIGHTS BACK

Park's and Carla's new house
San Diego

Park's eyes were wide and intense as he studied the security monitor, which showed three figures in dark hooded sweatshirts prowling around outside. The intruders had yet to breach the side gate, and the way they fumbled about with a pair of bolt cutters made him think they were either on drugs or mentally disadvantaged.

Carla threw on a pair of sweats and grabbed the phone to call 911 while Park crept downstairs and out the front door. Guided by a streetlight, he stalked to the side of the house with his Navy Sig drawn, stopping to slice the pie at the corner. As he rounded it, his sights fell on the bumbling intruders' backs. Two were carrying a pistol, and the third only the cutting tool. "Police!" he roared. "Drop your weapons, put your hands up, and turn around. Slowly now!"

When the hooded figures only complied with the last of those commands, eyeing each other with insanely determined expressions, Park was hit by a wave of confusion. They couldn't have been over twenty. "No!" he shouted.

All in an instant, the two who were armed shot the third, splattering the fence behind him with bloody paste. "Ave Satanas," they said in unison, then jammed the guns in their own mouths and pulled the trigger.

Before anything else, Park made sure the area was secure. That done, he took a knee over the fallen youths and hung his head.

***

"The police are on their way, ma'am," said a female dispatcher on the other end of the line. "I need you to stay on the phone until they arrive. Can you do that for me?"

"Yes ma'am," said Carla. "Thank you."

"Is there anyone else on the property? Are you safe?"

"I'll be fine," Carla replied, smacking a magazine into the grip of her G19. Then she cycled the action to chamber a round—click-clack.

"Did you say you're pregnant? You should lock yourself in the bathroom just in case."

"That's a good idea," said Carla, striding across her room and into the lavatory with the phone to her ear. Soon after that, she heard the bedroom window sliding open. Cold fear shot through her body as her pulse leapt up to prepare her for a fight.

"Ma'am?" said the dispatcher. "Are you still there?"

Carla didn't make any sound except for the tiny breaths she was taking, though judging by the two whispered voices heading straight for the bathroom door, her silence was unnecessary since she'd already been seen.

"Ma'am, if you're in trouble and can't talk, press a button on your phone."

Beep.

"We know you're in there!" a male voice boomed. "We're not here to hurt you, so come on out." They gave her five seconds before starting on the flimsy barrier with boot kicks and shoulder smashes.

"Tony!" Carla screamed, training her Glock at the door in a two-handed stance.

Then they came crashing in.

***

When Park heard her cries for help, he shot to his feet and charged into the house with his pistol leveled. The crack of a gunshot stopped him halfway up the stairs.

"You'll pay for that, you little bitch," came a male voice, followed by crashing sounds indicative of a struggle.

Park flew up the rest of the stairs and into the bedroom, buttonhooking left, ready to read and react to whatever he might find. Through his iron sights, his gaze fell on a man sitting against the wall outside the bathroom with a GSW in his belly and a gun in his hand. Then on a second intruder in the bathroom, who was using Carla as a shield while holding a pistol to her temple. Park whirled back to the first guy and pulled the trigger twice—BLAM BLAM!—hitting him once in the heart and once in the head.

"Drop it!" shouted the second intruder.

Park froze, then slowly turned his head an inch, looking into the bathroom out of the corner of his eye. Neither of these guys were college kids.

"Put it down or say goodbye to your wife," the second intruder insisted.

Park flitted his eyes to Carla's, and she gave him a subtle nod, so he instantly swung his sights onto the second guy's face and squeezed the trigger while she jerked her head out of both lines of fire. In one one-hundredth of a second, blood spatter materialized on the white tile behind the second guy and he crumpled to the floor.

Carla rushed into Park's embrace, but he could only hold her with one of his arms. With the other, he panned his pistol from corpse to corpse, scowling, staring hard with the wide-open eyes of a wild animal.

"It's okay, babe," Carla cooed, rubbing his chest to relax him. "I'm fine."

As his rage gave way to a rush of softer feelings, Park finally lowered his pistol. "I don't know what I'd do without you," he managed in a whisper.

With police sirens fast approaching, and then a fleet of cruisers crunching to a stop on the street, Park and Carla held on to each other, literally for dear life.

***

Los Angeles, California

Two of Tim Reynolds' followers had pulled on full-face ski masks, found the hotel maid, and promised not to hurt her if she'd call out to Amanda Boydon from the other side of the door. But once they'd gotten inside the room, they'd stabbed the housekeeper to death, then bound and gagged the fair-haired singer, whom they rolled up in a rug and stuffed into the trunk of their sedan. Miss Boydon bounced around in the dark, barely able to breathe for half an hour before the car came to a stop again.

"Not *now!*" Reynolds shouted over his shoulder, storming out of his mother's mansion to lead his initiates through his childhood home to the pool house, into which they carried the rolled-up rug and its contents.

"You've been acting strangely ever since the cruise!" Mrs. Reynolds screeched, having followed her son into the back yard. "Then again, you've always been strange. What's the matter with you?!"

"Nothing," Reynolds replied. "Nothing at all." Then he nodded to his devotees, who'd just come out of the pool house carrying an empty rug.

Reynolds felt nothing as he watched them roll her up, but he did appreciate the symmetry—the beauty—in the completion of the cycle. More than anything else, it had been a business decision; nothing personal, just like their relationship, which had always consisted of cold transactions. Now he was a wealthy man, free to fulfill his secret desires in his own home, where he was also planning to base the narcotics division of the Master's vast enterprise. He sauntered into the pool house to find his prisoner on the bed with her wrists and ankles bound with duct tape and her lips sealed in the same way. He ripped the tape off her mouth, causing her eyes to flash with anger. "Scream and I'll hit you," he said, showing her a fist.

The singer's rage melted into fear. "Please let me go," she whimpered, which was exactly what Reynolds needed in order to get an erection. Giddy with the anticipation of forbidden pleasure, the most exquisite he'd ever known, he couldn't stop himself from violating her mouth with his fingers.

She immediately chomped down on them.

"God *dammit!*" he screamed, jerking his arm back, but she wouldn't release her bite, so he punched her in the head with his left hand.

Miss Boydon was undeterred. She gnashed forward for better purchase, trapping two of his fingers between her molars.

Shrieking, Reynolds tried to hit her again as she shook her head like a pit bull and snapped his bones, then bit his fingers off. With blood pouring out of two jagged stumps, he staggered away and lowered his head to keep from fainting. As he did, she bounced off the bed and crashed into his legs, dislocating his knee with a grinding crunch.

Through the pain, Reynolds reached up for a lamp and smashed it into the singer's head, knocking her unconscious. After that, it took him twenty minutes of excruciating pain to inch his way across the floor to where he'd dropped his burner phone.

"Father John?" he said into the device, and went on to explain his predicament.

Half an hour later, the second-highest-ranking member of The Faith made his way through the back yard and into the pool house. He taped Miss Boydon's mouth shut again, then helped Reynolds into a chair. "This is going to hurt," he said, extending the leg while shoving the joint back into place.

Reynolds screamed, but the relief was immediate.

Father John looked down at Miss Boydon as she came to. Her face was covered in blood, and she strained against her bindings in vain, wriggling around on the floor like a worm.

Reynolds caught Boydon's defiant eyes and gave her a smirk, even though his spat-out fingers lay on the carpet beside her.

"It may be too late to get those sewn back on. They look pretty chewed up," said Father John, scrunching up his lips in thought. "Tell you what. The next gathering's in three days, as you know. It's in honor of the Master's birthday, and we still need a woman he can ravish for the invocation. Why don't I take care of her until then? You'd better get yourself to a doctor and take it easy."

Reynolds' lips twisted into a smile. Except for the disaster at Tony Park's house, everything was working out according to plan. "Perfect," he replied. "But I don't need any rest. I'll go back for Carla Park; that way there'll be one for you and one for the Master."

Father John shook his head. "She's not my type, if you know what I mean. But I'd love to hold her down while you take her."

22

LINDBLOOM GOES BELLY-UP

Duke's Bar & Grill
Embarcadero Marina
San Diego

A sizeable group of Harbor Police officers had gathered around a row of tables pushed together, joined by some of their colleagues and friends. In sharp contrast with the lively chatter of the people surrounding them, they spoke in subdued tones, with downcast eyes and no boisterous behavior. Every so often, one of them would propose a toast to the late Sergeant Cheatham, whose tragic death was the reason for the get-together.

"Sarge would have been happy about the raid," said Walker.

Next to him, Furious nodded slowly, studying his untouched beer.

"Any leads on Baker?" asked Walker, who hadn't participated in the execution of the search warrant at the meth lab because doing so would have blown his cover.

"No," said Furious, "but he and Pope are gonna be down a bunch of men, at least for a while."

Across the table from them, Ortiz and Park were having a heated conversation, so Walker and Furious tuned in to that channel.

"And I'll keep saying it till it finally sinks in!" Park was telling MARTAC's team leader. "It's irresponsible for you to let him get on that ship. By now Pope will have heard what happened to Daniels."

Ortiz looked mad as hell, ready for war as usual.

"I assume y'all are talking about me, but you're wrong," Walker said to Park.

"Why?"

"One of the last things Sargeant Cheatham did was to request a media blackout, so news of Daniels' death wouldn't get out."

Park stared at Walker with his mouth agape, saying nothing. Then, in exasperation, he almost yelled, "Pope could find out from one of the inmates, or from Chasquas himself! Are you kidding me?"

"It's only been three days, man," Walker said. "And Chasquas *hates* Pope. I appreciate the concern, but it's not your call."

Park lowered his eyes.

Ortiz crossed his arms over his chest and sat back looking smug.

No one said anything for a while, not until Furious asked, "Why not just arrest Locke now?"

"Because the charges won't stick," answered DAI Dom Taylor. "The ballistic report on Daniels' sniper rifle is open to interpretation, and Walker's testimony as to what Chasquas told him would be hearsay."

"Them's some fancy words, Dom," Ortiz quipped. "A little something must've rubbed off on you at the DA's office." His chuckles quickly trailed off as Park, Walker, Taylor, and Lynn Peters, the blond-haired chief deputy DA to whom he'd referred, drilled him with a hard collective stare.

"That was uncalled for," Ortiz realized. "Sorry, Lynn."

"Thank you, Steve," she said. "Anyway, back to Tony's question. There's another reason why we haven't gone after Locke—yet. He's just a puppet. I'd really like to take his donors to court."

"How do we know Chasquas was telling the truth about the bomb?" asked Dom Taylor. "Or anything at all, for that matter. He might be colluding with Pope and Locke."

"I don't think so," said Walker. "If he'd wanted me dead, I wouldn't be sitting here."

"If you see him, are you going to keep your word?" Lynn Peters asked.

Walker nodded.

"Not me. I didn't make any promises," said Furious.

"Me neither," boomed Ortiz, clinking his pint against Furious's with so much force that it was a miracle the glasses didn't shatter. "Cheatham was like a father to me."

"To me too," said Park.

Walker hung his head. "To me too."

"To all of us," said Furious. "May he rest in peace."

***

"Next on the docket," said Ronnie Locke into his microphone at the city council meeting held the following morning, reading from his notes as he and nine other well-dressed individuals presided over a large wood-paneled chamber from behind a semicircular bench. "Item six, proposed resolution number R-314576, Proclamation of a Local Emergency Related to the Downtown Riots for the Immediate Preservation of Public Peace, Property, Health, and Safety. Councilmember Lyons, if you would."

Lyons, a bearded man sitting to the mayor's right, looked around at his fellows, nodded once, and read the full text of the resolution to be voted on. Fortunately, thought Ronnie Locke, no one was listening—no one that mattered, anyway. Five minutes later, when Lyons came to the most important part, he read it in a quick and cursory manner (as instructed): "Be it further resolved that during the existence of this local emergency, the mayor shall take command of the police."

Once Lyons had finished, Mayor Locke called for the vote, which resulted in a final tally of eight ayes and two nays. *A very expensive final tally*, Locke thought as he leaned into his microphone again. "Excellent," he said. "Be it ordained by the Council of the City of San Diego. Moving on to item seven. Chief Deputy District Attorney Lynn Peters will now give us an update on the status of Bravo Security Services LLC versus the City of San Diego. Miss Peters?"

The flaxen-haired attorney strode up to a podium that was set much lower than the circle of local politicians. "Mayor Locke," she began coldly, making no attempt to disguise her contempt for him. "Councilmembers," she went on, twisting her features in a show of disgust. "Good morning to you all."

Ronnie Locke smiled down at the curvy blonde in her perfectly tailored pantsuit, undressing her mentally for several minutes. Yet as the woman blathered on and on about Pope's private security team's alleged perpetration of civil rights violations and felony murder, he rolled his eyes and exchanged conspiratorial smirks with most of the councilmembers. At one point, he even stifled a yawn. Finally, when he could stand her no longer, he leaned forward into his mic and said, "Thank you, Miss Peters. I'm afraid we're out of time. The recommendation of this office is to drop all charges with immediate effect. As you can see, our city is in a state of emergency and it is our opinion that Mr. Pope and his team had no choice but to act as they did. Are there any questions from the council?"

One member voiced her support for Peters' case, and another repeated his objection to the resolution just passed, but both were decisively interrupted by the well-paid majority and Lynn Peters stormed out of the hall.

"All right everyone," Locke concluded, looking around. "If there's nothing else, we're adjourned. Thank you for attending." With that, he hurried down to a private exit, where he was quickly surrounded by Pope and company, escorted to his blacked-out SUV, and driven back to the superyacht.

"How did it go, Mr. Mayor?" asked Joshua Pope from behind the wheel.

"Best day of my life, Pope," Locke replied from the rear, sandwiched between two giggling girls. "Best day of my life."

***

Followed by two other riders, Chasquas blasted off at the crack of dawn, delighting in his Dark Horse's spectacular power as the crisp morning air buffeted his body. It was a quick trip to the Mission Bay Marina, where he and his shaven-headed street soldiers strutted down the dock toward one of Stryker Lindbloom's new charter boats.

"Welcome aboard the Bass Hunter!" Lindbloom boomed as the three Latinos stepped aboard. "She's a custom Marshall flybridge sportfisher powered by a two-hundred-fifty-hp turbo diesel. Let me show you just how *custom* she is." The thick-necked ex-con led them down to the cabin, where he gestured toward a booth like one might find at a restaurant. He unbolted the base of the table, set the whole thing aside, and flipped a hidden switch to reveal a storage compartment one meter deep and twice as long and wide. Plenty of space to make the Mexican runs worthwhile.

"*Excelente*," said Chasquas, nodding in approval.

As the sunrise began to cast its colors over the eastern hills, they motored into the dark-blue swells of the Pacific Ocean, which stretched out to the horizon line off the bow. Chasquas and

Lindbloom stood at the forward helm station while the enforcers took a seat in the aft lounge, facing the trailing wake.

The wet, salty air reminded Chasquas of his home country. His memories of Honduras weren't generally pleasant, but one that he'd always cherished was working on his uncle's boat as a boy. He'd learned to fish at an early age, and he'd been good at it. He'd had to be, if he wanted to eat. "How you did ... in *Los Cabos*?" he asked in stilted English, glancing down at Lindbloom's holstered pistol.

"Not bad," Lindbloom replied, keeping his hands on the wheel and his gaze straight ahead. "I bashed Richards' head in."

"Record me who is Richards," said Chasquas.

"Remind me," Lindbloom corrected him. "Richards was my boss on the last of the casino jobs, when they killed my brother."

"Yes. Now I remember," Chasquas said, lighting a cigarette.

Lindbloom dropped anchor after an hour. While he was getting out the fishing gear, Chasquas drew the machete he'd concealed in his pant leg, crept up behind Lindbloom, held the long blade to his neck with one hand, and reached down for the man's gun with the other.

Thinking he had an ace up his sleeve, Lindbloom suddenly grabbed Chasquas's wrist, preventing him from taking his pistol. But when no help came, he knew he'd been deceived.

Chasquas's enforcers had met with Lindbloom, agreed to his plan, and accepted thousands of dollars in advance, but after that they'd told Chasquas, who'd let them keep the money. So, when they finally did take to their feet, it was to grab Lindbloom's arms as Chasquas relieved him of his gun.

"Down! On your face," Chasquas hissed, handing the pistol to one of his men, who held it to Lindbloom's head.

Chasquas's other enforcer got down on the deck with Lindbloom and brought the man's arm straight out, immobilizing it.

"Traitor," muttered Chasquas as he whipped the long blade down, chopping off the ex-con's hand.

Lindbloom writhed in agony as the enforcers danced around, whooping and shouting in celebration.

"Please," Lindbloom begged Chasquas. "You would have done the same thing to me."

"Hell no," said the Honduran, tossing the man a towel for his bloody stump. "Sit there."

One of the enforcers covered Lindbloom with the pistol while the other one tossed the severed hand overboard and went to raise the anchor.

Beads of sweat streamed down Lindbloom's face and his breathing came in gasps. "I'll sign all the sportfishers over to you. Please, Chasquas. Just tell him not to shoot me."

Back at one of the safe houses, after Lindbloom had relinquished his ownership of the new fishing boats, Chasquas smiled, patted him on the shoulder, and gave him two pills and a glass of water. "For the pain," he lied.

Soon after that, Lindbloom was unconscious, shirtless, and face up on a table with a crooked surgeon implanting a large explosive device in his abdominal cavity, while Chasquas sat nearby sipping on a cup of coffee.

23

BRENTWOOD

Park's and Carla's new house
San Diego
5:00 a.m.

"I'll be fine," said Carla softly as Park held her close. Her pink terrycloth robe and the curves under it were soft and warm. After a long moment, Park reluctantly pulled away, picked up his bags, and strode down the steps to the street, where he offered his hand to the SDPD officer stationed there.

"Don't worry, sir," the officer said. "We'll take good care of her."

"I know you will," Park replied. With a serious look and a single nod, he climbed into his big blue 4x4, brought it to life, and flipped on the headlights. Normally he'd have cranked up the stereo, too, but his active brain needed the quiet time.

He wasn't thrilled about leaving Carla, of course, given the incident that had occurred just a few nights before, but SDPD had offered to drive her to and from work, and a second cruiser would be stationed outside their house at all times. Plus, the reason Park was driving to LA in the first place was to stop the same crooks who'd come to kill them, presumably on Tim Reynolds' orders. *But why would Reynolds have given that order?* The only possible explanation was that he was trying to clean up the mess he'd made on the *Oasis*, which meant that the rest of the undercover team and, more importantly, Amanda Boydon would also be in danger. Park tucked away a mental reminder to ask Phillips about her.

For the third time in so many months, he was bound for the Wilshire Federal Building, home to the FBI's Los Angeles field office, where he'd be meeting with Phillips and Kerr before rolling up on Tim Reynolds' mother's Brentwood residence to serve a federal warrant for her son's arrest. Most of the credit was due to Walker and Sean Choi, who had tracked down the web server that hosted the satanic internet forum and had then subpoenaed all the data, which had been enough to file federal charges against Reynolds and his followers.

Park's thoughts next turned to Chief Richards' murder on the *Oasis* by heavy metal pipe. Had Tim Reynolds sent Lindbloom to do it? *No*, he decided. *Stryker Lindbloom lives in San Diego and works for Chasquas, who had nothing to do with the cruise ship murders as far as we know. That one was probably a personal grudge.*

Besides Carla, there was one other person Park wasn't happy about leaving behind: Jeff Walker, his best friend and partner, who was about to embark on a risky undercover mission. Park's fist shot out to punch the dash in frustration, but he'd had no other choice; he was assigned to the FBI, and much more importantly, Carla was his first priority. If stopping Reynolds and his followers meant leaving Walker on his own, then that's what had to happen. Jeff was more than capable of handling himself, and he'd have the rest of MARTAC watching his six.

Just as Park hit the long stretch of North County beaches to his left, the sunrise came peeking over the hills to the right, casting a golden sheen over the ocean. Now he did crank up the sound system.

Two hours later, the same attractive receptionist as before showed him in to Special Agent Phillips' office, where SSA John Kerr, the profiler, was the first to shake his hand. Naturally, Kerr was out of his padded suit, and his gray beard was filling back in. "How's the shoulder?" Park asked.

"I'm not complaining," Kerr replied. "But the bullet tore a ton of muscle." With his left index finger, he traced a line from his right collarbone down to his right flank. "I've still got my left hook, though," he jested, swinging a slow fist at Park's head, which Park dodged easily. Grinning, the two lawmen squared off in a simulated confrontation.

"Thanks for coming in so early," Phillips said, interrupting the horseplay by coming around his desk to offer Park his hand. Then he gestured toward the visitors chairs.

"How's Amanda doing?" Park asked as they all took a seat.

"Fine, I think," Phillips replied. "I haven't talked to her since she flew to Florida."

"How long ago was that?" asked Kerr.

"Just a couple of days. Thanks for the reminder, guys; I'll give her a call today. I've been really busy with this case. Speaking of which, there's a SWAT team waiting for us downstairs, so let's get to it."

Phillips drove Park and Kerr to Brentwood, a wealthy neighborhood in LA's Westside. They were escorted by two armored SWAT vehicles, one in front, one behind. "We'll have two snipers on overwatch, a five-man breaching team, and five more guarding the perimeter," he explained on the way there.

On arrival, they parked several blocks away and hustled to their predetermined positions. Once all fifteen men were ready, the entry team smashed the front door open to find Jessica Reynolds' sprawling residence deserted and the main building clean. But in a backyard swim shack between the pool and a well-tended lawn, the floor was stained with fresh blood, and there was a hair clip that looked like a claw.

"That's Amanda's," said Phillips with alarm, whipping out his cell and stepping away to make a call. He paced back and forth, looking increasingly frustrated, then hung up and dialed another number. After briefly speaking with someone, he hustled back to the group with a report: "She didn't pick up, so I called Excelsior. She never made it to her next gig."

Phillips hung his head and rubbed his temples with one hand.

"It's not your fault," Kerr assured him.

"Yes it is," said Phillips. "I should have driven her to the airport instead of leaving to work on the case."

Then the SWAT team leader strode up and said to Phillips, "Sir. I just got a call from the mayor's office ordering all available units to deploy to the riots. Are we available?"

"Go ahead, Bass," said Phillips. "We're good here."

As the SWAT team hustled off to their next assignment and the trio completed their search of the premises, Park couldn't shake a nagging doubt. Finally, he had to ask. "Is LA in a state of local emergency?"

Phillips nodded. "Yes, unfortunately. If you think the protests are bad in San Diego, you should see *our* nightly news."

"Did the city council pass a special resolution granting the mayor power over the police?"

"That's right," Phillips answered, looking mystified as they stepped out of the pool house. "Why?"

Just then, the grumbling, sputtering sounds of a pack of motorcycles grew louder as it pulled up to the mansion, then fell progressively quiet as the engines were shut off one by one. Park heard barked orders and boots stomping through the main house. By the time he, Phillips, and Kerr had retreated to the pool house and taken defensive positions, their assailants were in the back yard opening fire.

"Follow me!" Park commanded from behind the sofa where they'd all taken cover. Bullets shattered windows and snapped over their heads, sending glass and wooden splinters flying as they crawled through the kitchenette toward a bathroom window on the back side of the building. Park stopped at the stove to turn all four knobs to the "on" position without igniting the burners, checked the bathroom to make sure Phillips and Kerr had climbed out the window ahead of him, then pulled the pin on a frag grenade. Dropping it behind him as he sprinted into the restroom, Park jumped, landed with one foot on the toilet, and dove headfirst out the window. His eyes darted to the grass below—where Kerr and Phillips were scrambling out of his way—and he curled into a somersault to soften his landing.

BOOM! Glass shards sprayed and flames and smoke billowed out the bathroom window; Park, Kerr, and Phillips heard grown men screaming for help as they backpedaled toward the main house with their M4 carbines leveled. On Park's command, they all dropped to a kneeling position and trained their sights on the corner of the pool house, around which any surviving bikers were sure to come running with their guns ablaze.

Sure enough, after a very long couple of seconds, their assailants did exactly that.

Park pulled the trigger three times while sweeping his rifle slowly right, shooting three bikers in their center mass before he, too, was hit in the upper body. It was protected by a Kevlar vest, but still the impact was like that of a hundred-pound sledgehammer swung by a giant. Park was on his back before he knew what had happened. Then another round caught him in the helmet, blurring his vision. He turned dizzily to his comrades. Both were in the same situation: lying on the grass, disoriented, surrounded by a mob of men with blackened faces, singed hair, and pistols pointed straight at them!

Park, Kerr, and Phillips raised their arms as the angry circle tightened around them.

"Don't shoot!" someone commanded from inside the main house.

Park turned toward the sound. It was Tim Reynolds, flanked by five or six other guys, who all stepped into the back yard wearing street clothes. It was the first time Park had seen the killer in person; neither large nor small, he had boyish features and brown hair cut unevenly, probably by Reynolds himself.

"Tie them up," Reynolds said to his followers, who bound the lawmen's hands and feet with zip ties, stripped them of their gear, and covered their mouths with silver duct tape.

As a pair of bikers picked Park up and carried him through the main house, the pungent stench of propane gas made him wince.

"Thanks for giving me the idea," Reynolds gloated, walking beside the bikers and looking down at Park. He flicked open a Zippo lighter and stopped, turning back to face his house, then ignited the device and threw it through the front door.

The resulting blast shattered all the windows outward and set off a chorus of shrieking alarms in the neighborhood. And there stood Reynolds, with his arms crossed over his chest, watching his mother's house burn to the ground.

Park, Phillips, and Kerr were tossed into the back of a waiting van. On the way to wherever they were being taken, their butts bounced painfully on the floor and their backs against the interior paneling. Even if they could free themselves from their restraints, there was no chance of escape, since the cargo bay was sealed off by a steel divider and the rear doors couldn't be unlocked from the inside. So, for the time being, Park resigned himself to captivity and reflected on something he'd observed, namely the patches on the bikers' jackets, which identified them as the East County Warlords. He'd known about their connection to the new mayor, of course, through their leader, Stephen Baker, who was working with Joshua Pope, and Pope with Ronnie Locke. But now it seemed the bikers were associated with a satanic cult based in LA, where, as in San Diego, the city council had handed over control of the police to their mayor. This led Park to suspect that a conspiracy much greater in scale and far more sinister than he'd first believed was threatening the good people of Southern California and possibly the entire United States!

24

DESCENT INTO DARKNESS

Bayside District
San Diego

Walker pulled on a soft pair of slacks and buttoned up a short-sleeve collared shirt, leaving it untucked to conceal Daniels' Colt 1911. Then he mounted the late mercenary's dual-sport Honda and started her up, receiving an eager grumble in reply.

His first destination was the Harbor Police dock, where he spoke with the team who'd be watching his six all afternoon. Then, after exchanging nods with Furious, Sergeant Ortiz, Lieutenant Coffin, and others, he continued along Harbor Drive, circling the bay under a long row of palm trees. The sun was high, but cool air rushed into his open collar as he passed the twin towers of the Castlefield Waterfront Hotel, which brought back bittersweet memories of his last major case. Walker also blew by the Convention Center and a grassy park before passing under the Coronado Bridge, where Navy personnel in green fatigues stood waiting for their turn to cross the street.

He dismounted at the National City Marine Terminal, where Locke had built a custom dock for himself at the Pier 47 wharf. As he strode toward the superyacht, he spotted a Latino sitting low in the driver's seat of a catering van with a ball cap pulled down over his eyes. When the Latino looked up to meet Walker's gaze, he revealed an unmistakable assortment of dark-themed facial tattoos.

"Daniels," Chasquas growled, lowering his window and waving Walker closer. "The party finish at the six o'clock."

Why would Chasquas reveal his position by providing information I already know? And why did he speak in English? Walker concluded that the shaven-headed "caterers" in the van must have seen him get off his bike and recognized him as Daniels, and that Chasquas had had no choice but to wave him over because it would have seemed strange not to speak with such a close associate. Surprisingly, Chasquas had behaved honorably for once by not blowing Walker's cover, not even to his own men.

With their frowns less than a foot apart, they eyeballed each other for some time, then finally exchanged slow nods, fully aware that the following day—if he survived—Walker would be coming after Chasquas with everything he had, and that Chasquas would do anything to keep himself out of jail. Then the window went back up and Walker set off for the giant white yacht.

***

Chasquas felt his face curl into a wide-eyed scowl, a portrait of the murderous hate that so often held him in its clutches. Knowing he'd soon be adding tally marks to his kill count, he traced his finger over the knotted scar that ran through it, prompting him to re-live the fight with Walker in the crematorium. The only reason he'd lost was that it had been two against one; Murci, the young Mexican, had slashed both of Chasquas's forearms to the bone before the brawl. Even so, Chasquas lamented the defeat, recalling with embarrassment how he'd grown helpless against Walker's hammer fists as his life force drained out of him. In any case, he'd never met a white man as crazy as Walker and he wasn't eager for a rematch.

One of the few advantages of being Hispanic in San Diego was the extensive network of like-minded individuals to which Chasquas had access. By coincidence, one of his many contacts owned the catering company Locke's office had hired for the party, and that man had been more than glad to let Chasquas manage today's job in return for a hundred thousand dollars.

"In the unlikely event that your company should be blamed for the bomb," Chasquas had told his fellow Central American in their native language, "I promise I'll take care of you and your family. You'd never have to work again."

"Done," the caterer had replied. "I hate Locke anyway. He always shorts me when I send him the bill."

So as Walker headed for the superyacht, Chasquas made his way to the back of the van, nodding to his lieutenant and two enforcers. All three were wearing chef coats and tall white hats that were begging to be made fun of. But Chasquas headed straight for one of the heavy-duty catering trolleys and pulled out a stack of plastic tubs, then swung open a hidden lid to expose a long rectangular compartment at the false bottom of the trolley. There lay Lindbloom, bound, gagged, and semiconscious, with an unnatural bulge protruding from his belly. Chasquas prepared an injection and leaned down to administer it. "He'll be out for the rest of the day," he told his men. Then he led them in a prayer to Our Lady of the Holy Death, imploring her to grant them strength and courage enough for a successful mission. After that, his three supposed "caterers" wheeled their cargo toward the superyacht while he drove off to see about the next part of the plan.

***

Two days earlier, Amanda Boydon had been swearing like a sailor, but only in her mind, as there'd been a long strip of duct tape encircling her head and mouth. Huffing and puffing for air through her nostrils, she kicked out at the side wall of the trunk she was trapped in and fought against her bindings to no avail, then let out a muffled scream and trembled with fear.

The car slowed to a halt after twenty minutes. She heard two male voices. Then it moved forward again before stopping and the lid of the trunk popped open. The older man who'd come to Tim Reynolds' rescue at the pool house smiled down at her, but with violence in his eyes.

"I need to cut your feet free," he said, gently helping her out of the trunk. "But if you try anything, you'll regret it." After she nodded, he stooped to slice through the tape around her ankles.

As Miss Boydon scanned her surroundings, she saw she'd been taken to a gigantic cliffside residence with ornamental battlements, tall corner towers, and high walls made of massive stones. She would have been in awe of the medieval-style architecture had she not been filled with the desire to launch a knee into the older man's face, and prevented from doing so by a group of men standing near a row of motorcycles, all with suggestive bulges under their shirts or jackets.

"Don't worry," her aging captor said, guiding her along the path to the front entrance. "I'll make sure you're safe. For now, anyway, since we need you in top shape for the gathering."

The gathering? Then this man's a devil worshipper, like Tim Reynolds, Miss Boydon concluded, and she could only think of two reasons why they might need her to stay in good shape for the cult meeting, both of which filled her with dread.

"You may call me Father John," he said, swinging open a thick wooden door three times the size of a normal one.

As she followed him inside, she peered over his shoulder through picture windows, sweeping her gaze over an aerial view of the Pacific Coast. The sea was choppy and dark, with cold-looking whitecaps rolling in to a rocky shore, each wave meeting its inescapable fate.

"After you," said Father John, nodding toward a winding stone staircase that led down to a terribly dark place.

***

Two days after Miss Boydon arrived, a second contingent of East County Warlords showed up at the same cliffside castle, some of them leading and others following a cargo van driven by Tim Reynolds himself. Reynolds stepped out of the van, made straight for its rear doors, yanked them open, and leveled his gaze on Park, Phillips, and Kerr, who still sat bound and gagged. "Help me carry them in," he ordered the bikers.

Park felt some satisfaction when he saw the Warlords' soot-covered faces and their involuntary haircuts marked by scorched ends and missing hair, but in general he was enraged. As he and his fellow operatives were lugged into the castle and carried down the winding stone staircase, he thrashed about like a two-hundred-and-thirty-pound worm on a hook.

Just as he had done on the way out of his mother's mansion, Reynolds was walking beside the bikers who were carrying Park. "Hang on," he said, stopping the group, then drew back his arm and punched Park in the mouth. "Quit squirming," he yelled, with as much force as a man of his size could muster. Park barely registered the blow, however, since it had been dealt with Reynolds' non-dominant hand.

Passing the first subterranean level, they continued down the stairs to the basement, a high-ceilinged hall with a stale odor and steel lanterns designed to look like flaming torches running along the walls.

The bikers dumped Park and his fellows at the foot of the stairs with a painful smack, then dragged them through the long rectangular space toward what looked like an altar at the end. This was a church, Park realized, but not the holy kind, since on the near side of that altar stood a low stone platform roughly the size and shape of a king-size bed, and it was fitted with two sets of wrist and ankle shackles.

The bikers hauled the trio past the altar and through a door on the far wall into a smaller room. Park winced; his back was being scraped raw. Then, when he was thrown into a shallow cell built along the back wall of that smaller room, his expression of pain deepened into one of great dismay. The stone floor on both sides of the bars was stained with reddish-brown patches, despite the drains installed for easy cleanup.

"Scott!" Amanda Boydon cried out, rushing to peel off the tape over Phillips' mouth. She did the same for Park and Kerr and helped them all to a sitting position.

"I was looking forward to a chat," Tim Reynolds said as he slid the door shut with a heavy metallic clang. "But Father John and I are late for a party. We'll be back tomorrow with the Master and a big surprise for *you*, Tony Park."

As Reynolds turned to leave, his cackling laughter bounced off the walls, echoing throughout what could only be a torture chamber.

***

"Thank you, officer," purred Carla Reyes. Surprising herself, she flashed her young and muscular escort a suggestive smile, then closed the police cruiser's passenger-side door and waved goodbye. As she sashayed up to the offices of Executive Helicopters, looking and feeling irresistibly gorgeous, with a curly ponytail that swished back and forth, dark aviator sunglasses, tight-fitting black trousers, and a tucked-in white shirt and tie that accentuated her brand-new breast implants, she caught herself fantasizing about what she'd like that officer to do to her, and where, and how. And how *else.* He wasn't the sergeant stationed in front of her house, who had been nothing but a gentleman. *And he's easy on the eyes, too!* Carla thought with a grin. But that was as far as she allowed her mind to go. As she came to the double glass doors, she vowed to be faithful to Park in thought, word, and deed.

"Morning Mary," she said to the receptionist on her way to the front desk.

"Hey Carla," Mary replied. "Your passengers are already checked in."

"Thanks, hon. How are the boys?"

"Up to no good as usual. But I wouldn't trade 'em for anything in the world. You'll see what I mean," Mary said, dropping her gaze to Carla's swelling belly for an instant. "See ya when ya get back."

Carla smiled and nodded. She was right on time for her Surf & Turf tour, a route that would last an hour. A few minutes later, she stepped outside again, this time through a back door at the end of the hall. Smiling at the maintenance crew and a few other co-workers, she strutted across the apron to a red and white Airbus H125 and ran through her preflight routine. Then, as she settled in the cockpit, her passengers climbed aboard.

"Hi," she said, turning around to offer her hand to a couple in their twenties. "My name's Carla Reyes, and I'll be your pilot today."

"Nice to meet you," the woman returned. "I'm Liz and this is Mike."

Today's tour wasn't an ordinary one, Carla knew. Mike would be proposing to Liz as they flew over Lake Hodges, so when she shook his hand, she shot him a conspiratorial wink. "Buckle up and put on your headsets," she said, then "Here we go!" as she rolled on the throttle and raised the collective to start the hover. With a gentle right pedal turn, she took the chopper up to two thousand feet and set a course for the lake.

Carla had always had flying dreams. Usually she'd climb into the sky by swimming through the air as if it were water, then soar like a bird, sometimes performing acrobatics in the sky. And this, she mused, as she flew through the endless baby-blue sky at a hundred and fifty miles an hour, was as close as she'd ever come to that subconscious fantasy. It was literally a dream come true. *One that I worked hard to achieve*, she reminded herself. Overhead, a smattering of puffy white clouds drifted by, and below her, the dark-green foothills rose and fell. "You can see Lake Hodges straight ahead," she said into her microphone as the shimmering reservoir hove into view.

Mike unbuckled his seat belt to take a knee, and Liz let out a shriek of apparent delight. He reached into his jacket, for a ring, supposedly, but pulled out a pistol and whirled around to point it at Carla. "I'm a pilot, too," he growled. "So I'll have no problem shooting you if you try to call this in."

Carla nodded quickly and kept her thumb far away from the radio's toggle switch, offering no resistance at all as Mike clambered into the co-pilot's seat. It wasn't just *her* life he was threatening; her lifelong ambition, vastly more important than her dream of flying, was to be a mother, and she was only months away from becoming one.

25

FIGHT, FLIGHT, OR FREEZE

Harbor Police dock
Shelter Island, San Diego Bay
2:00 p.m.

Sergeant Ortiz stood on the deck of a patrol boat, watching Mayor Locke's superyacht motor out from the bay to the open sea. He didn't order his men to cast off, not yet, since they didn't need to keep an eye on the gargantuan vessel. They'd be following at a distance via the GPS tracker in Walker's keychain ornament, which, Ortiz hoped, would also provide a recording that could be used as evidence against the intellectual author of Mayor O'Connell's assassination. If Walker uttered the duress code, MARTAC would speed toward Locke's superyacht and forcibly come aboard, most likely under fire.

The blond-haired former soldier nodded to Furious and six other operators, who were all clad in green fatigues and busy stowing their equipment on the patrol boat. He checked his wristwatch. Walker had until seventeen hundred hours. Even if he hadn't said "cigarette" by then, MARTAC would still come aboard the superyacht and extract him before the bomb went off.

As Locke's ship grew smaller and smaller, a convoy of police cruisers and armored trucks pulled up in the parking area. Seconds later, a large and well-armed tactical team marched down to the dock and formed a semicircle around the patrol boat, each of them with his rifle at the collapsed low ready. "Sergeant Steven Ortiz!" their leader barked. "Sergeant Michael Shipley, SDPD SWAT. You and your team are coming with us." Like MARTAC, the arriving unit was decked out in full tactical gear, but their fatigues were dark blue and they were twice as strong in number.

"Negative," Ortiz barked back, stepping confidently off the boat, whereupon SDPD SWAT, as one, brought their rifles up to a firing position, sighting his head. "Whoa!" yelled Ortiz, who then whipped up his sidearm and panned it from man to man. All of MARTAC followed suit, resulting in twenty-five pairs of eyes staring at each other with deadly intent for ten seconds of very heavy silence.

"What the *fuck* are you doing?! Stand down, all of you!" bellowed Lieutenant Coffin, hustling down into the midst of the standoff. MARTAC's grizzled commander leveled his stern gaze on his own men first, then swung it onto SDPD with so much fury that everyone pointed their muzzles in a safe direction.

"Lieutenant Bill Coffin," he said to their leader, who couldn't have been over twenty-five. "Wasn't Chris Miller your team leader?"

"He was transferred. I'm Sergeant Michael Shipley, and you and your team are coming with us."

"On what charge?" Coffin demanded.

"You're not under arrest but you will be if you don't comply."

"But we've got an under—" Ortiz blurted out, referring to Walker, their undercover man on the superyacht, but Coffin stopped him in midsentence with a sharp look.

Sergeant Shipley whirled on Ortiz. "What was that?"

"But we've got a right to know why," Ortiz corrected himself.

Shipley nodded in agreement. "It's to keep you from going near the superyacht. Remember, Mayor Locke's your commander now, and ours as well. He believes there may be a traitor among you, someone paid by his opponents to assassinate him. And after what happened to Mayor O'Connell, he's not taking any chances. Leave all your weapons and gear and follow us. Easy or hard, guys, your choice."

***

Walker, posing as Daniels, stood in a circle of VIPs on the superyacht's sun deck close to the swimming pool. A clean, salty breeze tousled his hair.

"Rick Daniels, meet Tim Reynolds," said Joshua Pope to Walker. Walker forced himself to smile and shake hands with the cruise ship killer. Reynolds' hand was bandaged, and it felt like he was missing a few fingers.

"And I'm Father John," another man volunteered, beaming at Walker oddly and clasping his hand for too long.

"Father?" Walker asked. "Are you a priest?"

"Yes, I am," Father John replied. "I was actually hoping to talk to you."

Berg, Joshua Pope's right-hand man, the one whose computer had proven so valuable, turned to Walker and said, "His church needs a security specialist and I recommended you."

As Walker nodded in understanding, Mayor Locke and another man came strolling up to the circle of VIPs, carrying themselves like a pair of world-famous celebrities. All heads turned to face them. "What should we drink to, *Mayor*?" Locke jested, looking to his taller colleague.

"I don't know, *Mayor*," replied the other man with a winning grin, plucking a champagne flute off a waiter's tray. Every person in the circle laughed until he spoke again. "How about to prosperity?"

"To prosperity!" the group echoed, Walker included, and they all brought their drinks together.

Locke's protruding belly, his tacky golfwear, and his greasy black hair stood in sharp contrast to the clean and elegant features of the statesman standing beside him. In the conversation that followed, Walker learned that Locke's tall and virile companion was the Mayor of Los Angeles, whose perfect smile was reflected back to him by everyone standing around. Even Walker was swayed by his charm. "Bruce Whitaker," the man boomed, sticking out a hand. "I hear we owe you a favor."

Walker had to assume Whitaker was referring to Daniels' assassination of Mayor O'Connell, his close friend, so he puffed out his chest with pride instead of showing his anger. "That's not necessary, sir."

"Well, I appreciate it all the same," Whitaker said, producing a business card as if by magic. "Give me a call next week. We could use someone like you."

The circle grew in size as the rest of Whitaker's and Locke's well-dressed donors added their number to the group. Once everyone was present, Whitaker turned to Locke and said, with a theatrically formal air, "Shall we?" whereupon all twenty people, including Pope, Berg, and Walker (the security team), headed up to a private lounge. Looking back down at the pool through a window, Walker couldn't help noticing the arrival of a flock of females clad in thong bikinis, as if on cue. Many of them looked young enough to be skipping school.

"Not bad, eh?" said Berg, joining Walker where he stood. "Glad you could make it."

Then, as the donors pulled up chairs around Locke and Whitaker, Walker and the rest of the security team took strategic positions around the room and scanned for internal and external threats. From what Walker could overhear, Mayor Whitaker had not only organized this group of investors, but he was also expected to campaign for President of the United States, with Locke as his running mate.

After the meeting, with the festivities now in full swing, the security team headed back down to the pool and grabbed a seat at a table. Berg remained alert, scanning his surroundings, while Pope stared openly at the young females prancing about—those who weren't busy with a donor—and Walker tried to think of some questions that might lead to an incriminating recorded conversation.

"Have you seen Chasquas?" Pope asked suddenly, turning his drug-fueled stare on Walker.

"No," Walker lied. "Why?"

"We told that beaner to get the fuck out of San Diego, so if you ever see him in town, you know what to do. Hang on." Pope reached into his pocket and pulled out his phone. "Yeah," he answered, then said nothing as he listened to the caller. A minute stretched on and on with no more than an "uh-huh" or a grunt from the former Marine, whose features finally twisted into a violent scowl. When he clicked off, he whipped out his pistol, aiming it at Walker's chest from across the table.

"What's wrong, Pope?" Walker asked. "Want a cigarette?" He reached for his weapon as if it were a pack of smokes, but Berg was on his feet in an instant, pressing the hard muzzle of his own gun into Walker's head. "Hands!" he barked.

Walker complied.

"What I *want*, you fuckin' rat," Pope replied while relieving Walker of Daniels' Colt 1911, "is to kill you here and now, but I can't. So follow me." He took Walker's phone, but not his keys, and led him down to the main deck while Berg brought up the rear, prodding Walker along with his pistol. When they came to the galley, the ship's cooking area, Pope flex-cuffed Walker's wrists, opened the door to a walk-in freezer, and ordered him inside under the threat of death still posed by Berg's leveled weapon. "Now I remember you," Pope said. "You're the cop who came to see me at the training camp with that n—"

"I'm gonna fuckin' kill you!" Walker roared.

Pope snorted. "Good luck with that," he said, then slammed the door in Walker's face.

After his captors had locked him in and left, Walker fished out his keychain and reported his situation to his team. At first he was optimistic about the possibility of a rescue, but as the minutes ticked by, he started to suspect that MARTAC wasn't coming. *Okay, change of plan.*

"*Oigan,*" he called out, having seen Chasquas's shaven-headed "caterers" on the way in to the galley and hoping they were still around.

"*¿Sí?*" came a voice from the other side of the door.

In perfect Spanish, Walker identified himself as Daniels, the guy who'd approached the catering van earlier that day and spoken with their boss in the parking lot. He explained that Chasquas's original plan would have to be modified and gave several reasons why. Then he asked if they'd be able to trigger the explosive device ahead of time.

"Yes, we can," came the young Latino's reply. "Hang on."

After a long and very cold silence, Chasquas's henchman came back to say that the bomb would now be going off in thirty minutes, and that he and the rest of the caterers had been ordered to take certain other precautions.

"Can … you le-let me out?" asked Walker, whose words came out in a mist.

"No. There's a heavy padlock on the door. I don't have the key, and we need to get to work. Good luck."

Walker was out of ideas and too cold to think anymore. Just as he was starting to resign himself to a painful death, whether by ice or by fire, the padlock rattled and the door swung open. There stood Pope, with his rifle leveled, and Berg and the mayors behind him.

"Did you search him?" Mayor Whitaker asked.

Pope jerked his chin at Berg, who patted Walker down, took his keys, and stepped back to his original position.

"Jeff Walker," said Mayor Locke with a taunting grin. "I'm your boss now."

"Not for long."

"You're right about *that*," said Locke, chuckling. Then his features fell serious and he turned to Pope. "Shoot him."

Berg and Mayor Whitaker looked on in amusement while Pope took careful aim.

"You don't want to kill me," Walker blurted out. "There's a bomb on this ship set to explode in thirty minutes and I'm the only person who knows where it is. You won't have time to find it."

Mayor Whitaker frowned and shook his head dismissively. "Even if you're telling the truth, this ship is equipped with lifeboats," he said, turning to Locke. "Isn't it?"

"Absolutely," said Locke, but he didn't look eager to lose his superyacht.

"It *used* to be equipped with lifeboats," Walker returned, knowing Chasquas had told his guys to disable any means of escape. "See for yourself."

Berg left to check and came back with bad news, and even *then* Mayor Whitaker was confident in his response. "Then we'll jump ship, swim away, and my helicopter will pick us up," he said. "Fire at will."

Pope raised his rifle once again, but this time Locke stepped in his way and twisted Walker's ear till it popped. "If you're lying," he growled in Walker's face, "I'll cut off your arms and legs and throw you overboard." Then he smiled suddenly as if he'd been struck by a funny thought. "You'll have to change your name to Bob." That got him a laugh from his cronies.

"All right," Whitaker agreed. "Show us where the bomb is."

Walker didn't actually know where it was, but he figured it had to be somewhere in or near the galley. Yet he offered no resistance when they shoved him up the stairs to the sun deck; that's what he'd wanted them to do. As he emerged into the fresh air, he saw Chasquas's caterers standing on the portside rail. The shaven-headed Latinos took the leap and dropped, tipping into a vertical attitude, gaining speed, then brought their arms over their heads, knifed into the water, and swam toward a sportfisher that was keeping station nearby.

Pope and Berg rushed to the rail, letting loose a fusillade of bullets that drilled into the side of the fishing boat, but then they stopped shooting and seemed unsure of what to do. Walker peered over the railing to see Chasquas standing on the sportfisher with a rocket-propelled grenade launcher on his shoulder, aiming it up at the superyacht.

Pope, Berg, the mayors, and everyone else who could see what was happening scrambled to the far side of the superyacht, including Walker, but Walker didn't stop at the starboard rail. He leapt over it headfirst. BOOM! A hot wave of smoke and debris overtook him from behind as he dove overboard, careening toward the water just as the caterers had done, sucking in a huge breath before plummeting into the sea. Once under water, he held his zip-tied wrists straight out and whipped his body like a dolphin to put as much distance between himself and the ship as he could. On he swam, ignoring his burning lungs, but eventually he had to scramble to the surface. When his head popped out, Walker gasped for air and spun around to see if he was in danger.

His eyes climbed up the hull of the now-distant ship. No one was at the railing. But they could start shooting at any time, Walker knew, so he leaned back with his face up and kicked himself out of range while keeping an eye on the superyacht. As the salty water slapped his face, he heard a familiar sound: the rhythmic beat of rotor blades, which preceded the sight of a helicopter swooping in to land on the superyacht. A frantic group of passengers piled in to the aircraft, which lifted off immediately, and which was replaced by a second one in less than a minute. Another load of evacuees hustled aboard that helicopter, and it had just taken off when a thunderous explosion tore the superyacht apart. Clouds of fire billowed into the sky and the blast wave hit Walker like a slap, even from so far away.

Certain there were still innocent lives to be saved, he put his face down and started swimming back to the blazing vessel, but he was stopped by the whup-whup-whup of a chopper again, frighteningly close this time, and it grew into a gale-force wind on his back. Walker put his legs under him and treaded water while looking up at a red and white Airbus H125 hovering twenty feet over his head. As it drifted closer, he spotted Carla at the controls! At first he thought he'd been saved, but then the side door slid open and a scowling Berg threw him a rope. Pope was up there too, staring down at Walker through the sights of his pistol, and he maintained that threat until Walker was seated in the cabin.

In addition to the passengers already named, Walker counted two others as Carla took to the sky: a young man in the co-pilot's seat and a young woman in the cabin with the rest of them. It wasn't a pleasant ride, for many reasons, chiefly Pope and his pistol. The militia leader's shaven head glistened with sweat and his beady eyes showed deadly intent, while the tribal tattoos on his throat and face made him look like a Māori warrior. On drugs.

"Where are you taking me?" Walker asked, hoping against the odds that Berg still had his keychain, that the device was still operational, and that someone was still listening in.

"We're taking you to church," Pope replied with a smirk. He was sitting on Walker's right.

But Berg, to Walker's left, was feeling more talkative. "I've got good news and bad news," he said. "What do you want first?"

Walker just stared at him.

"The good news is, we're taking you and Carla to see Tony Park."

Walker stared harder.

"The bad news is you've got five hours to live."

Carla whirled around with wide, desperate eyes.

"Don't worry," Walker told her. "We have a plan for this contingency."

It wasn't true, of course. There was no plan, and, what was worse, MARTAC was out of commission for some unknown reason. That's when the co-pilot turned around to face Walker and looked him dead in the eye. A cruel grin spread on his lips as though it were feeding on Walker's fear.

"Ave Satanas," he hissed like a snake.

26

A KNOCKOUT BLOW

The Hall of Justice
Downtown San Diego

MARTAC wasn't able to receive the audio transmitted by Walker's keychain, but there was still one person who could. Sitting at his desk, District Attorney Investigator Dom Taylor heard Walker say, "What's wrong, Pope? Want a cigarette?" and he immediately grabbed his radio. "Ortiz, this is Taylor, how do you read? Over."

No response.

"Taylor to Ortiz, come in."

Silence.

Taylor dialed the number for the Harbor Police, but he hung up before they answered because Walker had begun to detail his predicament from inside the freezer. After that, he heard Walker and the caterer speaking Spanish through the door, which he understood well enough, and then the crooks confiscated Walker's keychain before letting him out to find the bomb. This was followed by crackling gunfire and an explosion, and the last thing Taylor overheard was that Carla and Walker were being taken to some kind of church, that they'd see Tony Park there, and that they'd all be dead in five hours' time.

Taylor double-clicked his mouse to open the tracking software Choi had installed on his computer, which showed Walker flying over the sea at a hundred and sixty miles per hour, headed north along the coast. Then he snatched up his cell and hit redial.

"MARTAC is being detained at SDPD headquarters," the Harbor Police desk sergeant told him. "All of them, including Lieutenant Coffin. And everyone else is out responding to the riots. Unfortunately, there's nothing we can do."

Taylor closed his eyes and drew a breath to hold back his rising anger. "Park, Walker, and Park's wife are about to be killed by a satanic cult up in LA."

"Well, LAPD has their own riots to deal with, on a much bigger scale, but I'll call the FBI. If they can't provide assistance, I'll get the governor to send the National Guard."

"I appreciate it. You can reach me on this number," Taylor said, then proceeded to call every other local agency, with no better luck.

With time running out, he flew out of his chair and down the hall to Sean Choi's office, where he said, "I need you ready to go in five minutes."

A half-Asian, half-Caucasian young man looked up from the far side of three computer monitors with a bleary gaze. "Hi Sean," he replied testily. "We haven't spoken in a while. How have you been? Are you sleeping enough?"

"Walker's mission's gone to shit. He, Park, and Carla need our help right now."

Choi's eyes snapped to the middle display and his fingers flitted over the keyboard in a blur. By the time Taylor had come around the desk to take a look, Choi had brought up a satellite map with an overhead view of the cliffside castle. "Got him," said the technology analyst.

Taylor studied the image and pointed out prominent details as Choi zoomed in and out. "It'll be tough to make entry from the front," he said. "How high is the cliff?"

Choi entered another flurry of keystrokes to pull up a topographic map. "A hundred feet."

Taylor considered his options in silence. Finally, he said, in a low and serious tone, "I really need you on this one, Choi."

"You can count on me, sir."

"Good. Then let's roll."

They took Taylor's SUV to San Diego Lifeguard Headquarters, where they met up with Marcus Crawford (Walker's fit and deeply tanned brother-in-law) along with two other members of Crawford's dive rescue team, and the group double-timed it down the hall to their supervisor's office.

"Please. This is an emergency," Taylor implored the lifeguard lieutenant, "and no one else is available. You remember Park and Walker, don't you?"

"No, I don't. They'd already left when I transferred down from Laguna Beach," the lieutenant replied from behind a desk. Then he turned to his lifeguards. "Look, guys, I'm sorry your friends are in trouble, but I can't give you the day off, especially if it's going to put you in danger. If something were to happen, I could be held responsible."

Crawford exchanged a three-way look with Fowler and Hall, his colleagues, and they all nodded in agreement before he turned back to his boss and said, "Park and Walker aren't our friends. They're family. We have to do this, Lieutenant."

"You do and you're fired!"

One minute later, the lifeguards climbed into Crawford's truck while Taylor slid behind the wheel of his SUV, with Choi sitting beside him, and they all barreled out of the parking lot, bound for Malibu, a two-hour drive at maximum speed. On the way there, the Harbor Police desk sergeant called to tell Taylor that the FBI couldn't send a team on such short notice, but that the National Guard was still a possibility.

Taylor wasn't optimistic about the National Guard, nor about his chances of bringing Park, Walker, and Carla back alive, but he'd be damned if he wasn't going to give it everything he had.

***

Joshua Pope shoved Carla and Walker into the bloodstained holding cell in the castle's basement and slammed the door behind them with a bang that echoed like the end of the world. Then Pope and Berg headed back out into the great hall and, presumably, up the winding stone staircase.

"Carla," Park called out faintly. As she came to him, he staggered to his feet, then wrapped her in his arms as tightly as he could manage. One of his eyes was swollen shut and purple, and his nose had been smashed into his face.

Park caught Walker's eye over Carla's shoulder. Walker gave him a worried look and trudged over to where Phillips and Kerr were sitting on the floor against the wall. The FBI agents' faces were bloody, black, blue, and every color in between other than a normal healthy shade, and they offered Walker weak fist bumps as he took a seat beside them.

Carla and Park were the last to ease themselves down to the bloodstained floor, forming a miserable row of six prisoners with their backs against the far wall. Strangely, the cell measured less than four feet from that wall to the bars—barely enough space to stretch out their legs—but twenty feet from side to side.

"What happened to MARTAC?" Park asked.

"I don't know," Walker answered. "Maybe Locke ordered them to stand down."

"And had them detained, since they wouldn't have left you alone on the superyacht."

Walker nodded glumly. "Sounds right to me."

"What about Taylor?"

"No idea."

Park introduced Walker and Carla to Amanda Boydon, who was the only one of the original four prisoners who hadn't been beaten.

"Father John says it's because the Master wants me in good shape for the gathering," she explained.

"Dere's a bla' mass forda Master's birday," said John Kerr, part of whose jaw hung at an odd angle; he grimaced in pain with each garbled word. "In jus'afewhours."

Phillips turned to Walker and asked, "Who do you think the Master is? Locke?"

"Locke's not smart enough," said Walker. "I bet it's the Mayor of LA, Bruce Whitaker. He's running for U.S. President in the next election."

"Not if I can help it," growled Phillips.

"I saw two sets of shackles out there," Carla moaned.

Park turned to her with fire in his one good eye. "I won't let them take you."

Phillips looked at Amanda with a similar expression. "They'll need an army to drag you out of here."

"Dere's a bigang a ... bikers upstairs," Kerr reminded Phillips as best he could.

"Tim Reynolds, too," said Amanda Boydon. "With all his followers."

After adding Joshua Pope and his militia to the count, everyone agreed that an army was exactly what they were up against.

The cell went pretty quiet after that.

***

"I can't believe those idiots actually *drink* this," Mayor Whitaker said to Tim Reynolds, while urinating into a silver chalice held by Father John.

"Shhh," Father John hissed. He shot Whitaker a pointed look and jerked his head toward Reynolds' devotees, who were huddled in a corner butchering an animal for communion.

"I love this place!" Mayor Locke declared, looking up from a table piled high with cocaine and gesturing grandly toward a picture window with a nocturnal view of the ocean: parallel beams of pale moonlight filtered through the clouds, illuminating its rippling surface like spotlights on a stage. "How much did it set you back, *Mayor*?" he asked.

"That joke's getting old," Whitaker replied as he pulled on his black robe. After his head popped out of the neck hole, he added, "But if you *must* know, I'm renting it from an Iranian princess."

BANG BANG BANG! Everyone tensed. BANG BANG!

Gunfire, Whitaker knew, *most likely from the beach at the base of the cliff.*

They all stayed quiet, listening for further noise, but there was none.

"It's probably just the bikers blowing off steam," Mayor Whitaker said to Mayor Locke. "But tell Pope to check it out anyway."

Locke rose from the table and marched out of the room.

"Are you excited, Master?" asked Tim Reynolds, adjusting his pointed black hood so that the slits were aligned with his eyes.

"Not yet, Brother Tim," Mayor Whitaker replied, now fully garbed as well. "But I will be. And so will you, if you know what I mean." He glanced down at his crotch and back up to his newest protégé. He and Reynolds laughed together like father and son.

"Happy birthday, Master. We'll get the 'virgins' ready," said Father John from behind his own black hood, making air quotes as he said the penultimate word. Then he nodded to Reynolds, who followed him down the winding staircase to the basement.

The great hall bore a strong resemblance to the sanctuary in Hacienda Heights, and this was by design. Both here and there, a circle of candles around the altar illuminated the evil symbols on display, rows of flickering torches set on the side walls made the shadows come alive, and recorded incantations and chilling screams played in the background while the satanists milled about before the ceremony. As Father John and Brother Reynolds glided up to the chancel in their robes, some of the worshippers approached them.

Reynolds chose to act as his elder did, nodding subtly to his admirers and condescending only once to accept an offered hand. As soon as they reached the altar, a massive table draped with a long black cloth, an initiate brought Father John a silver platter piled with bloody meat, which the father set next to the silver chalice.

Meanwhile, Reynolds continued past the chancel to the torture chamber. He spotted the prisoners at the far end, then turned to his right and stepped into the sacristy, a small room for preparation and storage, where he reached behind a wall tapestry to lift a hidden lever.

***

Before his wife was shoved into the cell with him, Park had been on the verge of surrendering himself to his desperate situation. But when he saw how frightened she was at the prospect of being dragged out of the back room and chained to a stone block for satanic purposes, his body came alive again, to fight for her life. *Why is this cell so shallow?* he wondered. There had to be a reason. Otherwise, it would have made much more sense to build it square. *What advantage does this shape give our captors?*

It hit him like a slap in the face.

Park scrambled to his feet and turned to face the wall. "Look!" he said to his cellmates, pointing out eight small holes set two feet apart, almost as high as the ceiling. "Knockout gas. That's why the cell's built like this, so we can't run away. Let's plug the holes."

Walker, who had already freed his wrists by wearing down his zip tie on the edge of a stone, tore his shirt into tiny strips and handed them out to Park, Carla, Amanda, and Phillips, but not to Kerr, who he thought was too badly injured.

"Gimme one," Kerr grumbled.

So the entire group set their feet on the bars and their hands on the wall and walked themselves up to the level of the nozzles. It took some time to stuff the fabric into the holes with their little fingers, but they all managed it, meaning six nozzles disabled and two to go.

That's when one of the doors to the great hall started creaking open.

They all took the drop, landing on their feet, and whirled around to see Tim Reynolds come in. He stopped to stare at them for a moment, possibly wondering why they had such innocent looks on their faces and why Walker was shirtless, but then he ducked into a room on his right.

Park instantly climbed back up to the seventh nozzle, and Walker to the eighth. While supporting themselves with one arm on the wall and two feet on the bars behind them, they held the shirt strips in one hand and were just about to push them in to the holes when a sickly-sweet fog jetted onto their faces and into their eyes. Blindly, they tried to plug the nozzles, but the outflow pressure was too strong and the drug too fast acting. As Park and

Walker crashed to the floor, unconscious, the rest of the prisoners hurried to the opposite end of the cell, where they pressed their faces between the bars and sucked in the freshest air they could, hoping they'd plugged enough holes to save themselves.

They hadn't.

27

THE GATHERING

"*In nomine Dei nostri Satanas Luciferi Excelsi,*" boomed the Master, whose rich baritone carried through the great hall from the chancel to the winding staircase. Brother Reynolds and Father John stood at his side, all three in their black robes and pointed hoods looking out at the hundred souls who had come to worship.

"Amen," the congregation replied as one.

"The grace of our lord Satan, and the hate that he provides, and the communion of the demons be with you all."

"And also with you."

The Master made a solemn two-handed gesture, cueing his followers to take their seats.

"Brothers and sisters," began Father John, as the Master and Brother Reynolds made their way down the set of stairs at the front of the chancel, leaving him alone at the altar. "As you know, it is our custom at every gathering to invoke the presence of our lord by the murder of a person or an animal. But the holy one can also be summoned by the rape of a virgin. So tonight, in celebration of the anniversary of our dear Master's birth, that is how we shall begin."

Every eye fell on Carla Reyes and Amanda Boydon, who were chained to the stone platform set between the chancel and the congregation. Face up and wearing only underwear, they stirred groggily in the flickering candlelight.

"In addition," Father John went on, directing the worshippers' attention to four drowsy men tied to chairs, two on either side of the stone platform, "to appease the legions of demons in the Devil's flock and initiate the newest members of our own, we shall set these sinners free." Father John proceeded to lead the congregation in a hymn intentionally sung in low and off-key voices while ten initiates, each with a knife, positioned themselves behind Phillips, Kerr, Park, and Walker in teams of two or three, and the Master and Brother Reynolds took their places beside Amanda and Carla respectively.

"Gloria Satanas," Father John pronounced after the grating tune had come to an end.

"Gloria Satanas," replied the worshippers, whose eyes were alight with greedy anticipation.

***

Two trucks crunched to a stop at Westward Beach, and DAI Taylor, Marcus Crawford, Jenn Fowler, and Ethan Hall piled out of them. They nodded to Sean Choi, who drove Taylor's SUV back up the hill to park near the cliffside castle, but not so close that a roving patrol might be likely to discover him.

By the parallel beams of moonlight filtering through the clouds to illuminate the coast like scattered spotlights, Taylor and the others double-checked their gear, then backed Crawford's truck and its trailer up to the surf and launched the Zodiac. Once the entire team had climbed aboard the inflatable craft, they motored south, skirting around Point Dume, and when the rocky shoreline widened into a sandy beach with a hundred-foot cliff and a castle atop, they lowered the anchor and killed the engine a half mile off the coast.

Camouflaged by their black wetsuits and the boat's dark color, the rescue team bobbed in the waves with little to go on; all they knew was that Walker was being kept in the castle with Park and Carla by a group of unknown size including Tim Reynolds, both mayors, Joshua Pope, Berg, Stephen Baker, Bravo Company, and the East County Warlords. But once Choi got the drone in the air, they'd have a better idea of what they were up against.

Taylor lifted a pair of night vision binoculars to his eyes and scanned the base of the cliff. "There's one sentry at the beach access stairs and another on the opposite end." Then he handed Crawford an HK416 with drain holes drilled into the magazine. "As you come out of the surf, remember to partially retract the bolt to allow any water in the barrel to drain away."

"Roger," said Crawford eagerly.

Is he too eager? "Have you ever killed a man?" Taylor asked.

"No sir."

"Hopefully you won't have to. Just watch my six and do what I say, *when* I say it."

Crawford made good eye contact and nodded gravely.

"Okay, we've got eyes," came Choi's voice in their amphibious in-ear headsets. "As you know, the cliff is steep, but it's craggy enough for holds. Once you reach the top, you'll come to a seven-foot fence, drop down to the other side, and see an empty swimming pool. The terrace is clear for now, and I'll keep you informed."

"Roger that," said Taylor, who extended his fist to each member of the team. After everyone had given him a knuckle smack, he and Crawford popped their regulators into their mouths, slipped into the chilly water, and kicked themselves toward the beach at a depth of ten feet. They used their large fins for propulsion and hand-held lights to illuminate their path. When the sea floor began to rise up below them, they ditched the scuba gear, including their fins, and ascended to the surface.

Taylor gave Crawford a nod and headed for the beach, equipped with rock-climbing shoes, a combat knife, and a Glock 19. Crawford, who was similarly supplied but with a rifle, not a pistol, began to count. At twenty, he'd make his way in to shore as well.

Taylor swam with his head up to keep an eye on the sentries, who stood a hundred yards apart on either end of the beach. He set a course for the right side, since that was the darker end, and when his feet hit the sand, he low-crawled to the base of the cliff. Once there, he rose to a crouch and stalked the guard from behind while carrying his pistol in one hand and his knife in the other. When Taylor was almost upon him, he dropped his pistol in the sand, freeing his left hand to pinch the man's nose and cover his mouth, while at the same time plunging his knife into the man's right kidney, twisting it, pulling it out, then plunging and twisting again, several times, as quickly as he could. The sentry's blood gushed and spurted out of his lower back, and his muffled shouts grew faint. Taylor caught the body as it fell and lowered it down to the sand. "South side clear," he whispered.

"Roger," came Choi's voice in his ears. "Looks like the one on the north side didn't hear you."

As Taylor acknowledged the transmission, he spotted Crawford sneaking up to join him at the base of the cliff. They traded firearms. Then Taylor peered into the assault rifle's night vision scope and confirmed that the sentry at the far end of the beach was not aware of their presence. "Let's move," he said. With their weapons at the ready, he and Crawford stalked down the beach in the dark. All was quiet save for two recurring noises: the waves crashing on the shore and Taylor's heartbeat pounding harder and harder as it prepared him for a second kill.

"Hang on. I think he *did* hear you," said Choi from his remote location. "He's moving toward you, fast, and it looks like he's got night vision."

No sooner had Choi spoken than a hot burst of rifle fire snapped past Taylor and Crawford.

"Fuck!" shouted Crawford reflexively.

"Shhh," whispered Taylor as they hustled forward to take cover behind a rock formation. "That was close. He's definitely got NODs."

"Thirty yards and closing," said Choi.

"Listen up, Crawford," Taylor hissed. "On the count of three, climb up here, pop out quick and shoot the side of the cliff fifteen yards out. Three rounds should be enough. Got it?"

"Got it."

"And keep your head down."

"Twenty yards," came Choi's voice in their ears.

Taylor locked eyes with his younger buddy. "One. Two. Three!"

On three, Crawford clambered up to do as he'd been instructed, firing at the cliff—BANG BANG BANG!—while Taylor left the protection of the rocky outcrop they'd taken cover behind. Advancing rapidly in a crouch, Taylor peered through his illuminated scope and spotted his target clear as day. The man was looking up at the load of rocks and dirt that Crawford's pistol fire had dropped on him. Taylor squeezed the trigger twice—BANG BANG!—then dropped his rifle and sprinted forward to shove his knife into the sentry's brain from behind with a wet *splitch*, preventing him from using his radio.

"North end clear," Taylor muttered. "Fowler and Hall, you okay?"

"I'm good," said Jenn Fowler from the Zodiac.

"Me too," said Ethan Hall.

"I've got bad news," said Choi. "We just lost the drone. They're jamming it. That means I have to get to high ground to get eyes on the terrace. It'll take me ten minutes."

Taylor checked his watch. "We don't have ten minutes," he said. "Is the terrace clear right now?"

"Last I saw."

"Roger that. Stay alert and keep us posted," said Taylor, who then slung his rifle across his back to scale the face of the cliff. As he climbed from hold to hold, he used his legs to step up and his hands for balance. At the halfway point, he made the mistake of looking back down at Crawford, the more experienced climber of the two.

"You're doing good," came Crawford's voice in his ears.

Fighting a growing sense of panic, Taylor returned to his ascent and clawed his way to the top, where he whipped up his rifle as soon as his feet were under him. The ledge was deserted. Once Crawford was standing next to him, he whispered, "Give me a boost."

Then, as Crawford interlaced his fingers and heaved him up to the top of the fence, a metal bat came whistling down from out of nowhere and smashed into Taylor's head.

***

As Taylor regained his senses, he slowly became aware of a blinding pain in his temple and a cold lapping at his legs. For a moment, he thought he was a boy in a bathtub, but why wasn't the water hot? And why was he wearing a wetsuit? Then he opened his eyes to find himself in the deep end of a swimming pool, lashed back-to-back with Crawford, who was still unconscious, and the ropes around their chests tied to a drain. Making matters much, much worse, seawater was shooting out of a fill valve at the shallow end, causing the chilly liquid to flow down to where they were and the water level to inch ever higher.

"Crawford!" Taylor screamed, thrashing around to wake his buddy up. "Crawford!"

Up above them at the edge of the pool, the East County Warlords were hurling insults and spewing off abuse, and when Pope's militia showed up, the mocking began in earnest. One of them shouted, "Crawford, save me!" and another "Oh my God!" in girly voices, causing the crooked bunch to explode into laughter as Taylor struggled in vain.

The water was up to his chest.

28

FINALE

After snorting another couple of lines, Mayor Ronnie Locke set off to do as he'd been told, careening down the winding stone staircase from the top of the castle. But instead of steeling his resolve to complete the mission, the cocaine produced the opposite effect. Having been afraid of the Devil since childhood, Locke was unable to stop his drug-fueled paranoia from producing visions of a horned red humanoid with a mocking grin; Satan, he felt, was coming to claim his soul.

He made it to the ground floor and knew he had to get outside, but the front entrance was proving elusive. With a stratospherically rapid pulse, he glanced in all directions, desperately looking for a way out. On the other side of the kitchen there was a side door. It would serve his purpose. Sweating profusely now as he burst into the night, Locke hurried along a walkway to the front of the house. To his left, the garden grew and twisted in his direction as if by magic, fed by a dark power that he knew all too well.

Get a grip! Locke berated himself as he came to the driveway, shaking his head to clear it and steadying himself with a breath. On his way down to the public road, he passed a row of cruiser bikes and a cargo van. Pulling open a door built into the front gate, he stepped out to find Berg leaning against the guard house and two of Berg's men inside. "Get down to the beach," he ordered Pope's second-in-command. "We heard gunshots."

"We heard them too," Berg snapped. "And we already caught the intruders."

"Just do as I say. All three of you."

"Who's gonna watch the guard house?"

"Your mayor."

"I'm going to have to call this in."

Locke flew at Berg and screamed in his face, "Just do as I *fucking say!*" causing the entire security team to scramble down the hill. Then he stormed into the guard house, grabbed a chair, put his head between his knees, and tried to catch a breath, but his body would not cooperate. With a dangerously high heart rate and his anger replaced by an ice-cold panic, Locke feared both life and death.

***

Weighed down by a backpack full of high-tech gear, Sean Choi hustled to the top of a hill and stopped to peer through a night-vision monocular, looking down at the edge of the cliff and the fence in front of the castle. What he saw plunged him into despair: on the ocean side of the fence, Crawford was giving Taylor a boost; on the other, the East County Warlords were crouched on flowerpots and benches, waiting for someone to show their face. Before Choi could warn his teammates, one of the bikers popped up to smash Taylor on the head with a bat, and the rest rose up to train their guns on Crawford.

"Taylor's down," came Crawford's voice in his ears.

"I know," Choi replied gloomily. "I just got up here. I can see you, but there's nothing I can do right now. Hang on. I'll think of something." Choi could only watch as the bikers hauled Taylor over to their side and forced Crawford to come over on his own. Fortunately, the Warlords weren't as smart as they were hairy, Choi thought as they tossed Taylor's and Crawford's headsets into the bushes. So he was sure no one was listening in when he said, "Fowler and Hall, do you read?"

"Loud and clear, unfortunately," said Ethan Hall.

"What should we do?" asked Jenn Fowler.

"I need a minute. Stand by." Choi sat down in the dirt to open his laptop. Hoping Walker's keychain was still operational, he accessed the audio feed, and with the added advantage of his monocular, he was able to hear and see Locke order Berg and his men out of the guard house and down to the beach. Then he swept the night-vision device back toward the pool area, where the bikers were tying up Taylor and Crawford and turning on the fill valve.

"Hall and Fowler," he said. "I need you to make some noise down on the beach."

***

Ethan Hall cut the anchor line and Jenn Fowler started the outboard motor. On his nod, she hit the throttle and headed for the beach. Salty spray stung their eyes, thrown up by the hull as it bounced on the waves. "Just drop me off!" Hall shouted over the engine noise.

"No way, man!" Fowler replied, standing aft with one hand on the tiller. "We're in this together."

Hall had gone to the shooting range with Park and Walker many times back when they were working together as lifeguards, and after Park and Walker had left to join the police, he'd continued to hone his marksmanship skills. He and Crawford both. He didn't think Jenn knew how to handle a gun, but even if she did, his first instinct was to keep her safe. "Please, Jenn," he said as she eased off on the throttle to stop the boat just short of the breaking waves. "Just keep station here and stay ready to pick me up. That way we won't have to fight our way past the surf if we have to make a quick getaway."

As their gazes caught and held, the moonlight hit her features just right. *God, she's beautiful,* he thought. *Go for it!*

"All right, I will," she said, flashing him a heart-stopping smile. "But you better make it back to me."

"I will," he promised, leaning in for their first kiss. Then he dove off the boat and popped up facing the beach, checking to make sure the coast was clear. Seeing nothing but the two dead sentries Taylor had taken out, he let the waves push him in to shore. As he ran up the beach, he pulled back the pistol's action to drain out the water, dropped the magazine to blow it dry, smacked the mag back in, chambered a round with a metallic click-clack, then headed toward the beach access stairs on the left, at the foot of which he found a dead guard, a rifle, and a set of night vision binoculars. Hall strapped on the NODs to see if they still worked, and they did!

His objective was to make all the men at the pool come running down to the beach, but before he could make any progress on that front, several sets of footsteps came clomping down the stairs.

"There's no one down there," he heard a man say.

"Fuckin' waste of time," added another.

Hall snatched up the dead guard's rifle and ran back to take cover behind a rock formation, watching as three men in army fatigues came trudging down to the sand some forty yards away. To his left, a crashing wave slid up the beach face. Then a second one. Then a third, slowly marking the passage of time as he took a knee and sighted his targets.

Once the militia men had seen their fallen comrade, they advanced much more carefully. Unlike Hall, however, they were not supplied with night vision, so as they swept their rifles back and forth, they didn't spot him.

Hall pulled the trigger when they were twenty yards away. CRACK! The first guy took a round to the face and instantly dropped, as though someone had flipped the switch to his brain. He shifted his aim and fired again. CRACK! Another head shot. Easy at fifteen yards. The man toppled straight back like a tree blown over by a hurricane.

Struck by sudden inspiration, Hall dropped his muzzle an inch and pulled the trigger repeatedly—CRACK CRACK CRACK CRACK!—catching the third guard in the legs as he tried to run away. With his rifle still raised, Hall stood, strode forward, and kicked the last guy's gun out of his reach. "If you can get your whole team down here, I'll let you live," he said. "Tell 'em a large tactical team is arriving by sea."

Hall held his breath as the wounded man weighed up his limited options, then blew it out as the man did as he'd been told. He couldn't believe things were going so well. Maybe Crawford, Walker, Park, and Taylor *did* have a chance after all. Then, with two hands, he lifted the rifle and brought its buttstock down onto the guard's head, but only hard enough to knock him out. Then he collected all three of the sentries' radios and hustled back into the waves, dropping them in the sea as he swam back out to the Zodiac.

***

Sean Choi had always been an exceptional student, but also always afraid of physical confrontation and thus a prime target for bullies throughout his life. Now, however, to save his friends, he was determined to overcome the all-too-familiar sense of terror that was threatening to freeze him in place at the top of that hill. *Not this time,* he swore to himself as he hurried down the slope, trembling so violently that a little brown surprise appeared in his boxer shorts. Stopping to shake it out of his pants before going on, he was comforted by the knowledge that no one would ever find out about it.

Not only was Choi afraid of violence, but he was also opposed to it on moral grounds, so it was with the greatest reluctance that he strode up the driveway toward the Mayor of San Diego with a loaded gun in his hand. Hugging the shadows, he crept toward the guard house, which stood outside a solid-steel gate topped with electric fencing. Since the interior lights were on, through a window he saw Ronnie Locke sitting at a desk, sweating profusely with his head down and his face cupped in his hands. *So,* thought Choi, *how can I get past the gate without firing this pistol?*

It was no secret that the businessman-turned-politician was a drug user (*incidentally,* Choi wondered, *why shouldn't public servants be subjected to drug testing when such is standard practice for fast-food workers and warehouse packers?*) At any rate, he remembered from a university lecture that cocaine can cause psychosis (hallucinations) as well as paranoia, and this gave him the solution to his dilemma.

***

Never in his life had Mayor Ronnie Locke experienced such a crushing sense of dread. He couldn't breathe, which made him dizzy, and his heart was so overworked that it hurt, as though the Devil himself were stabbing an embroidery needle into that vital muscle again and again. Deep down, Locke had always known that his misdeeds would come back to haunt him, but he had never thought that it would happen so soon. Then, a tapping on the windows snapped him out of his thoughts and plunged him into a reality that was infinitely more terrifying.

"Locke," growled Satan, scraping a long black claw on the glass with a screech. "LOCKE!"

The crooked statesman's mind was flooded with visions of all the people he'd ever cheated, stolen from, lied to, belittled, or killed. One by one, they glared at him with outrage and not a single shred of mercy. It was torture! There was only one way out. Locke pulled open a drawer and felt warm relief when his gaze fell on what he'd been hoping to see. He snatched up the pistol, jammed it into his mouth, and blew out the back of his head.

***

Having successfully impersonated the Lord of Darkness, Sean Choi let himself in to the guard house, gaped at the chunky red splatter on the wall, hit a green button to unlock the door in the gate, and sprinted through it to the castle's front entrance.

"Choi, this is Hall," he heard in his ears. "I'm back in the boat with Fowler and the beach is crawling with guards."

"Roger," Choi whispered, easing open the front door, then advancing with his gun held in a two-handed grip. "Well done. Now motor around the point and I'll meet you back at the beach."

Choi was still afraid but no longer trembling. After some exploration and a bit of doubling back, he found his way to the pool terrace. It was deserted except for Taylor and Crawford, who were still back to back in the deep end, gagging and coughing and tilting their heads to keep their lips above the water line.

With a splash, Choi jumped in, untied the knot on the drain—setting his buddies afloat—then towed them to the side of the pool where he freed them entirely, keeping the ropes in case they came in handy. Then, while Taylor and Crawford were catching their breath, he climbed out by the ladder and panned his pistol in every direction.

"Outstanding job, Sean," Taylor growled, clapping Choi on the back much too hard. He looked angry enough to murder every crook in the castle. "Now get your ass back to the truck."

"No sir," Choi returned as he handed over the gun. "Someone's got to keep your temper in check. Plus, three guys are better than two."

"Roger that," said Taylor. "Then stay sharp, 'cause this isn't over. You good, Crawford?"

"Yes sir."

Taylor led them into the castle and started down the winding staircase. Holding his pistol at the high ready, as he came around the central column he spotted a guard at the foot of the stairs, so he held up a fist to stop his team and took three steps back, moving out of sight. The guard was carrying an all-black AK-47 derivative and wearing a knife sheath on his belt. Two minutes later, the guard was unconscious and restrained in a remote corner of the basement, and Taylor, Crawford, and Choi each had a weapon.

After explaining his plan in a whisper, Taylor stalked into the great hall and up the middle aisle. The congregation surrounding him sat transfixed, staring straight ahead at a black-hooded priest up on the chancel. In front of the priest, to the left and right of a large stone platform, were four teams of men and women standing behind Walker, Park, Kerr, and Phillips, who were tied to chairs. At the priest's nod, two other black-clad figures clambered onto the stone platform and attempted to tear off Amanda's and Carla's underwear while the kill teams raised their blades in the air, but Taylor froze them all by firing his rifle into the ceiling—CRACK CRACK CRACK!—He charged up the aisle with his iron sights fixed on the kill teams, shouting, "Police! Drop the knives!"

"Down on the floor!" roared Crawford, who came storming up the left-side aisle covering the stone platform with his pistol, while Choi came up the right flank with his knife, ready to cut the captives free.

Taylor kept his rifle trained on the kill teams until they all dropped their blades. Then, as Crawford rounded them up, he strode over to the two men lying face down on the floor and pulled off their hoods. Strangely, the older one, who he figured had to be Mayor Whitaker, turned to the priest on the chancel. The priest gave Mayor Whitaker a reverent nod, then charged Taylor, running straight down the chancel steps while screaming bloody murder.

Taylor took aim and fired, piercing the priest's hood right between the eye slits.

* * *

Loser, thought Mayor Whitaker as Father John made the ultimate sacrifice, just as he'd commanded the man to do with nothing but a look. Yet Whitaker didn't watch him die; he used the distraction to unchain Amanda Boydon and drag her into the back room. "Reynolds!" he hissed on his way there, but it was too late for the cruise ship killer, who leapt to his feet, scooped up a knife, and tried to stab Carla, possibly thinking, Whitaker guessed, that if *he* couldn't have her, then nobody could. But one of the rescuers gunned Reynolds down before he could do her any harm, so Mayor Whitaker slipped into the back room and from there into the sacristy, taking Amanda Boydon with him and locking the door. He dropped her wrist to make a call. "Pope!" he hissed, opening a wall safe with his other hand. "Where are your guys and the bikers?"

"Last I knew, they were down at the beach, but no one's responding to my radio calls. I'm headed there now."

"No! Turn around," Whitaker barked while filling a black duffel bag with bundled stacks of hundreds. "All the prisoners have escaped ... except for one." He paused to leer at the fair-haired singer, who cowered before him on the floor. "Meet me at the helipad. Bring flex cuffs and the heaviest weapons you've got."

***

Walker rushed out of the back room and into the great hall carrying Carla's clothes. "The sacristy's locked," he said to Park. "With a heavy door and a solid bolt. There's gotta be an emergency exit in there."

"So we need to get upstairs," Park concluded.

"I'll stay here," said Taylor, handing Walker the AK-47 derivative he'd taken from the guard at the bottom of the stairs. "Me and Crawford can hold it down."

"Thanks, Dom," said Walker, smacking Taylor's knuckles with his own.

Then Sean Choi strode up. "I just talked to Hall and Fowler," he said. "They're down at the beach with the National Guard, who've rounded up Baker and the Warlords, as well as most of Pope's men."

"Come *on!*" shouted Phillips, who was already running up the center aisle toward the winding staircase.

So while Choi tended to Kerr's injuries and Taylor and Crawford cornered all the remaining satanists, Walker, Park, Carla, and Phillips hustled up the stairs, following the sound of a helicopter spooling up for liftoff. But by the time they made it to the helipad, Mayor Whitaker's chopper was too far away for Walker to shoot at it.

As one, they sprinted for Carla's red and white Airbus H125, which was parked nearby on a grassy clearing. Carla jumped into the cockpit to initiate the startup procedure while Park slid into the co-pilot's seat and Phillips and Walker shut the side doors with a clunk and a chunk. Carla then raised the collective lever, causing the thump-thump beats of the rotor and a whining noise to grow tremendously loud, and the ground fell away as she achieved forward flight, banking north to follow Whitaker's trajectory.

They soared through the night over the moonlit coastline, seeing no sign of the fugitives for quite some time. Then, from out of nowhere, a bullet pierced the front windshield, missing Park's face by inches!

"*Chingada madre,*" Carla muttered, diving down while rolling right. "They're not using their nav lights. Which is actually a good idea." So she switched off her own and circled back around.

With Phillips holding on to his belt, Walker slid open the right side door and sat on the edge, looking into his rifle's night vision scope. As the two choppers blew past each other a second time, he spotted Joshua Pope sitting on the cabin floor with a rifle, just like him. Both men fired and missed, so the rival airships looped around once more, lining up for a third and final head-on pass.

"Ready?" said Carla into her headset mic at a hundred yards away.

"More than ready," Walker replied into his, drawing a slow breath as he peered through his reticle to target the oncoming chopper's windshield, then pulled the trigger repeatedly—CRACK CRACK CRACK CRACK CRACK!—producing no appreciable result. As the other helo raced toward him at a hundred miles an hour, he next sighted Pope, who was protected by a tactical vest, so it had to be a head shot. Walker thought back to his SWAT training and to the crash course taught by Lieutenant Coffin before going undercover at Baker's rural compound, and that helped, but more than any instruction he'd ever received, it was the memory of Joshua Pope telling him to imagine shooting an N-word at the firing range that particularly steadied his aim.

As the choppers roared past each other, Walker let loose a barrage of semi-automatic fire and caught a glimpse of pink mist spraying out of Pope's head. Simultaneously, several bleeding wounds appeared in his right shoulder, but Walker held his rifle steady and fired again, this time at the passing tail rotor.

"Nice shot!" came Carla's voice in his ears as he crawled back into the cabin and flipped onto his back. The pain was terrible.

Park scrambled out of his seat to check on him.

"I didn't have to imagine he was anything," Walker mumbled to Park before passing out. "Just the crooked bastard he really was."

"He did it!" Carla exclaimed. "Whitaker's gonna have to attempt an emergency landing."

As the other chopper lost altitude, four yellow pontoons inflated at the level of its landing skids; then it plopped onto the sea and floated there in a normal parking position.

"Let's have a look," said Park, checking Walker's wounds while Carla took the Airbus down. The shoulder would need reconstructive surgery—again—but Walker would live. Park peeled off his shirt and held it against the affected area. "Firm and steady pressure," he told his buddy. "We'll be back in ten mikes." Then he checked the load in the rifle's mag, exchanged nods with Carla, and jumped into the ocean with Phillips right behind him.

Park propelled himself with his legs and left arm while using his right to keep the rifle—their only weapon—out of the water. Taking one-handed aim as he swam closer to the other chopper, he saw no one in the cockpit, but couldn't see into the cabin through the tinted side windows.

Phillips looked angry enough to tear open the mayor's helo like a tin can. Park turned to look him in the eye. "You ready?"

"Oh yeah."

After they'd agreed on a plan, Park pulled himself out of the water and threw open the co-pilot door. A bullet snapped past his head, missing since he hadn't gone into the cockpit yet. When he did, it was with his AK leveled, but he didn't have a shot.

In the center of the rear seats, with deranged agitation and deadly intensity twisting his features, Whitaker sat just out of reach with Miss Boydon on his lap, shielding himself with her body while holding a pistol to her head. The singer was pleading for help with her eyes.

Still peering through the reticle at the hostage situation, Park climbed into the next seat over, that of the pilot.

"Ditch the rifle or she's dead," growled Whitaker.

That's when Phillips clambered into the co-pilot's seat so that he and Park were both facing the rear cabin. "No, *you're* dead, if you don't let her go," he growled back.

Whitaker stared at Phillips while pushing his gun's muzzle into the side of Miss Boydon's head, causing her to yelp with fright.

If only I could trust her to move out of the line of fire, Park thought (as Carla had done with the intruder in their bathroom), *I'd have put this maggot down already.* "You win," he said. "I'll toss the rifle and you let her go. Same time." Still sighting the mayor through his scope, Park swung the pilot door open. He hoped Phillips was as ready as he'd said he was.

"Deal," said Whitaker, with victory gleaming in his eyes. "I won't kill her. Not today, anyway. But you two are fish food."

Park lowered the rifle and stepped out onto the skid to drop it overboard. In the five seconds it took him to do that, a blur of violent chaos unfolded in slow motion:

Whitaker swung his pistol onto Park.

Phillips scrambled over the co-pilot's seat to grab the mayor's shooting arm.

Miss Boydon clawed at the mayor's eyes while Phillips fought for control of the gun, but it fired accidentally and clattered to the floor.

Phillips drew back his fist and punched Whitaker in the throat.

Park clambered into the cockpit and dove into the rear cabin to scoop up Whitaker's pistol.

Phillips slid open the side door, looped an arm around Miss Boydon's waist, and jumped into the ocean with her.

Park pushed himself back into the cockpit, out of the mayor's reach, and lined up his sights on the man's heart.

"Go ahead," Whitaker hissed. His eyes were shining with hate. "I'll be a martyr to the cause. Someone else will take my place, and he'll be even stronger and smarter than I am."

"Smarter for sure," Park returned. "But as much as I'd love to pull the trigger, I'd rather see how a rich white guy like you fares in federal prison for life. I'm guessing not well."

"I won't spend five minutes behind bars and you know it."

Whitaker was right. The kind of money he and his billionaire donors wielded like a heavy weapon would be enough to buy him an unfair trial, a rescue by a tactical team of overwhelming strength while in transit *to* that trial, or any number of other means to illegally preserve his liberty. While Park was reflecting on the injustice of it all, he shifted in his seat, accidentally banging his elbow on the open door and losing his grip on the pistol.

As the gun fell into the sea, Whitaker flew at Park, who let the hateful man's momentum push him backwards, and they both tumbled into the ocean.

Unfortunately, one of them drowned in the resulting struggle.

And it wasn't the former Navy SEAL.

29

EPILOGUE

"You may now kiss the brides," intoned a black-clad priest—a God-fearing one this time—whereupon Marcus Crawford and Sean Choi lifted their new wives' veils to lean in and express their love, and the wedding guests clapped with hearty exuberance as a warm breeze blew through the observation deck of the MS *Angelica*, Excelsior's newest vessel.

Under a gentle sun, the ship continued to sail through the crystal-clear waters of the Caribbean Sea, and the cheering invitees rose to their feet as Sean Choi wheeled Dulce Garcia up the aisle followed by Marcus Crawford and Maggie Garcia.

Tina Garcia wiped her eyes as she watched her younger sisters go, and she turned to her own husband, Jeff Walker, who put his arm around her. Park, Phillips, and Kerr were also in the first few rows, which seemed fitting as it had been their undercover work that had saved the cruise line's business and resulted in the complimentary VIP suite package for fifty people with all expenses paid that was now being used.

Two by two, the guests followed the newlyweds into the Highpoint Grill, an exclusive dining room reserved entirely for the wedding party, where gleaming white columns rose out of plush carpeting, and long rectangular tables were set with white linen, premium silverware, crystal wine glasses, and Bvlgari porcelain plates.

As Walker waited behind Tina's chair for her to sit down, he asked his daughters to keep their shrieks of delight down to a reasonable level. This proved difficult for the two little girls as they stared open-mouthed through the windows at an island ringed with white-sand beaches and palm trees, the ship's current destination.

Carla Reyes, now quite far along in her pregnancy, and Tony Park sat opposite Tina and Walker, while Señor Garcia presided at the head of the table, keeping a stern watch over his clan. His wife, Señora Garcia, whose features were only slightly softer than his, looked upon their daughters with loving pride. All three were dressed in white, Dulce and Maggie in bridal gowns while Tina's dress was simpler, and all three had flowing black hair, shapely figures, and heart-stopping smiles.

At the same table of honor, DAI Dominick Taylor pulled out a chair for Chief Deputy DA Lynn Peters, who wore a royal blue dress with understated elegance, and had curled her hair so that it tumbled down in long golden cascades.

At a different table, former Supervisory Special Agent John Kerr was surrounded by his adult children, though his ex-wife was absent, of course. After demonstrating on this last assignment that he was able to work with others as part of a team, he'd taken his retirement and purchased a BMW R 1250 GS, in black and silver, the same elegant, ergonomic cross-country motorcycle he'd rented before the undercover operation, which he was planning to take on long road trips to visit his scattered family.

Ethan Hall and Jenn Fowler were also in attendance, holding hands and lost in each other's gazes, giddy with newfound love. Having been fired for leaving their lifeguard towers against their boss's orders, they and Marcus Crawford had been offered jobs as Harbor Police officers pursuant to Park's and Walker's recommendations.

Scott Phillips, previously a special agent with the FBI and now Chief Phillips, head of security for the very ship they were sailing on, took to his feet and raised a glass. "To the happy couples!" he bellowed, drawing a collective roar. As he resumed his seat, he blew a kiss to Amanda Boydon, who swayed to the beat as the ship's band struck up a tune. *Bésame mucho*, his favorite.

Back at the table of honor, Park caught Walker's eye and said, "Hey man, didn't you vow never to ride a motorcycle again, six years ago?"

"Affirmative."

"So how is it that on every one of our cases you always get to use a high-end bike?"

"Just lucky, I guess. It's always an emergency situation with no other way out."

Park nodded, apparently satisfied with Walker's answer. Then, as the band played on, he said, "We did it again, brother."

"Yes, *we* did, brother," Walker replied, gazing around at all the people he loved most in the world. It was official now: they were a family. For better or worse, in sickness and health, and in times of peace and war, they would sail on together until death did them part.

***

Following his conviction for narcotics trafficking and related offenses, Stephen Baker was sentenced to a long stint in a California state prison. He felt like an idiot for building the meth lab on his own property. Next time he'd do it right.

But that next time might not come for twenty years, he lamented, shaking his head at himself. Clad in an orange jumpsuit and full restraints, he shuffled onto the prison bus in a sad line of other high-risk prisoners under the careful watch of a team of sheriff's deputies. Once they'd all taken a seat, the bus grumbled to life and headed for an impenetrable facility from which Baker wouldn't be released until good ol' Uncle Sam saw fit.

While en route, the convicts' conversations rose in volume to an agitated buzz as a pack of motorcyclists came roaring up from behind the three-vehicle convoy, shot out the tires of the escort cruisers, and forced the bus to stop several miles down the road.

A lanky Honduran covered in tattoos strode up to the bus, raised an automatic rifle, and opened fire, killing the two deputies seated in the front before climbing aboard. Baker recognized him immediately and vice versa. On the far side of the wire-mesh divider, while his shaven-headed comrades were searching the downed officers for keys, Chasquas grinned at Baker and called out, "Anyone need a job?"

Afterword

Dear Reader,

I hope you enjoyed this third installment of *The Park and Walker Action Thriller Series*. If you did, I'd love it if you left me a review. Just a line or two would suffice.

Now, are you ready for more books? There are two others in this action series (so far): *The Mazatlan Showdown* (book 1), nominated for Best Action Adventure at Killer Nashville 2023, and *Bad Traffic* (book 2), Winner of the 2024 Killer Nashville Readers' Choice Award. You can check them out on my website, patrickweill.com.

"Do you have anything else available, Pat?" you might ask.

"Yes!" I'd reply. "Have you read my short story, "A Hell of a Spring Break"? It's available for FREE at all major online retailers. If you haven't, I'd start there, because it's a prequel not only to this action trilogy, but also to a new series I'm starting, of a different kind. *The Hall of Justice Series* will be a collection of legal thrillers, and the first one just came out! *The Southern Trust Conspiracy* was written for male and female readers alike, and it does feature some of the same characters from *Double Threat*, but generally it's a separate series. Below you'll find the cover and the book description, but not before I let you know about another free story.

Just head on over to my website, patrickweill.com, where you can download "Relentless," a fast-paced historical thriller written in British English that introduces the heroine of this new legal thriller series. To do so, you'll have to enter your email address, but you can unsubscribe from my newsletter at any time and still keep your free story.

Wishing you a good day,

Pat Weill

Life in sunny Southern California is darker than it first appears—at least that's true for the San Diego District Attorney's Office in this first installment of *The Hall of Justice Legal Thriller Series*.

Chief Deputy Lynn Peters has her hands full enough, what with her heavy caseload, her complicated romance with investigator Dom Taylor, and the many legal units she's responsible for. So, when criminal defense attorney Vincent Tyson enters the picture to represent Dr. Millie Haukea in a murder trial, Peters calls upon the Major Violators Unit to prosecute the case.

Yes, Millie Haukea has resurfaced, after flying under the radar since the events of "A Hell of a Spring Break." And yes, she's a doctor now, of pharmacy—a professional poisoner and one of many specialized assassins secretly working for Tyson, the aforementioned criminal defender. Yet Dr. Haukea is merely a small fish in a far-reaching conspiracy, with some of the wealthiest people on the planet supporting her defense.

Tyson's team of hired killers wreak havoc at the Hall of Justice, leaving young attorneys Cammie O'Mara and Johnny Roche to face Tyson in court, with a crooked judge presiding. Luckily, Cammie and Roche aren't working alone either. Flanked by veteran lawman DAI Dom Taylor and his gifted assistant, Sean Choi, along with SDPD SWAT led by Lieutenant Ragasa, and a few other surprise guests from past adventures, Cammie and Roche "suit up," so to speak, and charge into battle.

Weill's fourth novel delivers romance, mystery, tense courtroom drama, sharp legal maneuvering, explosive action scenes, a memorable cast on both sides of the chessboard, and even a trip to the tropics. Can Cammie and Roche beat Tyson in court even if the Honorable Andrew Toles doesn't turn out to be so honorable? And in the white-knuckle finale, will Choi solve his rival's puzzle before the last second ticks away? What will Millie Haukea's final verdict be? Is Tyson really going to get away with it all? The answers to all these questions and more can only be found in *The Southern Trust Conspiracy*.

ABOUT THE AUTHOR

Patrick Weill is an award-winning author, translator, and editor. His favorite activities include dog walking, coffee drinking, music listening, and family time. You can follow Pat on Facebook, LinkedIn, and Instagram, and don't forget to check out his website, patrickweill.com, to see what's new!